Madison's eyes widened. "Get down," she ordered, and at the same moment Terry felt a burst of air pass her by, accompanied by a strange, muted spit. "What the —"

Madison dove to the ground. Rolling towards Terry she grabbed her by the ankles and jerked her down.

"What's happening?" Terry asked urgently, feeling the panic roll over her.

Madison glared at her, the bright green eyes warning her as they darted about. "Shut up. Do not speak. Do *exactly* as I say. This is no game, Terry. Do you understand?"

Terry nodded, and Madison continued, "Good. Now, stay down and crawl, and I mean crawl, behind that tree."

Terry looked into Madison's wild eyes questioningly.

"Do it now."

Terry followed the instructions blindly. She inched her way along the ground on her stomach, trying not to believe the truth . . . Someone was trying to kill them.

CLUB TWELVE

AMANDA KYLE WILLIAMS

Withdrawn

CLUB TWELVE

AMANDA KYLE WILLIAMS

The Naiad Press, Inc.
1990

Printed in the United States of America
First Edition

Edited by Katherine V. Forrest
Cover design by Pat Tong and Bonnie Liss
    (Phoenix Graphics)
Typeset by Sandi Stancil

Library of Congress Cataloging-in-Publication Data

Williams, Amanda Kyle, 1957—
    Club twelve / by Amanda Kyle Williams.
        p.   cm.
    ISBN 0-941483-64-9
    I. Title. II. Title: Club 12.
PS3573.I447425C58   1990
813'54--dc20   89-48964
                                                    CIP

For Julie

About the Author

Amanda Kyle Williams was born in August of 1957 and grew up near Boulder, Colorado. At the age of sixteen she dropped out of high school and took a full-time job. By the age of twenty-eight she was vice-president of a sizeable textile manufacturing company.

At thirty years old she walked away from corporate America to pursue her true ambition and began writing espionage novels.

She now resides in Marietta, Georgia with her partner and their seven cats.

Acknowledgements

There are so many people to whom I owe thanks for their time and patient support while I was so deeply emerged in this project. I would like to now thank all of you and mention a few in particular.

Tricia Watson, Janice Brannon, Robbyn Wood, Susan Fischer and Sandra Lambert, who invested time reading the original manuscript and making suggestions.

Thanks go out to Angela Motter for her help and inspiration, and her promise to never let me embarrass myself too badly in public.

Thanks to Amanda Gable who took time out of an impossible schedule to read the manuscript and make suggestions that helped me re-work the beginning chapters.

Thanks to Pam Stacy, Max, Bill West, Tully Bascomb and Jeff Andrews who offered encouragement along with some much needed financial support so that I was able to complete my first novel with as little pressure as possible.

And special thanks to Julie who taught me that nothing is truly unattainable.

Prologue

In Glasgow, Scotland an old man struggled out of his chair to answer a knock on his door.

"Hello my young friend. This is a surprise. Please, come in."

"Thank you," answered the handsome young guest, walking into the old country home. His eyes swept the room suspiciously. "Marcus, it's vital that we talk. Are we alone?"

"Yes," Marcus Radcliffe answered. "Jeremy's in town. What's on your mind?"

The visitor took a seat on the couch. He began to

speak, the urgency in his voice clear. "I was followed when I left here yesterday."

Marcus Radcliffe sat straight up in his chair. "Followed? Who?"

The younger man took a deep breath. "I don't know. I lost them." He leaned forward, elbows resting on his knees. "Marcus, it's clear that someone is watching you, watching the house, and probably listening in on your phone calls. Someone knows about the list."

The old man sighed heavily and rubbed his forehead. "But how? It's true I'm getting old, my friend. I'm not so sharp anymore. But, I've told no one about the list."

"What about your cook? Couldn't he have overheard us talking?"

Marcus chuckled. "Jeremy is no spy."

"Maybe not. But are you willing to take that chance? What if I'm right? The minute you try to deliver that list to Washington they'll intercept and you'll be a dead man . . . Listen, they'll be waiting for you to pick it up and deliver, right? So, go somewhere. Make reservations and fly out of the country. Meanwhile, I'll get the list and deliver it to Washington safely."

Marcus, his eyes warm, sincere, looked up at the handsome face of his visitor. He touched the arm of his friend gently. "You are a brave man. You would risk your life to protect me?"

The young man smiled. "You overestimate me. You are the one at risk here, Marcus, not me."

The old man stood and walked to a desk in the corner of the room. He removed the top drawer and reached under the desk, pulling out a small piece of film taped to the underside. He returned to the couch and handed it to his guest. "When this is examined you'll find the numbers of a coded bank account in Zurich, a safe deposit box at the Unione di Banche Switzerland. Once you get the list, it must go to a man named McFaye in Washington, D.C."

The guest reached for the old man's hand and held it tightly for a moment. "I promise you," he said, looking into the old man's eyes, "I'll do everything I can. Club Twelve has to be stopped."

Marcus smiled faintly and sat back down. "It won't stop them, my friend. I've only managed to collect ten of the names. But, it will bloody well slow them down a bit. The bastards. It took me years to trace their steps. Years to document their activities —"

The guest interrupted. "Are you sure you've told me everything? You've left nothing out?"

"Yes. God help you. One day you may wish you never heard of Club Twelve," Marcus answered quietly.

The younger man stood abruptly and smiled. "Well then, there's only one more little detail to take care of now."

"And what would that be?" Marcus asked.

"You," his guest answered, taking an automatic weapon from his jacket and skillfully snapping a silencer in place.

The old man's eyes widened in disbelief; he brought a trembling hand to his mouth. "Oh, God. You're part of them," Radcliffe mumbled.

The gunman smiled coldly. "Yes. And you, old man, are the fool." He lowered his gun to Marcus's temple.

3

Marcus closed his eyes tightly. The killer fired twice, watched the old man's body slump over the couch, returned the gun calmly to his jacket, and walked out.

Chapter 1

March 1978

It was raining in Washington, D.C. and the wind gusted violently as Madison McGuire exited the grey corridors of the State Department Building. She raised the briefcase, which was cuffed to her right arm, over her head for protection and wished vaguely that she were one of those clever people who listened to weather reports and carried umbrellas.

Crowds rushed by, fighting the bitter March winds. Polished black shoes and high heels slapped loudly against the flooded concrete as Madison threaded her way to the dark green military sedan waiting at the curb. The driver standing at the rear door seemed oblivious to the foul weather, his cap anchored firmly under his right arm. As Madison approached, he nodded slightly and opened the door, his face expressionless, wax-like. Madison climbed in, dragging the briefcase behind her, and sighed heavily as the door closed.

It had been a hell of a day. For that matter, it had been a hell of a year. She was anxious to return to the seclusion of her hotel suite, a hot bath and a cool drink.

Only a few months ago, Madison mused as the sedan lurched forward in traffic, she had wanted to leave the National Operations Intelligence Service, sure that she could contribute no more. Already the business of government intelligence had cost the lives of the two people she loved most in the world.

However, leaving presented its own complications. What did one do after performing as a deep cover operative for nearly eighteen years? She had played too many roles over those years. Acted out too many parts. Was she really prepared to become just Madison McGuire?

A college would, no doubt, welcome someone with her knowledge of foreign affairs and the ability to speak several languages fluently. Yet somehow she could not envision herself attending faculty meetings and answering the inevitable questions: "Oh? You've never been married? How odd. One would think any man would leap at the opportunity of having an attractive woman like yourself." Madison smiled.

Several would have, had she ever presented them with the opportunity.

Deposited at last at the hotel, Madison crawled into bed and closed her eyes. Any hopes she had had of living a normal life had been destroyed by the merciless blast of an UZI, in London, one year ago.

On March nineteenth, 1977, Madison McGuire, code name Scorpion, had stepped off the military transport at Andrews Air Force Base, a detail of six field agents forming a human wall around her and escorting her to a government limousine. Each man and woman in the detail had been issued top priority clearance for his or her assignment because Madison's return to America, the first in years, was highly classified. Officially the attempt on America's most elusive operative had been a success. At least that was the report that rocked the London network and the intelligence communities around the world. Washington had responded immediately and took every precaution to make sure the reports were believable. Even the agents who protected her with their own bodies did not know her true identity. Only a handful of anonymous commanders, divisional heads and directors, who issued orders from unnamed, unmarked rooms leading off the corridors of the White House, knew that Scorpion was alive and operational.

The door of the limousine opened and Madison climbed in quickly. Inside sat the head of the NOIS, Andrew McFaye, Madison's friend, employer, mentor. Andrew's round face flushed as he held out his arms and Madison slid towards him, hugging him tightly, feeling his pleasant bulk surround her. His large full lips creased into a smile, the lines in his face deep like slashes in concrete. The slight sparkle in the pale blue eyes betrayed his concern. "It's good to have you home in one piece," he said. "I missed you, Madison."

Three of the agents piled into a lead car and the remaining three climbed into a tail car behind the limousine. The motorcade began moving slowly, defensively across the blacktop of the air force base.

"Madison," Andrew began slowly, "I got your letter of resignation two weeks ago. I hope you'll reconsider. However, under the circumstances I would understand if you —"

Madison broke in quietly. "All I know right now, Andy, is that I want to get the debriefing over with."

Andrew smiled slightly, remembering how unpleasant Madison found these procedures, how she had displayed her distaste for the routine polygraphs and long debriefing sessions several times over the years. Andrew had done what he could by ordering that all the standard sexual orientation questions be excluded, that the examiners were to stick with questions concerning her oath of secrecy and her loyalty to the agency.

Andrew smiled again, remembering her first polygraph after being in the field for a year. She had been brought back to NOIS headquarters after a leak had been discovered in their European network. Oh, she had passed the tests, but there had been an impressive display of temper when the examiner questioned her about her sexual preferences and frequency of masturbation.

8

The young operative had broken the straps attached to her wrist, threatened the examiner with bodily harm, and marched straight into Andrew's office. Andrew had attempted to explain that the questions were simply routine and that the sexual habits and preferences of their field agents were important to the agency. "Our policy," he had said, "has long been to eject any personnel suspected of engaging in homosexual activities. The theory is that homosexuals are known to have frequent and indiscriminate encounters. That poses a security risk. This is not a personal attack on you, Madison."

Young Madison's green eyes had blazed, he remembered. "It most certainly *is* a personal attack, Andy. How can you deny that? It's an attack on every man and woman who doesn't fit into what society calls the norm. Do you really believe what someone does in the privacy of their own bedroom has an effect on the quality of their professional performance? Has my performance been altered one bit since I discovered my own sexuality?"

"Madison, this is not my policy, it's an agency policy that would take years in our court system to rectify . . . Personally I believe that, as a woman, your performance could only be enhanced by your preference for women. You aren't subject to the same kind of temptations that a heterosexual woman might fall victim to. However, this new-found discovery, as you put it, does create a problem for both of us. We're going to have to break some rules."

He leaned closer to Madison, his elbows propped on his desk, and spoke quietly, almost in a whisper. "I can protect you up to a point, as long as I'm made aware of when you're going to be tested. But if you're called into a foreign station, for example, and I'm not notified of the screening, you'll have to find a way to beat the box. And there are ways, you know."

"I can't do that . . . I can't lie about this," was the answer after several moments of sulky hesitation.

"Jesus Christ," he had said, throwing his hands up to emphasize his frustration. "So what are your options here, huh? You want to announce it to the world? Fine. But you would be forced to leave the agency. And I think that would be a tragic mistake. You're doing what you've always wanted to do. You've already proved you can do the job. In a few years I can envision you making a real contribution to the agency and to your country. This kind of work takes a special type of person, Madison. And you've got natural instincts, a feel for it like I've only seen in a few people. Don't waste that talent."

Her decision had been to play the game . . . Another deception required in the secretive profession she had chosen.

Now, sitting in the limousine next to his veteran agent, it was hard for him to believe that seventeen years had elapsed.

"Since you've been gone," Andrew said casually, "we've moved into the new Langley headquarters. Sure beats the hell out of that old naval hospital we used to work out of. Remember that?"

Madison nodded vaguely, as she peered intently out the shaded window of the limousine, and Andrew knew her thoughts were far away. The balance of the journey was made in silence.

The debriefing lasted over thirty hours. After that an exhausted Madison McGuire requested a two-week leave. Andrew had gladly approved the time away, hoping that a vacation would help heal her wounds.

The operative who returned was much like the young woman Andrew had first trained. More contained, perhaps. More experienced, certainly, but as full of the passion and hatred that had consumed her so many years ago. One week after returning from her leave, Madison had told Andrew flatly, "I want back in the field. I can't sit in that radio room all day interpreting foreign radio broadcasts. You know that." Her tone was almost pleading.

Andrew leaned back in his chair and studied Madison for a moment. "Do you really think you're ready for another assignment? What happened in London was devastating for you. Too many lives depend on how an operative functions in the field. Whole networks could be destroyed with one mistake. Frankly, Madison, I'm concerned about your mental readiness."

Madison held up a hand. "Please, don't lecture me. I know how important it is." She lowered her voice and looked at Andrew, her gaze steady. "I appreciate your concern. But you must understand how important this is to me. Either you let me back out there, or I leave the agency and go it alone. It's your decision."

Andrew shook his head and sighed. "Give me a

11

few days. I've got something in mind for you. I'll have to get approval and work out the details first, though. No promises."

"Thanks," Madison answered with a smile, but there was no laughter in her eyes, only the sadness and anger Andrew had seen since her return to Langley.

Chapter 2

Surrounded by the wooded Virginia countryside, twenty miles from Williamsburg, sat the home of Andrew McFaye. Two of his guests had just arrived and the third had called saying he would be detained.

It was not unusual for Alexander Pratt, Secretary of State, to arrive late for meetings outside the White House such as this one. After all, it was not a social gathering, but a rather hastily called meeting at the end of what had already been a fourteen-hour day. The Secretary would have to brief the President, who, as agreed, would be the only other person to know the secretary's whereabouts on this evening. All the guests would come separately, using different automobiles and different routes in order to insure secrecy.

In the western-style den, Andrew McFaye got up from his favorite chair, which sat closest to the ever-burning fireplace. He was a stout man with a ruddy complexion and a large round nose. He took several short steps to the window and watched as the two limousine drivers who had delivered his guests leaned against their vehicles and talked quietly under the bright lights that shone on all sides of the McFaye home. He turned to his guests and asked, "Mark, Troy, can I fix you a drink?"

"Sure," answered Mark Hadden, Deputy Director for Operations of the Central Intelligence Agency. "I might as well get properly lit before the meeting starts. I'll have a bourbon, straight-up."

"How about you, Troy? You need a warm up? I've got a fresh pot on now." Andrew stood behind the heavy mahogany bar he had had custom-built several years earlier.

Troy Delcardo rose from the couch and crossed to the bar. "Thanks, Andy. I could use another cup. That ass Pratt will, no doubt, keep us up all night."

All three men laughed at this statement. It was no secret that Alexander Pratt loved the spotlight, and if called on to speak he could ramble endlessly. He was a performer and the press loved him. In this sense he had done a good job during his two years in office, managing to give the current administration a good old boy down-home image.

The intelligence community, however, regarded

14

Alex Pratt with little respect. When he took office he had demanded to know the details of all covert operations. He kept a close eye on the NOIS and the CIA. Shortly after the new administration was in place, Pratt had publicly denounced both agencies, citing them for several human rights violations and calling them a disgrace. Needless to say, there now was more than the normal amount of resentment between the administration and its intelligence agencies.

Andrew filled Troy's cup and returned to the window. The Director of Central Intelligence took a sip and studied Andrew over his cup. "Andrew," Delcardo began. "I couldn't help but notice that you seem a little preoccupied tonight. You've checked the window twice now."

Mark Hadden sat up on the edge of the couch and laughed quietly. "I think Andy's getting paranoid in his old age. After all, it is a syndrome common to our business."

McFaye turned and smiled, and at the same moment there were three loud knocks on the door.

"Evening, gentlemen," the Secretary of State said in the southern drawl he had made as famous as Lady-Bird Johnson's. He removed his coat and pitched it aside. Loosening his tie, he crossed the room to greet the men he had kept waiting.

Alex Pratt was not a particularly tall man and his pants always seemed a bit too long, making him look even shorter. He had thick silver hair neatly combed in place and a heavy grey mustache.

"Mr. Secretary," Mark Hadden said, standing to greet him. "It's always a pleasure, sir."

Pratt took his hand and shook it firmly. "You can drop the Mr. Secretary horseshit, Hadden. Call me Alex." Pratt turned and looked at Troy Delcardo.

"Good evening, Mr. Secretary," Delcardo said dryly, without offering his hand.

"Still don't like me, do you, Delcardo? Well, no one ever said we had to be best buddies in order to do our jobs." Pratt turned to Andrew. "Andrew, old buddy. It's always good to see you away from the pressures of Washington." He put his hand on Andrew's shoulder. "I'm sorry to hear about Marcus Radcliffe. I know you were close friends. Marcus was a great man in his time. The President asked me to offer his condolences."

"Thanks, Alex. That's very thoughtful. Now, can I get you a drink?"

"Hell, I know my way around," the secretary answered. "You just sit down and I'll rustle something up."

The three men waited while Alex Pratt poured himself a drink, drained it and poured another before joining them. He took the chair across from Andrew. Delcardo and Hadden remained on the couch which faced the two chairs.

Andrew McFaye began. "As you know, gentlemen, Marcus Radcliffe was murdered in his home in Glasgow. There is little doubt that the murder is directly related to the Club Twelve investigation. This complicates our position a great deal."

"Why?" the secretary broke in. "Radcliffe was an old man, an ex-British intelligence director. What does that have to do with our investigation?"

Troy Delcardo answered. "Radcliffe played a vital role in the operation, Mr. Secretary. We believe he

16

was going to provide us with a list of Club Twelve activities. He also indicated he could provide us with the names of at least ten of the twelve members."

Alexander Pratt raised a bushy eyebrow and Mark Hadden added in his precise Bostonian accent, "The evidence would have given us a strong foundation for our investigation. As you know, sir, to date we've been unsuccessful in producing any concrete evidence against the group. Our hope was that Radcliffe's files would give us enough information about Club Twelve's operation to infiltrate and expose them from the inside . . . Now, we're forced to examine alternative avenues."

"I see. And exactly what are these other avenues?" the secretary asked cautiously.

"We need Presidential approval, Alex, in order to conduct a complete investigation," Andrew answered as the secretary stood, returned to the bar and refilled his glass.

Pratt chuckled. "If you're talking about a covert operation, gentlemen, within the United States, you can forget it. We've just begun to recover from the disgraces exposed by the Rockefeller Commission hearings, not to mention the Church Committee findings. The seventies have been turbulent years for our intelligence community. Now is not the time to open a bucket of worms like this. We cannot and will not authorize this kind of operation. What if there's a flap? Hell, everybody from the FBI to Army Intelligence would be pissed off, not to mention what public opinion would do to this administration. The President hopes to be re-elected in nineteen eighty . . . No, it's entirely too risky, my friends."

The other three men exchanged frustrated glances

and Andrew began to speak, quietly, seriously. "Before you make any decisions, Alex, let me explain our reasoning. We've gathered intelligence that leads us to believe that at least one of the group's members is not only a U.S. citizen, but a top-level executive with one of our nation's largest defense contractors, Woodall Enterprises, Inc."

Alex Pratt nearly choked on his drink. "Why, that's impossible," he replied angrily. "Our government doesn't hand out contracts to a company that hasn't been fully investigated. And, I don't have to remind you that WEI contributed generously to the campaign which got this administration elected." Pratt paused and lowered his voice. "The function of the CIA and the NOIS is foreign intelligence. Let's keep it that way."

Andrew McFaye, a man who rarely lost his temper or raised his voice, found himself biting his own lip for control. "Damn it, Alex. You want foreign intelligence? I'll give you some right now." Hadden and Delcardo exchanged glances as Andrew went on. "Iran is currently in a pre-revolutionary state. Our sources tell us that plans are being made to overthrow the Shah. Many more friendly governments around the world are in the same position. We happen to know, without a doubt, that Club Twelve is helping to fund these take-overs. They're purchasing weapons, politicians, and whole armies in large numbers. Moving millions every day. What do you think is going to happen if the Shah, who we support, is overthrown?" Before the secretary could respond, Andrew added, "I'll tell you exactly what will happen. Every agent, every diplomat and every source we have in the Middle East will be

18

compromised and possibly even killed. Diplomatic relations will come to an immediate halt, and that fanatic bastard Khomeini will come into power. This is serious, Alex. It's no game, it's not some paranoid fantasy we dreamed up. I assure you that it is in the interest of national security that we want to run this operation. And, it is very much in your best interest that you agree to speak with the President and make a recommendation in our favor. We know you have a private interest in Woodall Enterprises."

"I resent that implication," the secretary roared. "How dare you hint that I would put my own personal interest before the interest of this great country?"

Andrew leaned back in his chair and smiled. "You'd resent it a lot more if others began asking questions. Listen, Alex. We don't give a shit about your financial investments. But let's face it, the press is hungry for copy these days."

"You bastards. Are you threatening me?" Pratt asked in disbelief.

Andrew reached for his pipe and lit it calmly before answering. "It's not a threat, Alex. It's simply fact."

Several moments of tense silence followed. At last, after what seemed an eternity, Pratt leaned forward. "Okay. I'm not here to argue with you. I'll make my recommendation but it will have to go through the regular channels. You'll have to have Congressional approval through the Appropriations Committees. And under the Foreign Intelligence Act which we just passed you must have a court order to perform any electronic eavesdropping within the United States. It's because your agencies tend to get out of control that we now have stringent laws to protect our citizens. You can't justify everything you do any more by saying it's in the interest of national security."

Troy Delcardo, director of the largest intelligence-gathering agency in the world, stood, his face flushed. "There are exceptions to those laws, Mr. Secretary. The CIA may infiltrate organizations if they are believed to be acting on behalf of a foreign power . . . Your new policy of openness sabotages our operations before they get off the ground. We cannot report every move we make to some goddamn liberal committee. There's too many people involved, and there's always a leak somewhere. Covert operations quickly become overt operations. It's not smart, and it's this kind of attitude and unwarranted restraints put on us, largely by this administration, that freezes our ability to collect accurate intelligence. This is a time of increasing danger to the United States, and you're making sure the intelligence community loses its ability to provide the President with necessary and intelligent analyses."

Delcardo waved a hand and continued. "Jesus Christ, we're a fucking joke overseas. They say that CIA stands for caught in the act. Public confidence has eroded to the point that American citizens won't even cooperate with their own intelligence agencies."

He bent down and looked directly into the secretary's face. "It's you, Pratt, and others like you that put us in the position of not being able to function properly, and then you crucify us publicly when we don't perform. How about showing a little backbone, and give us back the authority to make critical decisions so we can become a reliable and productive instrument again, instead of kissing the fat asses of all those committees." Delcardo finished his speech, his face still beet red, and walked rapidly to the bar. "To hell with coffee, Andy, I need a real drink."

The secretary turned and studied Delcardo for a moment before he spoke. "And you're suggesting that I obtain Presidential approval in order to override the laws of this nation?"

Delcardo threw his hands up, walked back to the couch and sank into it in quiet anger.

"Why, it would be political suicide," Pratt continued. "The President would never approve such an action." He paused and added, "Not in writing, anyway."

Chapter 3

It was a dangerous game. No court order would be issued. The Appropriations Committees and the Senate and House Intelligence Committees would not be aware that a foreign intelligence-gathering agency was conducting a covert operation within the United States.

Operation Accounting Central did receive a verbal approval from the White House. But it was made clear that the approval would be denied the moment any part of the operation became public. The President would seem appropriately shocked to discover that the CIA and the NOIS were at the heart of such an operation. Their lack of consideration for civil rights would be appalling. To think that they would, without his knowledge, place listening devices on the telephones of American citizens, open their mail and practice surveillance would be an outrage. Andrew McFaye and Troy Delcardo would be handed over to a Senate investigating panel on a silver platter.

In the heavily guarded, restricted access area on the fourth floor of the State Department Building, four people sat around a long conference table. Outside, two guards were posted, one at each end of the grey corridor. The four people inside the unmarked, bare-walled room, whose ages ranged from forty-five to sixty-eight, made decisions no one outside this room would ever know about. Decisions they would have to endure. Right or wrong. These four were the planners of clandestine activities, the highly concentrated strategists, the spymasters, the quintessential thinkers. All, save one, had practical experience in covert operations: a woman of fifty-five named Marge Price.

A specialist with a Ph.D. in human behavior, Marge had never served in the field — nor had she ever had the desire, for she had seen the kind of anxiety it produced. Her job did have its share of sleepless nights, but it was a controlled stress and Marge could deal with that. She liked knowing where her enemies were, rather than guessing who might next emerge from the shadows.

23

Marge Price was a specialist in manipulation. Others actually squeezed the trigger. Her job was to anticipate every variation, every action and reaction to a sensitive operation. On her evaluation an operation could be scrapped. With a nod from Marge Price an operative could be issued a deadly assignment, given more — or less — responsibility, taken out of the field completely, even terminated if it was in the interest of national security. The burdens of her decisions weighed heavily on her at times. Still she was thankful she had never actually performed the kill herself.

Gerold Rutledge, one of the three men in the group, was head of intelligence operations for the State Department. A thin man of forty-five with parenthesis-shaped gashes at the corners of his mouth and deep lines around his eyes, his lined face betrayed his young years. Rutledge had graduated from the Defense Intelligence College when he was only thirty, after spending four years at Yale and serving a short stint with the super secret National Security Agency. He was nicknamed Wonder Boy because of his rapid climb to the high ranks of Washington, D.C. Rutledge was one of the youngest and most respected strategists in the government.

The other two members of the group were Troy Delcardo and Andrew McFaye.

Today these four people had designed a plan for an operation aimed at infiltrating an anonymous and dangerous group, Club Twelve.

Club Twelve was not a new concern for the U.S. government, or for governments around the world. Most had been aware of the group's existence since 1952. However, all previous attempts to infiltrate the organization had failed miserably, and the cost had been high. American, British and Israeli agents had lost their lives. All four people in this room agreed that Operation Accounting Central was a long shot, but it provided more potential than previous operations. The first step was to place an "asset" inside Woodall Enterprises, Inc., which in nine years had become the government's largest supplier of weaponry of all kinds.

The person they needed to place inside the company must be able to enter at top level. Someone who would have immediate access to company records. The NOIS believed it had found that person, a law student from Harvard who had already been offered a position within the firm. The daughter of Edward Woodall, owner of WEI.

Andrew McFaye opened the manila folder in front of him and handed its contents to Marge Price. "I want you to go over this information, Marge, and give us a complete evaluation. It's everything we could dig up on the Woodall kid. I need to know your ideas on the best possible recruiting methods. Secondly, I want to know what you think about having Madison McGuire handle the recruitment."

Marge took the information and nodded.

Troy Delcardo looked at the three people sitting at the table with him. "Frankly, I just don't get it. Why would Club Twelve supply Syria, Iran and Libya with funds and weapons? Why support terrorist groups like Baader-Meinhof, the Red Brigades, Hizbullah and Islamic Jihad? They're stopping humanitarian shipments of food and medical supplies and replacing them with guns and explosives." He rubbed his temples. "Today we discovered that one of our finest

25

Senators has taken himself out of the nineteen-eighty Presidential race. We suspect he's being blackmailed and my sources tell me a large organization is behind it . . . Why? What do they hope to accomplish?"

Marge Price studied Troy for a moment. Her left eyebrow arched slightly and a faint smile crossed her stern face. "Come now, Troy. You're not that naive. I think there's only one real explanation. In a word, Chaos. When you drive a country's people into the ground, starve them, take every ounce of strength and pride away from them, control brutal governments and then give those same people weapons to fight back with, you have revolution . . . Chaos. Surely you understand that. The CIA has done the same thing."

"Bullshit," Delcardo answered. "The CIA has never starved people. We've never encouraged a Communist regime."

Marge Price shrugged her wide shoulders and lit a cigarette. "Maybe not." She pushed a stray lock of grey-brown hair from her forehead. "But you've helped begin revolutions. You've supplied arms, money, propaganda, whatever . . . Jesus, Troy, I'm not attacking your agency, I'm merely making a point. We do it when we want control. I'm just saying that Club Twelve does it for the same reasons: complete and total control. Maybe they promote revolution because it's the only way to get their own people into power. They can walk into the hell they've created and look like saviors. Suddenly the fighting and the horror will end. Wouldn't the masses be so goddamn glad to have someone at the controls that they'd welcome new leadership? Leadership that promises to end their struggling? It makes perfect sense to me. It's a clear case of manipulation. We do it every day in one way or another."

"I think Marge is right," Gerold Rutledge piped in. "It's happened before, and not so long ago. A charismatic leader takes control, rebuilds the economy, promises a decent life to his followers . . . Look what Hitler did."

Madison McGuire sat straight up in bed, her body wet with perspiration.

Elicia . . . No, wait . . . Oh, God, no . . . Please . . . Her own screams had shaken her out of a sound sleep. The images had been so real, so violent, that tears streamed down her face. In the total darkness one only finds in a hotel room, Madison reached under her pillow for her gun, a custom Smith and Wesson M686, and began to disassemble it. She went through the process several times, quickly, skillfully tearing it down and snapping it back together again. It calmed her somehow. It was familiar. It was something she understood and it helped to wash away the nightmares that had haunted her since that terrible day in London.

She turned on the bedside lamp and squinted in the sudden bright light to see her watch. "Jesus," she muttered aloud. "Only eleven forty-five. Going to be a long night."

She climbed out of bed, stretching her lean five-foot-seven-inch frame as she padded into the suite's living room and across to the wet bar.

Curling up on the couch, scotch in hand, she lit a cigarette and stared blankly at the wall. How lost she

27

felt in America, how lonely without Elicia next to her at night . . . She sipped her scotch slowly and fought back the tears.

In November of that year Madison had turned forty. The nightmares had become intermittent. She anxiously awaited her new assignment, the first undercover assignment since her return to America. Soon she would have her chance to strike back at the men who had turned her life into a living hell.

The assignment called for her to play several different roles. First she was to recruit a woman named Terry Woodall. Madison had handled dozens of recruitments during her eighteen years of government service, including two Soviet agents and a former member of the IRA. This recruitment, she was sure, would present no problems. Americans, she mused, were generally easier targets. The God and Country speech was nearly always successful. Especially when you believed it yourself.

The second part of the assignment had taken weeks of preparation. Her cover name: Paula Emerson, owner of a large international architectural design firm. In fact, Emerson Designs was a very real and flourishing business — one of the many front or "cut-out" organizations owned by the CIA. Other such businesses included research centers, printing companies, a well-known newspaper, car rental agencies and one major airline.

A year ago the CIA man who ran Emerson Designs suffered a fatal heart attack. Two months later the CIA made use of its newspaper to spread a rumor that the man's widow would soon be taking control of the operation, thus providing a convenient cover for Madison should she ever have to walk into the tight security offices of WEI, since WEI was one of Emerson's largest accounts. Hopefully, she would never have to actually go into WEI at all. She would merely act as back-up in case the new recruit ran into trouble.

Madison's third role, the most important to her, would be to perform surveillance on certain suspected members of Club Twelve and assist any law enforcement agency that could make an arrest once the necessary evidence was collected. How she looked forward to that day.

She felt better and more focused now than she had in quite some time. Her first two months after returning from England had been spent in the Langley radio rooms. It had been a lesson in patience.

Today, Madison had returned from Camp Peary where her last several months had been spent drilling new recruits at the Clandestine Planning Center by day, and drilling herself for her new assignment by night.

Camp Peary, nicknamed "The Farm," was a ten-thousand-acre complex that made boot camp seem like a vacation resort. The Farm was the main training center for the CIA, a thirty-million-dollar complex used for clandestine instruction, complete with its own airstrip and a restricted stretch of the York River used for maritime training. On its massive wooded grounds the CIA had created fake borders that included tank traps, mines, watch towers and dog-handling guards to train young operatives in clandestine entry.

This morning, upon returning to Langley headquarters, Madison had been given orders to go to the State Department. Waiting for her there behind an unmarked door was Marge Price, a woman Madison knew only by reputation. Price had shown Madison a thick dossier, locked it in a briefcase and cuffed it to Madison's wrist. She had then insisted that Madison have a military escort back to her suite.

Madison sat on the couch and opened the briefcase. Several eight by ten inch photographs tumbled out as she lifted the tall stack of papers neatly piled inside. Leaning back on the couch, she picked up one of the photos and studied it closely. Its subject: a young woman wearing jeans and a short tailored jacket. Her dark hair was pulled back loosely and several strands had broken free and hung around a triangular face. The eyes were dark, the brows thick, and she was laughing with another woman.

Madison lit a cigarette and turned the photograph over, reading the information printed on the reverse side. The dark-haired woman was identified as Teresa (Terry) Woodall. The second woman was reported to be Terry's homosexual lover. Madison involuntarily raised an eyebrow. This was a detail Andrew had neglected to mention. She looked at the photograph once more and smiled. "So, we meet at last," she muttered aloud before reaching for the other photographs.

In a matter of minutes Madison was deep into the dossier, poring over the background information. In two months she would travel to Colorado and approach Terry Woodall for the first time. By then she would know everything about Terry that could be documented from elementary school through college, from her favorite color to her political views.

Chapter 4

Madison McGuire sat in the back of a van parked in a wealthy Boulder, Colorado neighborhood. The van appeared to be a Mountain Bell telephone truck but was actually a sophisticated listening post. Beside her sat Robert Grier from the Office of Communications Division of the CIA. The OC's main function was to install and maintain communications equipment, including transmitters and receivers from the simple to high frequency and microwave.

Early this morning Robert Grier, dressed as a telephone repairman, had entered the home of

Virginia Woodall on the pretense of reported line trouble. He had produced identification supplied to him by the agency's Documents Division and had placed listening devices in several rooms of the Woodall home and on the telephones.

"Here we go," Grier said, seeing a line of dots appear on his computer screen. Madison heard several bleeps, and Grier noted the numbers that were being dialed from inside the house. He repeated the numbers aloud and Madison quickly typed them into her computer keyboard.

"Coming up now," Madison looked at the name and address appearing on the screen. "Michael Rubeck at six-eighty-two Golden Drive, Denver."

"Oh, shit," Grier said nervously. "The call's being forwarded to another number. I can't tell where it's going."

Madison quickly picked up a set of headphones.

"Library," a voice answered. "Michael?" asked the voice from inside the house. Madison had heard this voice several times during the last hours of eavesdropping, and knew it belonged to Terry Woodall.

The conversation continued. "I'd love to see you again," Michael Rubeck said. "Why don't you stop by tonight, around eight. It's slow then."

Madison began typing into the computer and her answer soon appeared across the screen: THE LIBRARY: 684 EAST BROADWAY-DENVER-MEMBERSHIP ONLY-HOMOSEXUAL NIGHTCLUB.

Robert Grier turned to Madison and smiled. "Well, it looks like tonight's the night. You're gonna have to socialize with a bunch of queers all night."

Madison glared at Grier for a moment, and then smiled. "It's a tough job. Come on. Let's go."

Terry Woodall walked through the dimly lit entrance to the nightclub and saw two levels with dark cherry wood tables. A bar sat in the center of the upper level and a lone pianist played softly in the northern corner. The carpeting throughout was a deep burgundy, and handwoven rugs decorated the walls. The lower level was filled with light mauve-colored couches and chairs, all in individual groupings. A bar, tended by a tuxedoed bartender, sat against the far wall, and two people played chess on a small table under a soft tinted light. Terry saw an adjoining room downstairs, filled with tall bookcases which were crammed with books. The center of the room was filled with long tables for reading.

She heard a voice behind her and turned to see her old friend Michael, handsome in his tuxedo. His sandy-brown hair was longer than Terry remembered, and hung a full inch below his collar, and he wore a mustache.

"Terry, it's so good to see you," he said, hugging her tightly, a broad smile on his face. "Well? What do you think?" He gestured around the club.

"It's beautiful, Michael, really. How did you get this place?"

"The old man helped me out with a loan." He took Terry's arm and walked her towards the bar. "Took a while to get it fixed up, we had some trouble with the zoning board at first. The neighborhood businesses weren't exactly thrilled about having a gay club down the street. But we worked it out."

Terry tried to hide her surprise. "This is a gay bar?"

"Absolutely," Michael answered smiling. "Do you think I'd have it any other way? Listen, how about coming to the house on Thursday. I'll take the night off. You can meet Daniel. But for now, catch me up. What's been going on with you? How's your love life, girlfriend?"

"Well, you know Cindy and I broke up. That's old news. We were just so different. She wasn't ready for a commitment." She shrugged. "Anyway, since then it's just been a few dates. Nothing serious. I'm still waiting for Ms. Right." She laughed.

Suddenly she found herself distracted by the woman coming through the entrance. She had deep red hair that waved slightly into a bun. Her slender figure was accented by a sleek black dress.

Michael smiled, and whispered in Terry's ear. "New member. Just joined today. Her name is Paula, I believe."

"She's beautiful," Terry answered quietly.

Michael laughed and waved a hand. "Some things never change. Go for it. I have to get some work done before the rush starts. Have fun, see you on Thursday."

Terry ordered a bourbon and seven, took a deep breath and sat on the stool closest to Madison. She was in the process of deciding her approach when the woman turned, as if she had sensed Terry's intentions, and introduced herself as Paula Emerson.

Terry was immediately struck by the fine aquiline nose, the chiseled features and a most disarming

35

smile. "It's nice to meet you," Terry said, taking the woman's hand. "I'm Terry Woodall. Could I buy you a drink?"

"Only if I buy the next round," Madison answered, and Terry noticed the British accent immediately.

"Woodall is a familiar name," Madison said, sipping her white wine. "I have a client named Woodall. Edward Woodall. Any relationship?"

"He's my father," Terry answered, surprised.

"He's a very interesting man," Madison added.

"You don't have to be gentle," Terry said with a laugh. "It's common knowledge he's a very difficult man. I don't envy you. I don't think I could work with him." Terry took a drink of the bourbon, feeling the steady gaze of Madison's bright green eyes on her.

Madison pulled a long brown cigarette from her bag, and Terry fumbled for the glass filled with matches on the bar. She was annoyed to see that her hand trembled when she held the match to the cigarette. Madison smiled as if she understood, steadied Terry's hand, and gently blew out the match. She took a long drag and Terry watched in fascination as the smoke curled around the full lips. Their eyes met and Madison held Terry's until finally Terry let her gaze drop shyly back to her drink.

"Do you live in Denver?" Terry asked, and again took in the wide green eyes and the full lips that turned down slightly at the corners. She watched Madison's thin fingers outlining the rim of her wine glass and wondered if the flush of heat she felt was obvious. Madison smiled. "Would you like to move to a table?" she asked, already knowing that Terry was a willing subject.

More bourbon and wine were delivered. The piano played soft jazz, the black dress raised and lowered with every breath that Madison took, and it was clear that Terry Woodall was quickly becoming intoxicated by the heady atmosphere.

Terry talked about going to school at Harvard, about her family, her likes and dislikes, all of which Madison knew from reading the thick dossier.

"So," Terry said at length. "Tell me about Paula Emerson."

Madison smiled and reached for Terry's hand. "I'm certain you would find me exceedingly dull, my dear," she answered quietly, and then added, "Terry, would it be possible for me to call you while you're in town? Perhaps we could get together."

Almost before Madison finished, Terry had managed to scribble her number across a cocktail napkin. Madison looked at the number with satisfaction, and stood. "I'll call," she said, stroking Terry's cheek before turning to leave.

Terry watched as Madison exited the club, then took a deep breath, and fell back into her chair.

The next morning Terry shook herself out of sleep enough to answer the persistently ringing telephone.

"Terry, Paula Emerson here. How are you this morning, my dear?" Madison asked pleasantly.

"Paula . . . ? I'm fine. I think. I mean, I was asleep, but I'm glad you called." Terry turned to see the bedside clock. Seven a.m. Jesus, she thought.

"I have a marvelous idea," Madison went on. "Would you like to join me in Vail this weekend? I have a condominium there. It seems a waste to let it sit unoccupied. We could leave Friday and return on Sunday. Sound good?"

Terry sat up in bed. "Sounds great. I haven't been in Vail for years. I don't have a car though. I'm spending my vacation at my mother's house."

"No problem, love. I'll pick you up around seven on Friday. See you then."

At the end of a secluded, tree-lined street in one of Denver's most exclusive neighborhoods sat a large old English Tudor-style home. From the outside it looked like any other home in the wealthy area. The grounds were impeccably kept. Weaving, wandering patterns of shrubbery could be seen leading back to the massive fountains guarded by stone figures.

Yet, inside, the old home was different. The windows were a full inch thick and capable of withstanding the impact of a high caliber weapon. The grounds, front and back, were wired and heat-sensitive. A quiet alarm and a series of light patterns and communication equipment would be activated should anyone enter the area, and video cameras would automatically begin operation. No one came in or out of seven-fifty-seven Aspen Drive without a series of photographs being taken. The computers inside would then process the data and within seconds a complete background file on any intruder would appear on the screen. Several of the rooms in the house were soundproofed and the entire house was swept for listening devices daily.

The old house was a fortress, a sterile location used for the sensitive business of government intelligence. More commonly referred to as a "safe house" it was used frequently for covert meetings, to house foreign visitors in secrecy and occasionally for interrogation purposes.

A man and his wife occupied one quarter of the house for appearance purposes. These trusted employees, who had been released from conventional government service in order to take their post here, often took walks around the neighborhood, and no one in the area had any reason to suspect that the house was anything other than what it appeared.

Inside, Madison McGuire leaned against the desk in the study, the telephone receiver in her hand. She walked around the desk and stubbed out a cigarette. She said in an annoyed tone, "Christ, Andrew, we've been through this before. Of course I can handle it, but I don't have to like it. It's too late to turn back anyway. The plumbing's already in place. We've developed a complete support structure, contacts, secure ways to communicate. Don't pull out on me now."

"You're having second thoughts, aren't you?" Andrew asked. "I know you, Madison, and I sense a change in attitude. What the hell happened? Everything was tits and diamonds before you met this kid."

Madison sighed heavily. "I like her, Andy. She's a very nice young woman. I suppose I'm feeling a bit

39

responsible for her welfare. I know those bastards at sixteen-hundred. They'll use her and toss her aside like a rag doll. What happens to her after the operation is over?" She paused and lit a cigarette. "Christ, I don't know what I'm trying to say. I realize the operation takes priority. I'm the one who pushed you to use me. You don't have to bring in someone else . . . Besides, I'm the best you've got."

His phone in his hand, Andrew McFaye leaned back in the wicker chair on his patio and took a deep breath. Madison was right. She was the best. For years she had contributed as much or more than any other single operative in the field. She had been able to penetrate front lines and gather intelligence that even the most experienced agents shied away from. Madison seldom rejected any assignment offered her, and at times she had surprised her male counterparts with her seemingly ruthless approach to her work. In truth, Madison was not ruthless, just very passionate. It was because her feelings ran so deep that she was capable of calculated revenge.

She's so much like her father, Andrew mused. Jake McGuire had also had a driving need to clean up the household of the world. He had been relentless in his pursuits and at times foolishly brave.

Twenty-one years ago Jake had been killed when his cover was exposed in a Middle-Eastern country. It was then that he extracted a promise from Andrew. "Take care of Madison," he pleaded. "She'll need someone now."

Madison had been nineteen then. Andrew had tried to be there for her, had tried to guide her, had tried to discourage her from following her father's footsteps, but he could not.

40

After graduating college at twenty-two, Madison officially entered government service. Andrew gave up on trying to discourage her and opted for teaching her everything he could about the profession she had chosen.

They had had their disagreements over the years. He had been horrified the day she announced to him that she was a lesbian, and she made no attempt to disguise her distaste over his reaction. "How can you be so self-righteous?" she had demanded. "There is so little definition between right and wrong in this business. Every day, Andrew, you cross over boundaries that would horrify the average person. Yet you have the gall to tell me this is wrong?"

He still wished that Madison had chosen another direction. He still believed that she had a choice in the matter, but he had used his considerable powers to shield her from the intractable homophobia of the U.S. government.

Now Andrew spoke quietly into the telephone. "All right, Madison. You know what to do. How you do it is entirely up to you. Just remember that we need that girl. And be goddamn sure you get her to sign that affidavit. Understood?"

"Yes. I understand. You'll have your asset before the weekend is over."

Andrew chuckled. "Well, don't sound so depressed. Everything is going our way."

"It's the methods I object to," Madison broke in. "It isn't fair."

"Fair?" Andrew shouted. "What is this *fair* shit? Don't tell me ole hard ass McGuire is going soft." He paused and lowered his voice. "Listen, I understand that you're a little gun shy after what happened in

41

London. But it wasn't your fault, Madison. You know how hard it is for people like us to maintain any kind of normal relationship. Jesus, we can't even leave a phone number when we take off on an assignment. Sometimes our professional lives spill over into our personal lives, and sometimes people get hurt. Nobody ever said it was fair, but it's the life we've chosen. Don't confuse this assignment with what happened over there. And, *do not get personally involved.* This girl means nothing to you. She is merely the vehicle we need right now. Keep your priorities in order, McGuire, or I'll see that you're put on permanent R and R."

"I'll handle it," Madison answered, and hung up abruptly. She reached for one of the eight by ten inch photographs of Terry Woodall that lay across the desk, and sighed. There was no denying that something stirred when she looked at Terry . . . She cursed aloud and tossed the picture across the desk.

The last thing that Madison wanted now was any emotional involvement with another woman. It had taken years of sexually and emotionally unfulfilling encounters before she had fallen in love for the first time, and then tragically lost that love. She was not willing to endure that heartbreak again. Not now. Especially not now when it was vital to the success of an operation that she stay focused.

Chapter 5

A stocky, slightly graying man sat behind his sixteenth floor desk in the tinted glass building overlooking Atlanta's Peachtree Plaza business district, a well-used cigar mashed between the fat fingers of his right hand, a gold pen in his left. Occasionally he leaned back in his chair, which barely allowed his feet to touch the floor, and stared out the window at nothing in particular. He was searching for the right words and absent-mindedly tapping his pen against the walnut desk top. He had never been good at letter writing. It made him feel inadequate, and inadequacy was a feeling that rarely touched the life of Edward Clark Woodall. Tossing his pen across the desk, he muttered, "To hell with it," leaned back in his chair once again and chewed on the soggy cigar.

Edward Woodall had made a fortune. His money had not always been made inside the law, but basically he was a man who believed that the end *does* justify the means. He had been successful at most every undertaking in his life, save one. He and his daughter were practically strangers.

The buzzer sounded, interrupting his thoughts. His short stubby fingers reached for the box next to his telephone. "Mr. Woodall," his secretary announced, "Mr. Guiseppe is here to see you."

"Send him in. Oh, and Anne, how about some fresh coffee."

Louis Guiseppe, Woodall's illegitimate son and a vice president of WEI, walked into the office, a broad smile on his handsome face. "Ed, it's good to be back," he said, extending his hand. "You look tired."

Woodall looked at Guiseppe for a moment. He was so different from the insecure young man of nineteen who had been introduced as his son twenty years ago.

Edward Woodall would never forget that day. He would never forget the nervousness he felt after receiving a letter from Maria Guiseppe, the first woman he had ever loved, telling him that he had a son of nineteen. He had wondered so many times why Maria had disappeared from his life so suddenly, why she hadn't told him that she was pregnant with his child.

Woodall was not a particularly introspective or sensitive man. It had never occurred to him that

Maria Guiseppe might be frightened of him. It never crossed his mind that she could not forgive him one drunken evening when he had forced himself on her, and she had become pregnant.

Now, nearly forty years later, he studied his son who stood in his office. "Sit down, Louis, and tell me about your trip."

Guiseppe smiled and crossed to the bar in the corner of Woodall's office. "I'm happy to say it went very well. The good Senator has reconsidered and decided not to run in the election."

Guiseppe was not a tall man. He stood five-feet-eight inches perhaps, but he radiated an aura of power, of complete and total confidence. His perfectly groomed hair was stylish and the soft brown eyes exuded sex appeal. Dressed in a Saville Row suit, he gave the impression he had just stepped off the cover of *G.Q.* Guiseppe was a likeable man, outgoing and friendly when he chose to be. One felt immediately comfortable in his presence. Unless, of course, one knew him well.

Woodall knew that the man behind the handsome face was a sly and cunning businessman. The inner Louis Guiseppe was secretive, cool, even cruel. In his sixteen years with WEI he had become a feared and respected force. His skills in negotiation had landed the company its first government contract several years ago and had enabled them to grow to one of the largest defense contractors in the world. In addition, Guiseppe had meticulously obtained information over the years that, if made public, would put an abrupt end to the careers of several top level executives in the White House and Defense Department.

Edward Woodall smiled. "What changed the Senator's mind?" he asked.

Guiseppe looked up from pouring his drink and answered casually. "A million dollars and some pictures of his wife in some, shall we say, compromising positions."

Woodall stood and crossed the room. "Pour me a drink, boy. This calls for a celebration."

The two men touched glasses in satisfaction.

Vail was as spectacular as Terry remembered. The view from Madison's balcony was breathtaking. The early morning sun cast a dim light across Gore Mountain Range and the snow-capped peaks of Vail Mountain shone in fluorescent beauty. Just a few hundred yards down Gore Creek Drive, Terry could see the lights of Vail Village coming on one at a time. The local storekeepers were preparing for another day of trade.

She smiled and leaned back in the patio chair. The morning air was thin and brisk. She warmed her hands on a hot mug of steaming coffee she had quietly prepared in the kitchen while Madison slept upstairs.

Paula . . . Beautiful Paula Emerson . . . Who are you? There was something mysterious, unsettling about the woman. An odd mixture of warm and cold. A sort of casual intensity. Yet Terry sensed that just beneath the surface a fire raged white hot. It was something in the eyes. She had seen it four nights ago in a candle-lit bar in Denver, and then again on the ride to Vail last night. Something just behind

46

those feline-like eyes had lashed out at her and then, in an instant, retreated behind the placid green ice. The eyes betrayed the woman. She was calm on the surface, the eyes were not. Terry remembered feeling weak under the strange gaze. There was something almost frightening about that gaze. Yet Terry was not afraid, only strangely drawn to the fire.

Madison's driver, Marshall, had driven them to Vail last evening, and once again Madison had managed to avoid any questions about herself and skillfully changed the subject. She had seemed distant, if not cool, Terry thought. It was odd, considering their first meeting. Then, when they had arrived in Vail, Madison had been careful to point out the spare bedroom and assure Terry she would be very comfortable there.

Terry sighed and took a sip of black coffee. She heard a sound behind her and turned to see Madison smiling down at her, the thick red hair falling recklessly just below her shoulders. Madison leaned over and gave Terry a quick kiss on the cheek, and as she did so the terry-cloth bathrobe parted slightly, exposing a hint of high, round breasts. "Good morning, my dear," Madison said cheerfully. "We're up bright and early, aren't we."

Madison edged her way around the small balcony and took a chair across from Terry. She sipped her coffee slowly and turned to admire the view. "It's quite beautiful here. Don't you agree?" she said, and when Terry did not answer she turned and looked at her. "Feeling all right? You seem rather pensive."

"I'm sorry," Terry answered, staring into her mug. "I guess I'm not really awake yet." She paused and looked up at Madison, and the bright smile

Madison had seen so many times during their first two meetings reappeared. "I can't tell you, Paula, how good it is to see that your eyes get puffy in the morning just like the rest of us mere mortals."

Madison laughed quietly. "Well, I must say, you have a rather strange sense of pleasure. Did you ever doubt that I was anything but mortal? I assure, I am reminded of my mortality quite often."

"Paula, tell me about you," Terry said seriously.

"What would you like to know?" Madison responded without emotion.

"I don't know. Where you grew up. Your parents, your life, your lovers. The same things you wanted to know about me. It's only fair, you know," she added with a smile.

Madison leaned back in her chair and crossed her legs. She held her cup of coffee close to her for warmth. "I've spent the biggest part of my life in England. My father was transferred there when I was barely crawling. He worked for the American government as their London Station Chief. My mother died when I was very young, only five years old, of leukemia. I barely remember at all. Although my father always said I am very much like my mother. I returned to America for a few years after my father died when I was around twenty, and since then I've traveled back and forth."

"Where did you study architecture? In England or in the States?" Terry asked cautiously.

Madison smiled. "Why I do believe you are grilling me, counselor. It's called pressing the witness, is it not?"

Terry laughed. "You're right. I'm sorry. The truth is, I find you very mysterious."

48

Madison leaned forward and touched Terry's hand. "I assure you, I am quite ordinary . . . Now, what would you like to do today?" she asked, once again skillfully changing the subject. The maneuver was not lost on Terry, but she was beginning to see that pressing the woman she knew as Paula Emerson would be futile.

Terry told Madison about the view from the top where one could see the whole of Gore Mountain Range covered with columbines, daisies and salsify seed in full bloom, and they decided on a hike up Vail Mountain.

Terry, having had a long shower, her dark hair wrapped in a towel, headed for the spare bedroom where she changed into jeans and a flannel shirt. She started downstairs, noticing that the voice she thought she heard from the bathroom was silent. It must have been Marshall, the driver. Halfway down the stairs Terry stopped and saw Madison sitting on the living room floor, wearing jeans and no make-up, humming to herself as she packed a few items in the backpacks that lay next to her. Then Terry saw the dark metal object and watched as Madison stuffed it into one of the packs. It was a gun. Terry stiffened and took a deep breath before continuing down the stairs.

"Hunting season is over," she said sarcastically, standing behind Madison.

Madison was not even startled by Terry's sudden appearance. Terry wondered if she had known that she was there all along.

"You never know when you may need one of these," Madison answered calmly. "And, by the way, I don't hunt. I take no pleasure in killing." She *had* killed, she reflected grimly, more times than she wanted to remember. But in self-defense. In desperate protection of her own life and for her country, *only* for her country.

Terry sat next to her, and asked, "Well, then, why would someone carry a gun if they don't want to kill something or someone?"

Madison turned and looked at Terry, her eyes serious. She spoke quietly. "There is so much I want to tell you, Terry. Perhaps one day I can. But for now you'll have to trust me. This gun is merely a precaution. I've made some enemies in the corporate world. Angry competitors and that sort of thing, but I assure you there is nothing to be concerned about. I should tell you that Marshall is a bodyguard of sorts. He'll be walking with us today. I'm afraid he insisted. However, I've instructed him to keep his distance."

Terry looked at her, unsure, and Madison continued, "Please believe me. I carry it more out of habit than anything else. Come on, old girl, relax."

Terry relaxed a bit and attempted to lighten the conversation. "I shoot a little. When I moved to Boston alone, my family insisted I buy a gun and learn to use it. I don't know much about them though. I've never seen one like that."

Madison pulled the weapon out of the backpack and efficiently emptied the chamber. "This is a Smith and Wesson M686 with a four inch barrel. It's very compact, but it's chambered for a three-fifty-seven magnum cartridge, so it's also powerful. It has a non-reflective finish and a round butt. And, right here, I had a custom grip adaptor made, which supports the second finger and keeps the weapon from sinking too far down in your hand from the heavy recoil." Madison paused and ran her index finger gently over the smooth finish. "It's really a very nice little weapon. Don't you agree?" she asked, grabbing the barrel and handing the gun to Terry.

Terry's jaw dropped in astonishment. Her eyes were slightly glazed. Madison had rattled off the weapon's specifications so quickly, so efficiently, that Terry barely had time to digest the information or its meaning. The room was totally silent for several moments, while the two exchanged eye contact. Finally, Terry muttered, barely audibly, "That's incredible."

At length Madison inquired, "What do you find so incredible?"

"I'm going hiking with Dirty Harry," Terry stated flatly, and after several seconds both women broke out into laughter.

It was almost noon. The two women climbed the mountain, carefully side-stepping cactus, jagged rock and an occasional patch of shaded snow under a vast western sky. Terry had already shed her flannel shirt in favor of the light undershirt she wore underneath. About a hundred yards back she became winded and fell behind. Madison, several yards in front, stopped and smiled. "Want to stop for a while and enjoy the scenery?"

Terry looked grateful. "Please, I could use a break. Jesus, it must be the altitude." Madison leaned against a small aspen and handed Terry a bottle of water. Terry accepted and drank quickly. "You could have told me you were in such great shape, you know."

Madison simply smiled and slid down into a horizontal position, taking off her flannel shirt and using it as a pillow. She closed her eyes to the warm sunlight.

Terry turned and studied her. The arms were tan, the muscles well defined by long circular lines around the biceps. The forearms were strong with an equal amount of definition, yet deliciously feminine. Madison's hands were slender with short, well-kept nails. This, Terry mused, is not the body of someone who sits behind a desk all day in high heels.

Madison turned and caught Terry staring. "What are you thinking about?"

"About you," Terry answered seriously. "About who you really are. About why you're so damn secretive. Tell me why you wanted me here. If you wanted a lover we would have slept together. You know as well as I do that you've been in complete control."

Madison rolled over on her back again and looked at the sky. "Come on. Let's walk. We have a lot to talk about."

The two women stood and slipped back into their flannel shirts and backpacks. As they walked, Madison began, her words measured. "I want you to try and keep an open mind. I have something important to say, but first I want you to know that I have enjoyed every moment I've spent with you. You're smart and witty and beautiful. You make me feel interesting and alive. It's just that —"

Madison stopped in mid sentence and tilted her head. "Sssh, I heard something . . . No. Don't turn around. Keep moving."

"What is it? What's wrong?" Terry asked, seeing the expression on Madison's face and quickly becoming alarmed herself.

Then, another sound. A twig snapping under a foot. A falling rock. Madison's green eyes darted about wildly . . . Another sound. This time Terry heard it clearly, and Madison turned enough to see Marshall waving an arm from a hundred yards back, trying to signal her.

Madison's eyes widened. "Get down," she ordered, and at the same moment Terry felt a burst of air pass her by, accompanied by a strange, muted spit. "Paula, what the —"

Madison dove to the ground. Rolling towards Terry she grabbed her by the ankles and jerked her down. "Stay down, dammit, and be quiet."

"What's happening?" Terry asked urgently, feeling the panic roll over her.

Madison glared at her, the bright green eyes warning her as they darted about. "Shut up. Do not speak. Do *exactly* as I say. This is no game, Terry. Do you understand?"

Terry nodded, and Madison continued, "Good. Now, stay down and crawl, and I mean crawl, behind that tree."

Terry looked into Madison's wild eyes questioningly.

"Do it now."

Terry followed the instructions blindly. She inched her way along the ground on her stomach, trying not to believe the awful truth . . . Someone was trying to kill them.

Madison spoke again, this time without turning around. "Don't move and don't make a sound."

She began moving away from Terry, and Terry understood that Madison was trying to get her out of the line of fire, using herself as a decoy, and in the seconds that followed she also realized that Madison had managed to withdraw the gun from the pack and attach a silencer. She watched in astonishment as Madison went about her business in a detached, mechanical, almost rehearsed manner, handling the weapon like a professional.

Then, another sound. Terry's heart pounded out of control. She heard footsteps. Running, fast, quiet, then stopping. She saw the shadowy figure running up the trail towards them, low to the ground. Her eyes widened, her breathing stopped. And then she saw that it was Marshall running towards them. She breathed a sigh of relief before once again hearing the sickening spits of an automatic weapon firing.

Marshall reeled, grabbing his left shoulder. He hit the ground and crawled, searching for cover. Terry saw the blood oozing from his shoulder, running between his fingers as they reached to cover the wound. She heard herself mutter, "Oh, my God."

Madison jerked her head around and glared at Terry. At the same moment the quiet cracks of the weapon were heard again. This time rock and bark flew wildly in all directions as the bullets hit the tree inches from Terry. She felt a slight pain as some of the flying bark penetrated her skin. She raised her arm to protect her eyes and caught a glimpse of Madison, who raised from a crouching position, aimed the M686 in the direction of the shots and waited a split second. Then *pop . . . pop . . .*

There was a horrible gasp, followed by a scream. Terry watched in horror as a man fell from behind a clump of rock no more than thirty feet away. Blood trickled out of his mouth, his eyes glazed in death as the last bit of air passed through his body.

Terry felt dizzy. Her vision clouded. It was the last thing she remembered.

Chapter 6

Madison McGuire and Marshall Stratton sat in the living room of the government-owned condominium in Vail, Colorado, while Terry slept upstairs after being given a mild sedative.

Madison was on the telephone with Langley. "Thank God you're all right," McFaye said.

"What did you find out about the sniper?" Madison asked.

"His name is Carlucci. He's a paid killer, an

independent not associated with any particular organization or government," Andrew answered, the concern in his voice clear.

Madison thought for a moment, and then asked, "Who knew where I was going this weekend?"

"Troy Delcardo and Mark Hadden."

"Well, that's a dead end," Madison answered wearily.

After a moment of silence, Andrew said, "Tell Stratton I want him back in Langley by morning. We'll put him on the box and find out if he's involved."

Madison turned and looked at Marshall and then spoke quietly into the telephone. "Surely you don't believe he's turned."

Andrew sighed. "Things change from day to day in this business. You know that. Let's check him out. It can't hurt. All we know right now, Madison, is that someone is trying very hard to kill you."

A well-dressed man in a business suit approached a public telephone on a corner of Pennsylvania Avenue in Washington, D.C. The creases had long since fallen out of his pants, and his coat was quite wrinkled. He picked up the receiver, inserted a coin and dialed carefully. After several rings a sleepy voice answered. The man in the suit spoke quietly. "I paid you to have a job done. What the hell happened?"

"What are you talking about?" the sleepy voice asked, annoyed.

"Carlucci blew it, asshole. He's dead. I thought you were sending someone who knew what they were doing. What are you going to do about this?"

After a long pause the voice answered, "I ain't gonna do nothing about it. I don't want the government crawling all over me. It ain't worth it for one hit. Sorry."

The man in the suit began to pace angrily, forgetting momentarily that he was on the end of a very short telephone cord. It jerked him back, and he cursed aloud, and then raised his voice. "Listen, you piece of shit. You better come through for me or I'll —"

"Or you'll what?" the man on the other end broke in. "Or you'll start talking? I don't think so. You got too much to lose, boy. Now if you're real sweet I'll see to it that you get your fifteen grand back. And by the way, if you ever call me at one o'clock in the morning again I'll cut your nuts out."

There was a loud click and the man in the suit stared blankly at the telephone.

It was nearly eleven o'clock in Vail when Terry Woodall walked slowly down the stairs, rubbing her eyes. She wore a long nightshirt, and Madison couldn't help but smile when she saw her. Terry looked so much like a child.

"Oh, God," Terry said when she reached the bottom of the stairs. "I thought it was a bad dream."

"How are you feeling?" Madison asked.

Terry looked at her for a moment and then

crossed the room, arms outstretched. "God, are you okay? And Marshall? He's okay too?"

Madison nodded and hugged her stiffly, offering as much comfort as she could. She pulled away and, putting her hand under Terry's chin and lifting it gently, looked her directly in the eyes. "We're all okay. Come and sit down. I'll get you a cup of coffee."

Terry sat quietly for a moment, then raised her voice so she could be heard in the kitchen where Madison was clanging cups loudly. "What happened?"

Madison came out of the kitchen with two cups. "You passed out cold, my dear. But not before you got a little skinned up and gave yourself a nasty bump on the head. The doctor was here. He put some antiseptic on the arm and administered a mild sedative. You've been sleeping for hours." Madison handed Terry a cup and sat down beside her.

Terry looked up from her coffee and asked, "So, can we talk now or should I just dive under the couch for cover?" When Madison did not answer, Terry continued, "Listen, I'm no detective but that man on the mountain was no goddamn angry competitor. I think it's about time you told me what's going on . . . Did you make a police report?"

"It will be taken care of with the proper authorities," Madison answered casually. "There's no need for us to get involved."

Terry looked at her in disbelief. "We're already involved. Good God, I was a witness to a shooting, Marshall was a victim, and you, I assume, were the target. I understand the law. We'll have to make a signed statement."

"I'll handle it with the proper authorities," Madison repeated. "You're going to have to trust me."

Terry laughed aloud. "Trust you? I did that before. Remember?" She paused in thought, and then added, "Who *are* the proper authorities, Paula? And who the hell are you guys anyway? Bonnie and Clyde? Jesus, you knew exactly what you were doing up there. You didn't hesitate. Hell, you didn't even seem surprised."

"Terry, I'll explain everything. But not until you calm down a little."

Terry raised both hands in submission. "I've never seen a man die before. I've never been shot at before. It makes me a little uneasy, okay?" She took a deep breath. "Screw it. I don't really want to know what's going on. I don't care and I don't want to get involved. I just want to get out of here."

She stood abruptly and felt her knees buckle under her. Madison helped her back down onto the couch. Terry went on, "I'm serious. I won't ask any more questions and you won't give any answers, and we'll just forget any of this happened and you'll get me back to Boulder."

Madison repressed a smile. "Terry, let me ease your mind a bit. I'm not a criminal. I work for the United States government." Madison handed Terry a small billfold with her identification. "My name is Madison McGuire. I'm with the National Operations Intelligence Service Clandestine Planning Unit. The NOIS is an arm of the CIA. I've been sent here to try and enlist your help. I want you to understand that what happened today had nothing to do with you. It was aimed at me and only me. You are in no danger."

Terry stared at Madison, stunned. At length she said, "Is it always this easy for you, Madison, or whatever the fuck your name is?" Her eyes filled with tears, but she fought them back. "So, tell me what the government could possibly want with me." Before Madison could answer, Terry raised both hands and said, "Okay, okay. I confess. I've been carrying a tiny camera in my notebook and selling Harvard secrets to the Soviets. I knew you'd find me one day." She held out both wrists in a dramatic gesture and added, "Take me away. I'll talk, I'll talk."

Madison rubbed her temples and sighed heavily. It was going to be a long night.

An hour later the two women sat at the kitchen table. Madison pulled a stack of papers from her briefcase and began to read. "Teresa Clark Woodall, I must inform you that the information you are about to receive is of a classified nature. Revealing this information to anyone would be against the interest of national security."

"Woo," Terry said, leaning back in her chair, raising both hands. "This is so unbelievable that I'm actually tempted to let you go on. But, I can't agree to anything like that. Jesus, Madison, this puts me in a very delicate legal position. I don't have the benefit of counsel here. I haven't been issued a subpoena. You know as well as I do that if I agree to these terms I also become indictable. I have certain rights, you know, and as far as I'm concerned several of those rights have already been violated. First, you bring me here under false pretenses, and then you endanger my life by involving me in a violent situation without my consent. I won't agree to your terms and I certainly will not relinquish my right to bring suit against your agency."

A faint smile crossed Madison's face. So, she thought, the lawyer makes an appearance.

"Terry, no one, certainly not your government, wants to take away your rights. I have answers to all your questions, but I cannot continue until I'm sure you understand that this is highly sensitive, top secret information. If you agree, we will proceed in this manner: I'll give you some information in general terms, no specifics. You will not be held to secrecy, nor can you be prosecuted, until I give you specific info like names, places, etcetera. Of course, we hope you would choose to remain silent out of love and loyalty to your country."

"All right," Terry agreed reluctantly. "Just go easy on the love and loyalty stuff. Okay?"

"I'll get right to the point," Madison answered. "Our government has been involved in an investigation for some years now that centers around a group involved in highly illegal activities. Activities that threaten national security. As far as we know the group has a small power base of only twelve members, but their influence reaches into governments around the world. We believe they may have thousands of followers, or soldiers."

"So what do they do that's illegal?" Terry asked.

"Importing drugs into this country on a large scale, manipulating stock and bond markets, sales of armaments to terrorist countries. Our biggest fear is their power to manipulate entire governments. Tensions are especially high in the Middle East right now, for example, and some governments may be in a take-over position. For instance, if the Shah is taken from power in Iran, friendly relations with the U.S. will come to an abrupt halt, and hundreds of agents, diplomats and informants we have in that country will be in danger. And now we have intelligence that leads us to believe this group is trying to infiltrate our own system. Top officials, Senators, Pentagon personnel may be under the threat of blackmail."

Terry reached for one of Madison's cigarettes, lit it, took a long drag and coughed the smoke out. Her need to ask questions would not allow her to stay quiet for very long. It is, Madison mused, the way the legally trained mind operates, sometimes questioning in order to satisfy that persistent inquisitiveness that accountants and lawyers possess, sometimes questioning for mere pleasure. And, she knew by now, Terry did love to weigh the differences between the evidence and speculation, constantly searching for some discrepancy.

Terry asked, "So, they use the funds they raise from drugs and armaments to finance these takeovers?" Madison nodded. "Amazing. I mean we're talking big bucks here. So why blackmail?"

"The blackmail is aimed at gaining political influence rather than money. For example, a senator who has a romantic interest outside his marriage may be persuaded to provide some political influence under the threat of exposure. Once he consents, he's theirs. He's in too deep to get out. Or a top level general who has something in his past, or just becomes

63

greedy, may be persuaded to involve himself in a bid-rigging scheme."

Terry shrugged and smiled at Madison. "I'm sorry, but I just don't have much sympathy for senators who cheat on their wives, or generals with skeletons in their closet. I would think people like you would be more interested in getting rid of those assholes than some obscure group of twelve people."

Madison took a deep breath. She had underestimated Terry Woodall. It would not be the simple recruitment she had anticipated. "Terry, this group is a very real threat. Soon they expect to have their people in control all over the world. They will kill indiscriminately for little more than financial gain. They will be capable of issuing orders for mass murder without concern or guilt."

"Why?" Terry insisted, frustrated. "What do they hope to accomplish?"

"Control," Madison answered simply. "Control of world finances, world policy, national reserve systems, national treasuries. We already know they're developing a computer network so sophisticated they'll soon be able to tap into the world's major banks. Try to imagine the chaos. Stock and bond markets crashing. Major banks closing their doors. Whole economies falling apart. The disciples of this group are in place right now waiting for their chance to take control. Do you understand how this could affect us? We, as Americans, could lose the rights we cherish so much. The rights that separate us from the Communist countries."

Terry looked at the woman across from her who spoke so easily of mass murder, blackmail and terrorism. Could it be possible? It was insane. Terry

64

felt chills running up and down her body. She felt weak, sick . . . It was all too impossible.

It had been quiet now for several moments in the Vail, Colorado kitchen. Madison understood that Terry needed time to digest the information. She felt Terry slowly unraveling, felt her defenses slowly breaking down.

"Madison," Terry began slowly. "Aren't you over-dramatizing a little? I just can't accept all this. It's too fantastic."

Madison leaned forward, her green eyes hard. "I wish I were being overly dramatic. Do you read the papers, Terry?"

"Rarely," Terry answered, confused by the question.

"Sit down one afternoon and read them. What I've just told you is not really so fantastic. It's happening every day, in every part of the world. Violence, terrorism, military coups, children fighting children in the Middle East. It's all there, and it frightens me more than I can tell you. I've seen it up close, Terry. I've been in the field for eighteen years, and I've seen what these people can do. Already too many lives have been lost, and it's just the beginning. I told you earlier that my father worked for the government, that he was Station Chief in London. Well, he was Station Chief for the Central Intelligence Agency there. He foolishly agreed to meet a contact in the Middle East rather than sending one of his agents. It was a set-up. He was exposed and killed. So, you see, I have first-hand knowledge of the danger that every one of our agents could be exposed to."

"God, I'm sorry." Terry said quietly. "All right,

you've succeeded in totally freaking me out. Now, tell me what it is that you people want from me."

Madison extracted more papers from her briefcase and began to read. "Up to this point you cannot be prosecuted for revealing the information I've given you. However, if you do reveal this information we will have no choice but to deny it in the interest of national security. You have the right to decline any further information. If you decide to receive more information you will be bound by the laws of this nation to remain silent under the National Security Act of nineteen forty-seven. Should you reveal this information to anyone, you can and will be prosecuted under the same act. Do you understand?"

Terry sighed. "Yes. I understand."

"Do you wish to continue?" Madison persisted.

"I don't know . . . I just don't know. Jesus Christ, I need some time to think."

Madison was trained to recognize this kind of stress and she could see that it was taking its toll on Terry. "Take your time. It's a lot to consider. I'll leave you alone." Madison stood and started out of the kitchen.

"Madison, wait, please. I have to ask you a question. All those feelings I thought I was getting from you, was it all part of the act?"

"Come on," Madison said, putting her arm around Terry's shoulders. "Let's go out onto the balcony." Terry reached to flip the outside light on, but Madison stopped her. "I'd prefer we sit in the dark. I wanted to come out here because this is a government condo. There are listening devices in most every room. What I have to say is just between you and me . . . I know you feel betrayed by me. I

understand that. But, you have to understand that this is my job. I won't try to justify it. I take orders. I'm fairly low in the chain of command. Terry, how could I have known we would have these feelings? It wasn't part of the act. I feel something every time I look at you, but we have to find a way to deal with it. I have a job to do and it takes priority over any personal feelings. What we're discussing here tonight has nothing to do with you and me. It's simply business."

"I know you have a job to do, and, by the way, you do it very well. You should be proud of yourself, Madison. I was convinced . . . You'd say anything, wouldn't you? Whatever it takes. Would you have made love to me too?" She waved a hand. "Fuck it, and fuck you too. I should just walk out right now."

Madison stood up angrily. "No one wanted to hurt you, Terry. Can't you see this is not about you? Are you so self-involved that you think the whole goddamn universe revolves around Terry and her needs? Go ahead. Walk out. Just remember, you're not walking out on me, you're walking out on your country."

Madison turned, opened the glass door and returned to the kitchen where she immediately reached for the bottle of scotch in the cabinet, and poured a tall drink.

Fifteen minutes later Terry walked back in quietly, sat down and said, "Okay, tell me everything."

Madison studied her for a moment. Terry had been right. She should be proud of herself. She had pulled off a very difficult recruitment. But she wasn't proud at all. Instead everything inside her wanted to

tell Terry to leave, walk out now before she was in too deep. Madison remembered Andrew's words, *Do not get personally involved,* and she reached in her briefcase and withdrew a single sheet of paper. "I have to ask you to sign this affidavit. It's merely a statement outlining the nature and penalties of the National Security Act." Madison watched as Terry scribbled her name on the bottom line. She wondered how many more times in her life she would have to sacrifice love for her government. Was it worth it? She wasn't sure anymore.

By the end of the evening Terry knew that the NOIS wanted her to accept the job with WEI and act as a spy, funneling out information. They wanted copies of shipping manifests, purchase orders from the Defense Department and copies of bids.

"Tell me about your brother," Madison said at one point, after Terry had not seemed surprised to discover that Louis Guiseppe was the suspected member of Club Twelve.

Terry thought for a moment. "Louis is manipulative, arrogant, deceitful, cold, and unfortunately also very charming. A real pretty boy too. You know the type. Very Wall Street, slicked back hair, looks like he puts his blow dryer on kill." She paused. "Madison, if I agree to do this, is it dangerous?"

"If you were exposed, yes. It could be dangerous."

"When would I start?"

"This is what we want you to do. Go back to Harvard. You should be finished by the end of June. Tell your parents and friends you're going to Europe for the summer. Tell your father you're reconsidering his employment offer, but you want the summer to

think it over. We'll arrange everything. We'll even supply you with postcards, and take care of having them mailed with the proper postmarks . . . However, you won't be in Europe. You'll be in Camp Peary, Virginia. It's our main training center. There we will teach you what to expect once you're inside WEI, teach you how to communicate with us and give you direct access to our computers. We'll teach you code systems for written messages, even give you some physical training, if you'd like. It may help boost your confidence level. I'll make periodic contact with you during the summer also. When this is all over, Terry, if you decide to pursue a career in intelligence, we'll be happy to have you full time. Think of it this way. You're not only performing a service for your country, but you're opening up a whole new field of career opportunities."

Terry smiled, and shook her head. "That's some sales pitch you've got. A little sappy here and there, but pretty good. Now, let's see, the government probably pays about seventy-five thousand less per year than I could make with a corporation in international law. Some career move, huh? Maybe you should have left that part out. I don't know. I need to sleep on it."

Terry stood up and added with a smile, "I'll take the spare bedroom. Good night."

"Good night," Madison answered, sure that the NOIS had its newest recruit.

Chapter 7

The stainless steel doors of the elevator opened and three figures stepped out. Troy Delcardo, Director of the CIA, followed by Andrew McFaye and Madison McGuire of the NOIS. They were on their way to the private screening room in Langley headquarters to view the video tapes of Madison's interview with Terry Woodall in Vail.

Madison and Andrew followed Delcardo down a long narrow hallway to the entrance of the screening room, its heavy double doors held open by a man in a conservative brown suit who nodded without smiling as they entered. The room looked much like any small theater one might find in a shopping mall on the outskirts of a sparsely populated town in middle Virginia. Rows of rust-colored fabric seats filled the room in typical theater fashion.

Troy Delcardo took a seat in the center row between Andrew and Madison. Delcardo pushed a black button on the arm of his seat and the wall in front of them parted, exposing a large white screen. He then pushed the red button on his seat. "Can you hear me, Fred?"

"Loud and clear," answered a booming voice from above.

Troy turned to Andrew. "Fred Nolan works with most of the film we get here. He knows how to cut through the bullshit. Been doing it for years. Say hello, Fred."

Fred Nolan answered with a weary hello, and then added, "I think you'll find this film interesting. The subject is a real pisser."

The lights dimmed and the first light hit the screen, followed by the six-foot image of Terry Woodall sitting at a round table facing Madison. The three figures watched the film in silence. Fred Nolan had edited and shortened the film by hours. Occasionally he broke in, stopping the film, to offer some comment he felt relevant, pointing out important aspects of the subject's behavior and reactions when given new information or put under extreme stress. He noted that when she was frightened she responded with caustic indignation, yet when details were outlined and explained honestly she seemed to remain reasonably calm and ask intelligent questions.

At one point during the screening, Delcardo, McFaye, Madison and Fred Nolan all burst into laughter. Their hidden video cameras had recorded something that took place after the interview had concluded and both women had gone to their separate rooms for some much needed sleep. The film showed Terry sitting on the bed writing on a legal pad. She sat quietly for some time: then suddenly, Terry Woodall did something her surveillants never expected. She stood up, walked directly to the hidden camera, raised the middle finger of her left hand, and covered the lens with a sock. The screen went dark. Nolan rewound the tape twice and each time all four people collapsed into laughter.

Madison shook her head. "Terry never indicated to me that she was aware of being filmed."

Troy Delcardo's long face pulled tightly into a smile. The short grayish hair was cropped closely in military fashion and the boyish blue eyes gleamed. Delcardo was a tall man with long legs, and when he leaned back and crossed them, Madison noticed that his pants rose just above the sock line, exposing dark curly hair on very white skin.

The film rolled on. This time it showed Madison sitting on the living room couch and Terry pacing in front of her, the legal pad in her hand. "I made some notes after we went to bed. I thought it would help me clear my mind," Terry said. "I want you to know that I'm flattered you think I could handle a job like this. I also want you to know that I'm grateful to people like you who work to make the world a safer place. But, I have this built-in mistrust for the government, especially the intelligence agencies. The way we met and the deception surrounding it didn't help much, you know. What I need from you is total honesty. No more bullshit. If I'm to put my butt on the line, if I'm the bait, then I have to feel pretty sure you guys aren't setting me up for a kill." Terry sat down, and paused for emphasis. She leaned forward and looked into Madison's eyes. "I'll agree to do this, but you're going to have to make a small investment. Shall we say a gesture of good faith?"

Madison permitted herself a smile while watching the film. She remembered the scene all too well.

The film gradually got to the point where Terry Woodall announced her terms with complete resolve. It would cost the NOIS five hundred thousand dollars for her "loyal and devoted assistance." She requested the sum be delivered within thirty days in two payments. Two hundred and fifty thousand in cash, and two hundred and fifty thousand to be deposited in a coded Swiss account . . . Madison had been astonished by the request and by the cool efficiency with which it was delivered. It was not the first time she had underestimated Terry Woodall, who was proving to be a very worthy opponent.

Andrew McFaye sat up on the edge of his seat, his eyes wide, his face creased into a smile. "Extraordinary," he exclaimed. "She is perfect, by God. Good work, Madison."

"Holy shit, Andrew. I don't see why you're so goddamn thrilled," Delcardo said angrily. "The little bitch just hit us for half a million bucks. I don't believe this."

Fred Nolan leaned forward and spoke into the microphone from above. "Looks like she has you by the short hairs, boss."

Five days after her weekend in Vail with Madison McGuire, Terry Woodall returned to Boston. She never thought she would be so glad to get out of her home state, never thought the crowded city streets of Boston would be such a welcome relief. The entire weekend still seemed like a dream, and she went over those incredible two days again and again in her mind. She thought about Madison. It all made sense now, those strange feelings she had had about the mysterious Paula Emerson, and the secrets she had sensed.

Fumbling with her keys, Terry opened the front door of her one-bedroom apartment, set her luggage inside and reached for the light switch. For the first time since she had lived in Boston the apartment, with its white walls and antique gold carpeting, seemed like home.

Terry considered this as she tossed her keys onto an end table and collapsed on the couch with a deep sigh. She was entering a world that she could not pretend to understand. A world she had never been a part of. A world that frightened her to the core, yet somehow offered a perverted interest for her. She could not deny the mixture of fear and excitement she felt, and she was astounded by the fact that she was actually intrigued.

* * * * *

74

In the CIA headquarters in Langley, Virginia, Mark Hadden walked into the small cubicle where Madison sat methodically punching at the computer in front of her. She looked up and smiled. It was amazing to her that she had never seen the Deputy Director in anything other than a three-piece suit.

"Can I come in?" he asked.

"You're already in, but you can sit down if you'd like."

Hadden smiled and leaned forward over the desk. "Madison, have I ever told you that you are one of the most stunning women I have ever seen?"

Madison stopped typing and looked up, amused. She leaned further towards him and answered, "Yes, you have. And have I ever told you that you are one of the most stunning dressers I've ever seen?"

Hadden looked at her a moment, unsure, cleared his throat and sat back in his chair. Madison returned to the keyboard and asked casually, "What did you really come here to say?"

"I just stopped by to see how Accounting Central is going."

"Everything is rolling along, old boy. How are things with you?"

"So, you have your new recruit?" Hadden asked.

"Yes. Indeed we do."

Hadden shifted in his seat. Madison never volunteered any information. It annoyed him. "So, who is this recruit?" he persisted.

Madison looked up from the keyboard and studied him. "Correct me if I'm wrong but it's my understanding you're not cleared for all the details of this operation. It's strictly a 'need to know' project."

"I'm the DDO goddammit." Hadden raised his voice. "I deserve to know what's going on."

Madison returned to the computer and answered casually. "If you have a problem with your security clearance level I suggest you take it up with the Director. Now, if you'll excuse me . . ."

Hadden got up and walked out. Madison smiled as she watched him disappear down the long corridor leading from her office.

It was Sunday, and Terry felt rested for the first time in over a week. The fitful sleep she had experienced in Colorado had finally given way to pure exhaustion. She had a quiet breakfast after running two miles and relaxing under a hot stream of water. She then purchased a large stack of newspapers and spread them out across the coffee table. *The New York Times, Chicago Sun-Times, Washington Post, Los Angeles Times* and two local papers. She made a pot of coffee and sank into the couch.

An hour later she sat up, astounded at what she had found. She remembered Madison's words: "Sit down one afternoon and read the paper. It's all there." Madison had been right, it was there. All the madness she had managed to ignore. Killings in Iran, brutal murders in Southwest Asia, seemingly senseless wars between Israel and Jordan, hell in Ireland. Terrorism again and again. Terry was amazed by how little she knew of world affairs. It was always so easy to detach herself from the pain of a world on fire.

Then something caught her eye. At first she wasn't sure why, but she went back to it over and over again. The article on the second page of *The New York Times* began: "Senator Eugene Pascel (R) Virginia announced today that he would not seek the Republican nomination for president in the 1980 elections." The article went on to say that in "a shocking speech" the senator had announced to a group of constituents that because of health-related problems he would be unable to run in the campaign. According to the reporter, Pascel would most likely have been the Republican nominee. "It is expected," said the report, "that the younger but highly electable congressman from Tennessee, Patrick Mitchell, will now seek the nomination."

Suddenly it hit Terry, and she heard Madison's words again: "Blackmail . . . A senator who has a romantic interest outside his marriage . . . Their people will be in place all over the world waiting to take control." Terry wondered if Congressman Mitchell was one of those people. It was frightening. She sipped her coffee and thought for a moment before reaching for her sweater.

The air was cool after a brief morning shower, and Terry pulled her sweater higher around her neck. She climbed into her car and drove straight to the Cambridge library where she spent the next hour reading a book entitled *Covert Surveillance*.

By the time she left the library she knew that any important phone calls she needed to make would be made from a public telephone. After all, Big Brother had traced her movements once before. They knew she would be in a Denver nightclub that night where she so conveniently had met Madison McGuire. This time she wanted no interference. She returned to her apartment complex and used a telephone next to the leasing office. After two short rings a male voice answered.

"Jonothan? Hi. This is Terry."

"Hey. When did you get back?" Jonothan Shore asked.

"Last night. Listen, Johnny, I need your help with something. You know those computer shortcuts you're always offering to teach me?"

"Sure. You behind on your studies? I hope you're not asking me to pull up your next exams."

Terry laughed. "No. It's nothing like that. It's personal."

Jonothan Shore, a Harvard instructor of computer analysis, breathed an audible sigh of relief. "You had me worried for a minute, sweetie. I'm trying to stay clean until I leave here in the fall."

"You're leaving that soon?"

"I hope so. I applied to the NSA cryptography department and I have every reason to believe I'll get the job after the investigation is over."

"Who is the NSA?" Terry asked. "What investigation?"

"Jesus, Terry, you don't know who the NSA is? The National Security Agency, dummy. When you apply for a government job like that they run a seventeen-year background check. Stuff like, am I a Soviet spy, do I do dope, who I sleep with, etcetera."

Terry was silent for a moment. "We need to talk, Johnny. When can I see you?"

"My door is always open to you. You know that," he responded tenderly.

An hour later Terry knocked on Jonothan Shore's door. He had been her friend since Terry came to Harvard several years ago. Her Johnny, as she called him, was a gentle bear of a man with strong shoulders, large hands and thick sandy-colored hair. He preferred thick-rimmed glasses to contacts, which promoted his academic look. Terry had come to Jonothan several times over the years when she needed a friend, someone to hold her, and he had always been willing to provide whatever support she needed. Jonothan Shore was one of those rare people who Terry knew would be a lifelong friend.

The apartment door opened and Jonothan stood smiling down at Terry. She stepped in and hugged him tightly. "God, it's good to see you," she said without letting him go, and the tears began to well up and slowly spill over.

He pulled away and lifted her chin. "Hey, what is it?" He wrapped a long arm around her shoulders and walked her to the couch. He pushed away a stack of papers and computer manuals to clear a place for them to sit. "Listen, I have some water on the stove. How about I fix us some tea? Herbal stuff. Very hip."

Terry smiled and wiped away the tears. Soon Johnny returned with her tea, prepared just the way she liked it with lots of milk and honey.

"Now," he said, putting a hand on her knee. "What's wrong?"

"I didn't even realize how upset I was until you hugged me, and then it just came out," Terry answered and then proceeded to tell Jonothan everything she could about her visit to Colorado, everything that the NOIS operative had told her before she was required to sign the affidavit.

Jonothan Shore listened quietly. When she was finished he sat for several moments, apparently stunned. Finally he asked, "What do they want you to do?"

"That's part of what I can't tell you."

"Terry, the NOIS is one of the big boys, a quiet arm of the CIA we don't hear much about. Secret agent types, spooks. You be careful. I know enough about them to know they wouldn't give you all this information unless they want something. They tried to recruit you, didn't they?"

"Don't press it, Johnny, please."

Jonothan Shore looked at Terry in disbelief. "Oh, Jesus, you didn't say yes, did you?" Terry did not answer. Jonothan went on. "Okay. No more questions. Just tell me what you need from me."

"I want to find out if an organization named Club Twelve is anywhere in our data banks."

"Is that the group the NOIS talked about?" Shore asked. "If it is we won't find them listed anywhere."

Terry thought for a moment. "Maybe they have a legitimate cover of some kind. You know, a front company. They must be moving tons of money all over the place. There must be a paper trail. I want to find it and see if there's any link between them and my father's company."

"You think your father's involved in this?"

"I'm afraid Dad's involved in something he doesn't understand. I want to find out. If he's in danger, if he isn't directly involved, I have to warn him. Can you get into the WEI computers? I want to know about anything that looks unusual in the financial records. Can you do it?"

Jonothan Shore sat back on the couch and rubbed his chin in thought. "It won't be easy, kid. It means

80

breaking security codes to get into the computers." He paused and smiled. "But, I'm about the best there is in the private sector for this kind of work. I'll use the computer rooms at school. That way if someone traces the link, they can't run it back to me. Don't worry, sweetie, we'll find out everything we can. Now, I want you to go home and take a long nap and don't even think about any of this again until tomorrow."

Terry smiled and hugged the big man again. "Thanks, Johnny. I knew I could count on you. But I'm not the least bit sleepy. I slept in this morning. How about we hang around here for a while and then I'll buy your dinner."

Jonothan smiled slyly. "You're offering to buy my dinner? Wait a minute. Let me find something to write with. I want to record the date you actually offered to let go of some of that money you have squirreled away."

Jonothan and Terry had dinner that evening in a small Italian restaurant in Cambridge. Jonothan marveled, as he did each time they ate together, at the enormous amount of food Terry was able to pack into her lean frame. "You're a damn pasta machine," he said jokingly, watching as she finished her meal.

When they arrived at Jonothan's apartment, Terry got out of the car and walked around to say good night. He held her tightly for a moment, a little too tightly, and said, "Would you like to come up for a while? We could see an old movie or something."

Terry smiled knowingly. "Its the 'or something' that worries me. No thanks, Johnny. I should be getting home. It's back to the old grind tomorrow."

"Okay. I'll just stay here all by myself and watch television alone."

Terry gave him a quick peck on the cheek. "You'll be all right."

She thought about Jonothan Shore on the ride home. It was no secret that Jonothan loved her. It was pleasant to think that someone wanted to hold her, wanted to make love to her, especially when she felt so rejected by Madison. But she could not envision ever being anything other than a friend to Jonothan.

The telephone was ringing as she walked into her apartment. She checked her watch. Eleven p.m. Probably her mother. She had forgotten to call her when she got back to Boston. She rushed to the phone.

"Terry?" It was Madison. Terry sat down slowly. "I just wanted to know how you were. I wanted to hear your voice . . . I don't really know what else to say. I suppose I shouldn't have called. It's very unprofessional."

Terry laughed quietly. "So, there is at least one spontaneous bone in that beautiful body of yours. I'm glad you called. I've been thinking about you."

"Terry, I wanted you to know I'm truly sorry about last week. I do hope we'll have another chance at it."

"I'd like that," Terry answered.

* * * * *

The computer room was empty when Terry walked in — with the exception of Jonothan Shore, who sat slumped over a keyboard, his fingers moving with grace and speed. Terry walked up behind him and wrapped her arms around his neck. "How's it going, Professor?"

Jonothan turned and smiled. "Okay, I guess. I've only been at it for an hour or so."

"Find anything yet?" Terry sat beside him.

"Nothing yet." He paused. "Listen, maybe we shouldn't be seen together after today here at school. I mean, I've got this thing going with the NSA and you have the NOIS, and we have to remember that what I'm doing is illegal . . . What do you think?"

"I hadn't really thought about it," Terry answered. "But you're probably right."

"Okay, and let's avoid lengthy phone conversations too."

"Agreed. Well, I'd better hit it. I have a ton of work to do. Talk to you later?"

Jonothan smiled. "Sure. I'll stop by."

It was nearly ten o'clock when Terry heard the knock on her door. Jonothan walked in, his heavy eyebrows slightly wrinkled, a stern expression on his face. He was out of breath and he held a computer printout in his hand. He rushed past Terry and sat down excitedly. "I found something. It's not great news I'm afraid, Terry. It implicates your father."

Terry sat down beside him. "What is it?" she asked cautiously.

"The last defense contract your father's company got was a gimme. A two hundred and eighty-nine million dollar gimme. WEI did not submit the lowest bid, but somehow they got the contract. A company named McDonald and something submitted a bid nearly seven million dollars less."

Terry stared at him, stunned. "Good God, Johnny. How did you find out?"

"A friend in the Justice Department managed to slip me an access code and I took it from there."

"What do you think it means?" Terry asked.

"It means your daddy's company is involved in bid-rigging most likely." He paused. "Terry, do you have any idea what would happen if this went public? Your father's company probably would never get another contract, plus they'd have to repay the money, and someone would have to talk to keep from going to jail. The entire Pentagon would be under investigation. People would lose jobs, the administration would be embarrassed. This is big stuff, and these people are powerful. It scares the shit out of me."

It was incredible. Terry wondered just how many other schemes Edward Woodall was involved in that she had never known about. Could he be the Club Twelve man rather than Guiseppe? And, if he was, how could she walk into his company as an informant and set up her own father? She shuddered visibly. "Johnny, did you get into the WEI computers yet or find anything about Club Twelve?"

"No. I tried but had to pull out. They have a sophisticated tracing system for unauthorized access. I'm sure alarms went off all over the place when I tried to get in. But tomorrow when I'm back at school I'll give it another try. I stumbled on this at home."

Terry sat straight up. "What? You did this from your apartment? Are you crazy?"

Jonothan smiled. "Don't worry. There wasn't enough time to run a trace. Besides, I didn't want to print out this stuff at school. What if someone walked in and saw it?" He stood. "Well, I'm exhausted. I'll see you tomorrow. Why don't you stop by my place in the afternoon?"

"Wait. Don't you want this printout?" Terry asked.

"Oh, no. You keep it. I don't want this stuff at my place."

Terry struggled through her morning classes the next day, finding it hard to keep her mind on her work. She had a late lunch in the cafeteria and then spent three hours in the massive Harvard library. She left the library with the strangest feeling. She tried to shake it, but could not. Something told her that Jonothan was in trouble, and she went looking for him, knowing she was breaking their agreement to not be seen together.

It was nearly five when she walked into the huge computer room. It was dark and empty. A silent alarm exploded in her mind and she quickly headed down a long hallway towards Jonothan's office. Finally she saw the office door. It was closed, but dim light escaped from underneath. More and more fearful, her heart racing, she walked faster and faster, hearing her own footsteps echo through the empty hallway. She was nearly running by the time she reached the door and pushed it open with all her force. It swung back and slammed against the wall.

"Jesus H. Christ!" Jonothan uttered, his eyes wide. "You scared the shit out of me, woman. What are you trying to do?"

Terry ran to him. "God, I'm so glad you're okay. I had the weirdest feeling. I thought you were in trouble."

Jonothan stood and hugged her, patting her back reassuringly. "The next time you get one of these feelings, how about calling before you storm the office? I'm not sure my heart can take another rescue attempt." Still visibly shaken, Jonothan sat back down at his desk.

Terry walked around the desk in front of him. "I want you to stop now. No more. It's not safe. You're right about what you said last night. These are powerful people. We're in way over our heads." She began to pace. "I must have been insane to ask you to do this. It's too dangerous. I want you to promise me, right now, that you'll stop. I don't want to lose you Johnny, and a while ago when I was running towards your office I realized just how important you are to me. I need you, Jonothan Shore. I want you to promise me you'll stop."

Jonothan leaned back in his swivel chair and looked at her. "This stuff is making you paranoid. I told you no one will find out as long as I'm careful. I'm too good at this."

Terry glared at him. "You arrogant bastard. You really think you're that good? I don't care. I want you to promise me. *Now*, Jonothan, today. You have to stop."

Jonothan raised both hands in submission. "Jesus, okay, I'll stop. I promise."

Terry looked at him suspiciously. He laughed, and added, "I promise. Okay? No kidding."

It was almost midnight. Terry had just fallen asleep when the telephone rang. Mother, she thought. I still haven't called Mother. She fumbled for the phone in the dark room.

"Terry, I found something." It was Jonothan's voice. "I have to see you right away." The urgency in his panicked voice was clear.

"Johnny? What are you talking about?" Terry asked sleepily, and then it hit her. She sat up in bed. "Oh, God. You didn't stop, did you? You kept banging that fucking computer. I can't believe this."

"You can scold me later. This is important. Can you come over?"

"Are you all right?"

"Yes, sweetie, I'm fine, but I need to see you. Okay? We can't talk about it on the phone."

Jonothan Shore hung up and wiped the beads of sweat from his forehead. He turned in his chair and faced the computer in his living room. What he had just uncovered sent chills up his spine. A fifty-million dollar weapons shortage reported by the Defense Department on an order received from Woodall Enterprises. The next day a ship would sail for the Gulf of Oman, a ship said to be carrying pipeline steel. Jonothan was sure that it was actually carrying the very weapons reported missing by the Defense Department. The most interesting aspect was that the manifest and customs forms had been signed by an official at WEI. Louis Guiseppe's name appeared again and again.

The telephone rang, interrupting his thoughts as he typed furiously at the keyboard.

He lifted the receiver. There was no answer. Instead he heard a series of short tones, a long pause, and then Jonothan Shore's world exploded. And with it his apartment went up in a mass of flames. Papers, drapes, clothing, and body and computer parts flew wildly in all directions. Alarms sounded, and moments later residents of the apartment building began a desperate escape from all exits. Some held their faces crying, running, crawling, screaming. Others covered their eyes to protect themselves from the chain reaction of explosions that followed the initial blast. Gas lines erupted and electrical boxes popped in a sensational display of spark and fire.

Chapter 8

Twelve-thirty a.m. Terry was within a block of the apartment. She turned south on Newport Drive and saw the flames leaping from the roof. She stopped her car and desperately ran towards the burning building. It was a scene that would be forever embossed on her memory.

Running and running, her legs would not move fast enough as the panic spread over her. A man in a uniform stepped in front of her. Struggling wildly, she fought to get past him, but he held her firmly. "Lady, hey, lady. You can't go in there," he insisted, but Terry continued to fight, and the officer finally slapped her. The stinging blow was effective.

"What happened?" she asked, barely above a whisper.

"Not sure yet." He pointed to the top right hand corner of the building. "There was an explosion in that apartment."

Terry dropped to her knees. Jonothan's apartment. She cupped her face in her hands. "Oh, God. Why?" she whispered incoherently, pounding the ground and sobbing. But no crying, no tears could bring her Johnny back to her now. "God, what have I done?"

The policeman leaned over her. "You gonna be okay? You need some help?"

Terry stood up slowly and attempted to wipe away the tears. A strange numbness came over her, and she began to stumble back towards her car. The world seemed a blur as she walked down the block which was bathed in lights of red and blue from the fire engines and police cars. She climbed into her car and slumped over the steering wheel.

It was almost dawn when she returned to Boston. She had been driving for hours with no particular direction in mind. Just driving anywhere away from the horror, away from the charred ruins of Jonothan's apartment.

Digging deep in the pocket of her jeans, Terry found a coin and walked to a pay phone. After what seemed an eternity she heard the distant ringing. "Yes?" answered the slightly British, unmistakable voice.

"Madison, I need the money today."

"What is it, Terry? What's wrong?"

"I want the money you guys promised me and I want it today."

"Terry, my dear girl, calm down. I've made arrangements to fly up next week. I cannot get you the funds on a moment's notice. I couldn't possibly fly up today."

"Then send someone else, goddammit. Do you understand?"

"Yes. I'm afraid you've made yourself quite clear, but I suggest you explain yourself. You owe me an explanation at least," Madison said, her voice calm.

"I owe you nothing," Terry retorted. "Get me the goddamn money or forget about our little arrangement." She hung up and leaned against the side of the telephone booth, her head in her hands.

Just outside Washington, D.C., Madison McGuire picked up the mobile phone in her black Porsche and dialed seven digits. After several clicks and two short beeps, she dialed five more numbers, sure that the scrambling devices on Andrew McFaye's private number were operational. "Sorry to bother you so early, old man," Madison said after Andrew answered. "But something rather unusual has come up." Madison went on to give Andrew some of the details from her conversation with Terry.

Andrew sat up in bed, alert now. "Who do we have in the area?" he asked.

"Spencer Teal. He's a bureau man, but he's good. I've had him keeping a twenty-four hour surveillance

91

on her. He's still trying to piece the whole thing together. We talked about two a.m. I didn't hear from our friend until five."

Andrew chuckled. "Poor baby," he said in a hoarse voice. "You didn't get your beauty sleep."

Madison smiled. "When have I ever since I've worked for you?"

"Are you on your way?" Andrew asked.

"I'll be there in forty minutes," Madison answered, looking at her watch and gunning the Porsche.

At seven a.m. Madison sat across from Andrew as he poured them both coffee. Madison studied him, noticing for the first time that the bags under his eyes were full, and that the already large, W.C. Fields-type nose was redder than usual. Andrew was known to drink on occasion, and Madison guessed that last night had been one of those occasions.

He said, "So, all we know is that she's been spending time with this guy, Shore. Then Shore gets blown away, the kid calls you nearly incoherent and demands the goddamn money today?"

Madison smiled. She had been working with, or against, professionals for so long that she found them to be incredibly predictable. Terry, on the other hand, was refreshingly amateur, unpredictable, and followed no set pattern.

Andrew squirmed in his chair. "What about the bugs on her phone?"

Madison shook her head. "No good. She's been using public telephones. Last night Shore called her and insisted she come right over. Teal said they didn't say anything else," Madison lied. She had intentionally neglected to tell Andrew that the bureau man had heard Terry say something about the work Jonothan was doing on a computer. Why she withheld this information, she was not sure. It was a gut feeling and she would go with it.

"Extraordinary," Andrew muttered, looking over his cup at Madison. "Do you think the phone call this morning and the thing with Shore are related?"

Madison thought for a moment. "Indirectly. I think Terry is simply responding to the loss of a friend. Plus she's been under a great deal of stress since Vail. My guess is she wants to get the money and get away for a while. Go somewhere to heal. I think it's all very innocent really."

"If it's all so innocent then why has she been using pay phones?"

Madison smiled. "It's a game with her, I think. She has obviously done her homework on our operations. Teal said she's checked out several books about surveillance techniques. She wants to beat us at our own game. Play with us a bit." Madison paused. "I did discover something interesting about Shore. He'd just been hired by the NSA. He probably never even had time to get the acceptance letter."

"The NSA? What could it mean?" Andrew asked, more to himself than Madison.

"I haven't had time to follow up," Madison answered.

Andrew yawned and stretched. "Okay, if the kid is in a panic let's not push her over the edge. I'll have the bank in Boston release the funds to her today. You just be goddamn sure we have someone on her every minute. If she tries to leave the country make sure we don't lose her."

Madison shook her head. "Christ, Andrew. She's a

93

frightened young woman, not a double agent or a thief . . . Listen, I'd like to handle this myself. Can you do without me for a few days?"

"What do you have in mind?" Andrew responded wearily.

"Once we know where she's going I'd like to pick up the surveillance myself. I have a feeling that Shore's death wasn't an accident. I want to be sure Terry's not in danger. I'll need some fresh I.D. I don't want to use mine."

"No problem. I'll set it up with the documents division at Langley."

"No," Madison answered. "Until we know where our leak is in the agency, I'd feel better using an outside counterfeiter."

At twelve-fifteen Terry Woodall was at the First National Bank of Boston. She was operating on automatic, mechanically going about her business, afraid to stop, afraid to slow down enough for the grief to seep in. She produced her identification and within twenty minutes left the bank with two hundred and fifty thousand dollars on her person.

On the way to her car she noticed a brown Ford parked across the street. Had she seen the car before? She could not be sure, but the man inside looked vaguely familiar. During the ride home she checked her rearview mirror several times, and saw the brown Ford in the distance.

Once inside her apartment she added one more item to her suitcase: a conservative blue suit that her mother had insisted on buying for her, a suit Terry had never intended to wear. She then called a taxi and asked to be picked up in an hour. Next she walked across the hall to her neighbor's apartment. Sheila reluctantly agreed to loan Terry her car for a few minutes. Terry accepted the keys gratefully, returned to her apartment, found a floppy hat, installed it on her head, and walked out.

As she exited the apartment complex the man in the brown Ford looked up, but did not recognize her or the car.

Twenty minutes later Terry returned the keys to her neighbor and walked back into her apartment with the short brown wig she had just purchased.

The brown Ford followed the taxi to the airport. When Terry was just inside the terminal she saw the man get out of his car and hurry towards the entrance. She picked up her small suitcase and went into the restroom where she changed into the blue suit, tucked her long hair up under the short wig and installed a pair of fake eyelashes. On the way to the Eastern ticket counter she saw the man who had been following her. He seemed somewhat panicked as he rushed from airline desk to desk, showing I.D. and demanding to see the passenger list. She allowed herself a faint smile as she waited for her ticket.

At three p.m. Madison received a call from a very frustrated Spencer Teal, Special Agent, FBI. "She lost me. I don't know how in God's name she did it. Shit, Madison, I thought I was dealing with an amateur. It was the damnedest thing. I followed her to the airport and then the little bitch just disappeared."

"She *is* an amateur, Spence old boy. You should have been able to keep up with her," Madison replied impatiently. "Did you go back to her apartment?"

"Yeah, I talked to a neighbor, one Sheila Patterson, who said the kid used her car for a few minutes around noon. Hell, she must have driven right past me. She told her neighbor she'd be gone for a week or two."

"Get to the point, Teal. Where is she now?"

"She used her neighbor's name and bought a ticket to Norfolk. Flight number three-fifty-seven, to arrive in Norfolk at four-fifteen."

Madison hung up and immediately dialed a private investigator she knew in the Norfolk area. Within minutes the arrangements were made. He would be waiting for Flight three-fifty-seven to arrive in Norfolk, and would inform Madison as to Terry's whereabouts shortly after.

It took Madison nearly six hours to make the drive to the resort off the North Carolina coast. At one a.m. Madison pulled into the Hatteras Resort at Rodanthe Island and immediately spotted the rented car Terry was said to be driving.

Exhausted, Madison walked into the registration office, checked in, and asked the man behind the counter for the guest list while sliding a crisp fifty-dollar bill across the counter. But it wasn't until she upped the offer to one hundred dollars that the man handed over the registration book. Terry had used her own name this time and was registered in a beachfront cottage, C-4.

Madison's assigned cottage was only two doors from C-4. She decided to leave the inside lights off while she unloaded the two small suitcases she had brought from Washington. Madison rarely went anywhere without the smaller case, which was crammed with cosmetics, temporary hair color rinses, sunglasses, plastic facial masks and a grey wig. During her years in the intelligence business she had used several methods of disguise, and found this to be a critical part of her craft. She set her travel alarm for five-thirty, sure that Terry would sleep in, and was asleep within minutes.

By five-forty-five Madison was out of the shower and futilely searching the cabinets in the small kitchen for coffee. "Shit," she muttered aloud before throwing her bags in the car and walking through the brown sand to the leasing office.

The man at the counter had been replaced by a rather large woman, who smiled and immediately offered Madison coffee. Madison accepted, and the woman began a search for a clean cup. "Hang on, hon. I'll have to go in back," the woman said, and Madison smiled, wondering how the large woman would negotiate the narrow doorway. Madison raised her voice to be heard. "Any activity this morning? Did you notice anyone coming or going?" The woman's voice came from the back room. "There was one person. Said she was checking out. Just got here last night too. I think she was in C-four."

The woman returned, a smile on her round face, a clean cup in her hand, only to find the leasing office empty. "Oh well," she said as she balanced herself on a stool behind the desk and looked at the empty cup in her hand. "Damn good coffee too," she muttered.

Madison pulled out of the Hatteras Resort, tires squealing, cursing herself. What had she been thinking? She had been too tired last night. Andrew had always told her that food and rest were weapons, that without them one quickly became ineffective. Unfortunately, she had proven his theory correct. She had made the mistake of thinking that Terry would sleep late, as one does on a vacation. It was a serious error in judgment. She should have known that Terry was in her own private hell right now. She would experience fitful sleep, nightmares.

Madison reached the stop sign at the end of the long drive that led away from the resort. She would turn south on Highway Twelve. It was the only logical route. Going north would only cover ground that Terry must have traveled. She turned left and the hunt began.

Terry parked the rented car on the side of Highway Twelve and walked a hundred yards to the beach. It was a chilly morning. The wind whipped off the green water and packed the brown Carolina sand firmly against the earth. She sat quietly for a few moments, and then mechanically returned to her car. Not even the beauty of a sunrise on a deserted stretch of island stirred her now.

Twenty miles further down the quiet blacktop Terry found what she was looking for: a strip of beachfront property with a For Sale sign out front. She turned onto a gravel driveway and drove to the house, a two-story with gray-brown weathered wood, and a deck overlooking the ocean . . . Perfect.

Several hundred yards away, Madison stood leaning against her car, peering through binoculars, watching Terry in fascination. What was she doing?

Fifteen minutes later Madison's question was answered. She watched as Terry walked into the Outer Banks Real Estate office.

It looked more like a small artist gallery than a real estate office. All but one corner in the main room was devoted to paintings, pastels and wood burnings of local scenes.

"Hi."

Terry spun around. "Hello," she answered. "I was just admiring the work. Are you the artist?"

"Yes. I'm Ann Newlin. You'll have to excuse the mess. I usually don't get anyone in here so early," answered a small woman with a broad smile, sparkling brown eyes and hair that looked as if it hadn't been combed yet.

Terry suddenly realized that she had no idea of the time. She felt as though she had been wandering for days. "Oh, I'm sorry. The door was open and . . ."

"It's okay," Ann Newlin said, tucking a strand of light brown hair behind her ear. "I live upstairs. I usually unlock the front pretty early. Can I help you find something?"

"Actually, I was interested in a house I saw up Highway Twelve a few miles, in Buxton, I think. Are you the real estate agent also?"

Ann Newlin studied Terry silently for a moment, taking in her jeans, T-shirt, and the worn tennis shoes, before walking to a small corner desk which was littered with property brochures. She ran her finger down the page of an open notebook, and looked at Terry. "Yes. I'm the agent, but you should know that property is high in this area. Especially on the beach. What did you say your name was?"

Terry smiled. "I didn't. It's Terry Woodall."

"Are you married, Terry?" Ann Newlin asked casually.

"Is that a requirement for buying property in Buxton?" Terry asked flatly.

"No, of course not. It's just that you look young to be —"

"Ms. Newlin," Terry broke in, annoyed. "I assure you I am serious about buying a house. Now, if you have some reservations about doing business with me I'm sure I can find another agent interested in making a cash sale today."

Ann Newlin smiled. "We're asking one seventy-nine."

Terry thought for a moment. "Are you interested in making an extra commission? I need something I can move into immediately, and I need the services of someone familiar with the area. I want the gas and electricity cut on right away, I need a couch and a bed, some blinds for the windows, kitchen utensils, stuff like that." She paused and looked around. "And, I suppose I could use some art work. I'll pay your asking price and put in another five thousand for you. But I want everything done today. Are you interested?"

* * * * *

100

Madison McGuire spent most of the afternoon trying to assess the situation, as best she could, from afar. She had watched Terry leave the real estate office, drive to Buxton and remove the For Sale sign from the front yard. Three hours later she watched as a large truck backed into the driveway and unloaded furniture and appliances. The real estate agent followed.

Madison smiled and shook her head. "You are quite extraordinary, Terry Woodall." She climbed into her car. There was one stop to be made before she made her appearance.

Terry's jaw dropped in astonishment when she opened the door and found Madison McGuire standing on the threshold. Madison smiled and pressed by her casually. "I thought you might need some groceries," she said, finding her way to the kitchen. "It appears you've thought of everything else." She set the groceries on the counter and turned to see a smile slowly forming on Terry's face. "How are you, my dear?" Madison asked seriously, moving across the kitchen towards her.

"How did you find me?"

"I must say, you executed quite a clever escape. It wasn't easy," Madison answered smiling.

Terry lowered her head. "You know, when I left Colorado, I wasn't sure I ever wanted to see you again. Then you called and I wasn't sure of anything. But God, I'm glad to see you now."

Madison held out both arms and Terry fell into

them. She held her there tightly for several moments, and then asked quietly, "Do you want to talk about it?"

"No," Terry answered, pulling away enough to look into Madison's eyes. "I want you to make love to me."

Madison touched Terry's face gently, slowly running her fingers over the parted lips. She began to kiss her and Terry guided Madison's hands under the T-shirt and around erect nipples. Terry moaned and pressed harder against Madison, and suddenly Madison was overcome by the need in both of them, a need so great that she pulled Terry to the sofa.

They frantically reached for each other, stripping off clothes in frenzied excitement, touching, kissing, learning. Madison hooked her thumbs in the belt loops on Terry's faded jeans and pulled them off her.

Terry came out of her T-shirt and Madison cupped the small, firm breasts in her hands, gently biting brown nipples. Willing herself to go slow, she traced the curves of Terry's sides and stomach with her fingertips, running her tongue up Terry's calves, the back of her knees, inside her thighs, watching the shudders that followed. She ran a finger up the inside of Terry's arms and across her lips.

Terry closed her eyes and held Madison's hand at her mouth for a few moments, first kissing, and then outlining each finger with her tongue. It was Madison's sigh and the sound of her breathing that ignited Terry and told her she could wait no longer. She pressed urgently towards Madison, guiding her mouth, wanting her, until, at last, she felt Madison's lips. She whispered in her ecstasy as Madison's tongue continued probing her, expertly moving in a circular motion.

Madison felt Terry's body under her touch, first pushing, then tense; and finally in an erotic spasm she felt the warm, creamy release of Terry's excitement.

Terry pulled Madison up to her, kissing her deeply, holding her tightly. Madison could feel her own tears on her face. It had been so long since she had allowed herself to feel the love and the passion that only two women can share . . . So long since she had lost her beloved Elicia.

Terry rolled over and kissed away the tears, somehow knowing what Madison was feeling. Moving slowly, now that some of the urgency had faded, she studied Madison's body with the fascination of a child, taking in every curve, every reaction. She ran her fingertips along Madison's lips, her breasts, her stomach, her thighs. And then she was lost. Lost in the blazing green eyes. Lost in the smooth olive skin. Lost in the thick red hair . . .

Chapter 9

It wasn't until the sun went down that the groceries were unpacked and supper was made. Madison and Terry finished a bottle of wine on the beach.

Madison stretched out across the sand and rested her head in Terry's lap. She looked up into the dark eyes and asked, "Darling, do you want to talk about Jonothan?"

Terry sighed and looked out over the water. "I don't know what to say. I made a horrible mistake, Madison, and it killed him. I told him about Vail, about you and the NOIS. I asked him to help me find out if my father was involved. He found something."

"What did he find?"

"The last contract my father's company got from the Defense Department was rigged."

Madison sat up and asked urgently, "Terry, when did he discover this?"

"The day before he died," Terry answered sadly.

"Do you know how he got this information?"

"He said he had a friend at the Justice Department who gave him an access number. I don't know who the friend was, but he used the number and found out about the contract. He said he tried to get into the WEI computer system but they had some kind of tracing system. It scared him and he backed off."

"My God," Madison muttered.

"Oh, Madison, I killed him. He'd be alive right now if I hadn't asked him for help."

"Listen to me, Terry," Madison said firmly. "We have people up there going through the wreckage from the explosion. So far we've found nothing to indicate it was anything other than a terrible, unfortunate accident."

Terry looked at Madison hopefully, the brown eyes wet with tears. "Do you really think it was an accident?"

Madison wrapped her arm around Terry and pulled her close. "I have no reason to believe anything else," she lied. "We're both tired. Let's go inside."

* * * * *

105

Edward Woodall's office door opened and Louis Guiseppe stepped in, his handsome face beaming. "Good news," he said cheerfully. "I waited to tell you until the situation was under control. It wasn't an internal security break. Our tracing system led us to Cambridge, Massachusetts, a professor there named Shore. At least that was his cover."

Woodall looked at him impatiently, fingering one bushy eyebrow. "What the hell do you mean, his cover? He was more than a hacker?"

"Yes," Guiseppe answered. "We ran a check on this guy Shore. He was with the NSA. Their files say he was only hired recently, but I think that was part of the cover. He was probably working undercover trying to nail Defense for doctoring bids."

Woodall's middle finger was pulling rapidly at one eyebrow, as it so often did when he was in deep thought. It was a habit that annoyed Louis Guiseppe. "I trust you've taken steps to be sure this won't happen again?" Woodall snapped.

"We're having our security systems checked out and entry codes changed," Guiseppe answered, and added with a smile, "And we won't have any more trouble with Mr. Shore. He's quite dead."

Woodall looked at his son for a moment. A faint smile crossed his full lips.

Madison had trouble falling asleep. Finally, after Terry drifted off, she carefully pulled back the sheet and walked to the window, which was cracked enough to hear the roar of the water beyond. She sighed and lit a cigarette, allowing the smoke to curl around her

106

lips before inhaling deeply. Aware of the dreadful pounding in her chest, she made a conscious effort to slow her heart rate. It was odd, she thought. The last half of her life had been spent in and out of life-threatening situations, yet none frightened her as much as what she now faced. Because love terrified her. She remembered Elicia lying in the front seat of her car, so still, so lifeless. Elicia who had died for no other reason than that Madison had loved her.

Everything within told her to collect her things and walk out now, while Terry slept. But she could not, and she cursed her own indecision as she stubbed out the cigarette. Watching the fire glow in the ashtray before slowly burning out, she remembered that day in a vivid flash of memory.

She had returned home late one afternoon, after being gone for over a week, to find Elicia curled up on the couch in their London flat, a romance novel in her hands and tears in her eyes. Madison smiled and hung her coat on the rack near the door and stuffed her keys in her coat pocket. Elicia put down the book, wiped away the romantic tears, and ran to Madison, hugging her tightly. She took Madison's hand and led her to the couch, chattering happily about what had happened at school during Madison's absence.

Elicia Peabody was a teacher at a school for children with learning disorders, and as she talked about her "babies" and some great obstacle they had overcome or something wonderfully charming they had said, the small, round face lit up and the dark eyes sparkled with pride. Elicia had spoken so often about the children that Madison knew them by name, knew their handicaps and their accomplishments.

Then Elicia asked how Madison was doing, always careful not to ask too many questions and always ready to accept a vague answer. She knew that Madison worked undercover and that Madison never wanted that part of her life to touch Elicia.

Sometimes Madison stayed away from home for days and weeks at a time, only coming home when her secret life did not interfere with her personal life. Elicia knew that it was a dangerous life deep inside the underground intelligence network of London, and she knew that Madison stayed away for Elicia's own protection.

After they made love, Madison drifted in and out of sleep as Elicia padded naked around the small flat. Watching through sleepy eyes the soft round body and full bosom as Elicia hurried about, chattering about a house she had seen in a real estate magazine that was so beautiful, Madison promised again that she was leaving the agency that year, and they would find that house.

"It's a lovely cottage with a green lawn just made for fat children to run in," Elicia said, sticking her head in the bedroom door. Madison, half asleep and half drifting to that cottage, smiled.

"I wasn't sure you'd be in tonight, love, so I didn't go to the market," Elicia went on. "I'm going to run and find us a bite to eat." She walked to the side of the bed and laughed quietly as she leaned over to give Madison a kiss. "I'm going to wrap up in your raincoat. Do you think anyone would ever suspect that the nice teacher is completely nude underneath?"

Madison smiled as Elicia walked out of the bedroom and left the flat, cheerfully humming to herself. A few seconds later she stuck her head back in the door and said, "I'm taking your car, love. Be back soon."

Madison yawned and stretched and closed her eyes sleepily. Suddenly she sat up in bed. A silent alarm sounded in her mind. Something was wrong, she could feel it.

Jumping out of bed, she struggled into her clothes as she moved to the window. The wood frame was swollen with humidity and she could not push the window open. Still climbing into her pants, she saw Elicia on the street below. Madison yelled and banged on the window.

But Elicia just smiled and waved as she climbed into Madison's car. Madison ran through the apartment, zipping up her pants, and burst through the flat door. She took the stairs two at a time, and just as she reached the bottom, she heard the sickening gunfire, heard Elicia's screams, heard the shattering glass and the roar of a car rushing away.

Then she was there. One side of her car had been sprayed with bullets. Bullets that had been meant for her. Elicia had fallen into the passenger's seat, her body horribly twisted, her head lying in a pool of blood, her eyes wide open, filled with the fear and pain of violent death.

Madison opened the door and gently lifted Elicia's body up into the passenger's seat. She felt for some sign of life, but there was no pulse. She leaned over and touched her face, softly closing the wide eyes, unable to bear the constant, frozen stare on her lover's face.

A crowd was beginning to gather, and from somewhere deep within, under the pain, the professional in Madison told her she had to move. She couldn't stay there. She drove to the American Embassy, barely able to negotiate the road.

The next day there had been a few paragraphs on the front page of the *Times* dedicated to the incident. The NOIS had managed to manipulate the report. An American deep cover agent had been shot to death on the streets of London. The agent was known to be one of America's most elusive spies, who worked under the code name of Scorpion.

There were no kind words about Elicia Peabody. Nothing about her untimely death, nothing about her life. Nothing about her wonderful accomplishments with the children she loved, nothing about the children who would miss her warm smile and kind face.

Elicia's life had ended and even the newspapers could not know. Elicia's family had been told that it had been an automobile accident. Perhaps they had wondered who the woman was at the funeral with the dark glasses . . .

Madison turned from the window now and looked at Terry, trying desperately to push the violent images away. Moving to the edge of the bed, she saw Terry's breasts rise and fall in sleep, and she knew she wanted her, needed her now. She pulled the covers away slowly. Terry moaned as she pulled Madison to her.

Chapter 10

Fifty-five miles from Stuttgart, where the more mountainous regions of Germany rise majestically over the countryside, sat the estate of Peter Mueller, neatly tucked away near the banks of the Danube. The land belonging to the wealthy German consisted of over three hundred acres, much of it surrounded by a great wall of rock erected by the Wehrmacht soldiers in 1935. The house was a grand example of the luxury in which some Germans had lived before the last desperate days of Germany under Hitler.

Inside, Mueller sat at the head of his dining room

table contemplating his single guest, a cognac in his hand. An elegant-looking man, Mueller was tall with a dash of gray at the temples. His sharp features could have been freshly sculpted from clay. The eyes were a clear gray, and the chin jutted forward in a stern expression he had adopted during his time as head of the Abewhr, Germany's intelligence agency.

Mueller had never forgotten the old days before Hitler lost control. He and a few others had been part of Hitler's demise, of an assassination plot that had nearly been successful. Hitler's right-hand man, Himmler, had suspected that such a plot existed and had done his best to discredit Mueller. It was ironic, in a way, that Mueller, the head of what was the greatest intelligence network in the world, had ended up working with enemy agencies, British and American, until he saw the end of the war coming in 1945 and Germany's inevitable surrender.

It was in that year that Mueller met Stewart Lawrence for the first time. Born to a wealthy family and sent through Eton College, a school exclusively for England's great sons, Lawrence, who eventually became Sir Stewart Lawrence, was destined to become the head of the British Secret Intelligence. He served for many honored years in the military and then under the great "C," spymaster to Winston Churchill.

Peter Mueller, who fancied himself a man of great vision, believed that he and Lawrence shared many goals. They both believed themselves to be men of peace, men who saw the madness in the world and wished to free the world from its burden. Mueller often said passionately, "One must tear down before one can rebuild and reshape the world."

With that goal in mind, Mueller and Lawrence

formed an alliance, and by 1947 they had included an Israeli named Islom Jabril. Together the three had worked out a complicated scheme to attain the finances they needed to build a secret network of men around the world who believed as they did, men who were unhappy with the way their own countries were run, men who believed they were all destined for greatness.

Their first endeavor had been highly successful. Mueller, being a highly placed official in the German government until 1946, was well aware of the millions that had been put aside to aid the escape of Nazi war criminals. The renegade Nazis were panicked by the end of the war, and Mueller had let it be known that he was sympathetic to their plight. He sheltered and fed them, and guaranteed that he could get them out of the country to begin new lives with new identities. Soon Mueller knew where the millions were hidden and was given control of the funds, of how they were transferred and divided.

In 1948 when Israel officially became a Jewish state, at the request of the third member of the group, Islom Jabril, the remaining Nazis were loaded onto a plane and told they were going to a neutral country where the law could not find them. The airplane landed in Israel. They had discovered that not only were they penniless, they would have many years in an Israeli prison to contemplate their crimes.

The scheme netted the men twelve million dollars, and they began calling their group Club Twelve. By 1952 they had chosen nine other members from around the world to join their alliance.

The group was pleased with its accomplishments, and the rest of the world seemed to be cooperating perfectly with their plans. Israel's West Bank was on fire, terrorists roamed Europe in search of a cause, Iran, Iraq and Syria were constant battlegrounds, and America was unwittingly allowing itself to be infiltrated by the soldiers of Club Twelve. By 1980, Mueller mused, the President of the most powerful country on earth would be handpicked by Club Twelve.

Mueller, sitting at the head of his table, took a sip of cognac, and spoke. "In two days a few of us will meet at the request of our newest member. He has something urgent to discuss."

Islom Jabril, sitting across from Mueller, permitted himself a chuckle which quickly turned to an agonizing cough, sending his frail body into a violent spasm. When he regained control, he said, "Everything is urgent when you are so young. Let us hope that his urgency has not caused him to be careless."

Mueller looked at Jabril and smiled. "He is very young and probably very foolish at times, but he can supply us with the steel and weapons we need. I believe that as long as he continues to make enormous amounts of untraceable money on the shipments he will not be too foolish." He added casually, "If at some point we feel that he is not performing to our satisfaction, he can easily be disposed of. But, for now, we need our handsome young friend."

Louis Guiseppe walked into the Atlanta home of Edward Woodall.

"What brings you here so late, son?" Woodall asked, looking up from the television. "How about a drink?"

"No thanks." Guiseppe pulled a chair close to Woodall. "I came here to tell you I'm leaving for Frankfurt tomorrow. Those damn textile workers at the plant are talking about a strike. I thought I'd fly over and calm their nerves. I'm sure it's nothing a few extra Deutsche marks can't take care of."

Woodall looked at him curiously. "I thought you were in Frankfurt last month."

Guiseppe hesitated and then answered stiffly, "No. It was the steel mill in Glasgow. Remember?"

Woodall shrugged. "So, how long you gonna be gone? I asked that idiot Congressman Patrick Mitchell to come down this week and discuss his campaign plans. I thought you'd want to see him. You were the one who convinced me we needed him in order to insure WEI's standing in Washington."

"I'll be back late Thursday night. Think you can do without me for that long, old man?" Guiseppe asked with a smile.

"Who you calling old man? I could still take you out anytime."

"All right," Guiseppe said, backing off playfully. "Just kidding around, Dad."

Woodall smiled. Louis rarely called him Dad. "Be careful over there. I hear those Frauleins will fuck your brains out."

Guiseppe stood. "Gute nacht, Herr Woodall," he said in a perfect German accent. He walked out thinking what a crude man his father was.

* * * * *

115

Madison picked up the small box lying beside the bed and pressed the button on the face. Andrew's code lit up the beeper. Madison and Terry looked at each other; both knew what it meant. The three days they had spent together was coming to an end.

Madison turned and kissed Terry gently. "I'll be right back. I need to call in."

She picked up the mobile phone in her car and listened to the distant clicks of the call being routed through city after city on the scrambling system.

Andrew answered. "You have to move right away, Madison. Guiseppe booked a flight to Frankfurt tonight. Can you be at the air base by five?"

"I can be on the motorway by two. I'll do my best. Will you have papers for me?"

"Stratton will be there to brief you on the flight, he'll have your papers. What else do you need?"

"Some operating capital and a few things from my place. Send Marshall over and have him get some clothes for me. I'll pick up whatever else I need in Frankfurt."

"You've got it." Andrew hung up.

Madison walked back to the house slowly and found Terry waiting at the front door, a knowing look on her face. "You have to go, don't you?"

"Yes," Madison answered, and walked upstairs.

Terry followed and stood at the bedroom door watching Madison pack. "Is it dangerous?" she asked quietly.

Madison turned and smiled. "No. It's very routine. Merely some simple surveillance. I should be back in a few days. Will you be here or in Boston?"

"I don't know," Terry answered, as her chin began to quiver and the brown eyes filled with tears.

116

Madison walked to her and put a hand on each shoulder. "I want you to be brave, darling. I'll be back very soon. I'm going to leave you a phone number. If you have any problems, or if you just need to talk, call this number and ask for Andrew McFaye. Don't talk to anyone else. Andrew is a good man, he's been like a father to me. You can trust him."

Terry nodded, her head down.

"Cheer up, sweetheart," Madison said. "We still have a few hours together."

At two o'clock Madison walked down the stairs, a towel wrapped around her neck, her bags in hand. Terry stood staring blankly at her for a moment before saying, "Jesus, what happened to your hair?"

Madison laughed. "Just a bit of color. What do you think?"

"I don't know," Terry answered. "You look so different. Even your eyes look different. Why?"

"Well, you can't send an operative into the field with red hair. It attracts too much attention. You see, the idea is for me to blend in. I think this is a nice typical brown color, don't you agree?"

Terry nodded, still staring.

Madison smiled. "Good. Between the hair and these annoying brown contacts I doubt seriously anyone will look twice. People don't really look at one another, you know. Instead they tend to group people into certain classes or stereotypes. For example, when you see a female stranger, if you remember her at all, you remember her as a certain

117

type of person, rather than by individual characteristics, unless her features are outstanding, like red hair and green eyes. You would naturally remember red hair before, say, brown or sandy. People may remember the businessman, the policeman, the waitress, but they won't remember the face. If you ever want to melt into the crowd, my dear, remember this little lecture. It only takes a few minor changes to make yourself look completely different."

Terry smiled. "God, I'm going to miss you, Madison. I don't know how I managed without you for all these years."

Madison tossed the towel aside and hugged Terry tightly. "I should be off now, darling. I'll call you over the weekend." She stroked Terry's cheek lightly. "Don't worry. Everything's going to be all right."

Madison tossed her bags in the rear of the car before turning to take one last look at Terry standing at the door. She looked so alone, so small, so sad, that Madison couldn't bear it. She ran back to the house, and Terry met her with outstretched arms. "I love you, Terry Woodall. I'll be back," Madison whispered.

Terry watched as the Porsche disappeared down the long blacktop. She stood there long after the car was out of sight, gazing aimlessly towards the road.

"Please come back to me," she whispered to herself, as she turned and walked back inside the empty house.

Chapter 11

Marshall Stratton sat in the high-backed seat on the private jet, facing Madison McGuire. "If you have any information to transmit, use the regular drop sites," he said.

Madison leaned back in her seat, absorbing the information. "Who is the principal agent in Frankfurt now?"

"Sugarbaker. His base is in Zurich, but he runs agents in Frankfurt." Stratton shuffled some papers on the small table between them and looked at

Madison, who was smiling. "Do you know Sugarbaker?"

Madison shook her head. "Only by reputation. I've seen his file. He's extravagant, excessive, a hopeless womanizer and one of the highest paid operatives in the field. His real name is Anthony Cane. He's around forty-six years old, and credited with stopping the Baader-Meinhof bombing of a West German U.S.O. last year. In fact, some of his contacts helped me get out of London in one piece last year."

Marshall Stratton looked at Madison with frank admiration. Her uncanny ability for total recall amazed him. Everything she saw, read, or wanted to commit to memory was forever locked away in her mind until she needed it. He said, "We can't find any hotel reservation for Guiseppe. That may mean he's planning to move on." He picked up a sheet of paper. "Sugarbaker's people will make contact at the airport. They'll address you as Scorpion. Their listening post and whatever else you need will be at your disposal." He held up the sheet of paper to Madison. "Take a look at these numbers. Memorize them. The sheet goes back with me."

Madison studied the sheet until she was sure she could remember all the numbers. There were several names and numbers on the sheet, including a direct line to the elusive Sugarbaker, a doctor she had worked with in the past near the Swiss-German border, and several other agents of influence.

Marshall stuffed the sheet in his briefcase. "I wonder what this guy Sugarbaker looks like. I understand he's a chameleon type, like you."

Madison smiled. "Yes. He is very good, isn't he?"

"Yeah," Stratton answered, a hint of resentment

in his voice. "A real James Bond. Now, back to business." He handed her two briefcases, one filled with American currency, the other with tools of the trade.

Madison laid the second case on the small table and opened it to find a wide array of materials. She began taking each item out and checking its condition.

Several small canisters looked like simple 35mm film canisters. However, when a tiny pin at the top was pulled the canister emitted a non-lethal vapor of Oleorsin in isopropyl alcohol which induced choking, nausea, and caused the mucous membranes to swell within twenty seconds. Madison had used the stun grenades before and knew they generally discouraged any aggressive behavior for at least thirty minutes. Also, she found a small electronic device she had seen used by the Israelis, which defeated any attempts at telephone bugging. Nicknamed the bug smasher, the small box hooked directly to any telephone, needed no batteries, and scrambled the voice to such an extent that any third party listening in would hear nothing but gibberish. There was also a tiny camera, neatly tucked inside a gold cigarette lighter engraved with the initials P.E., for Paula Emerson. And, a fountain pen with a tiny vial and syringe hidden in its chamber. The vial held a powerful tranquilizer. There were several lock-picking sets, complete with double-sided disc tumbler picks, and padlock and shim pick sets. They would insure that Madison could open most European locks if necessary.

She closed the briefcase and smiled. She spent the balance of her trip studying personal information about the subject of her surveillance, Louis Guiseppe.

One hour before the scheduled landing in Frankfurt, Madison took her make-up bag into the restroom. After nearly forty minutes she returned and Marshall stared at her, stunned.

Louis Guiseppe stepped off the plane in Frankfurt, a small carry-on bag in one hand, a raincoat draped over his shoulder. A line of passengers walked behind him, couples chatting; others hurried past towards baggage claim. Guiseppe did not notice the elderly woman behind him, hunched over as if her tired old feet were aching. But it was not unusual for Guiseppe not to notice women of any age. He generally had little use for them except as a complement to him at social functions. Guiseppe was fond of walking into prestigious environments where prominent individuals looked on in awe as he entered with a striking female on his arm.

Guiseppe did not exit the Frankfurt airport as expected. Instead he made his way to the ticket counter and purchased a ticket for Zurich on the next available flight. He then picked up a newspaper and strolled to the gate where he would wait for another hour to board his flight. It neither excited nor disturbed him that several of the young West German women took notice as he walked by. Guiseppe was accustomed to receiving unsolicited glances from persons of both sexes and, in truth, he had no real preference, except in social status and physical attractiveness.

In Zurich, Switzerland, Guiseppe walked out of the airport and signaled a taxi. He remembered his third trip to Zurich when he had felt confident enough about his knowledge of the lakeside city to rent a car and drive himself around. It had been a nightmare he would not soon forget. The streets, he was sure, were designed as a European plot to confuse Americans. Though pleasing to the eye, most of them ran only one way and then, for no apparent reason, changed names every few blocks. It was then that Guiseppe made a commitment to remain loyal to taxicabs.

A taxi pulled up and the driver hurried around the cab and gathered up Guiseppe's luggage. *"Dos Dolder Grande, bitte,"* Guiseppe said, in excellent German. He climbed in the back seat and started to close the door when an elderly woman approached. She leaned forward and looked at Guiseppe, who was astounded by the number of wrinkles in the old face. He shuddered at the thought of ever being that old.

The old woman smiled, her dry lips creasing and parting slightly. "Young man, please forgive the intrusion. My son was supposed to meet me here but I can't find him anywhere, and you look like such a kind man. I heard you mention the Dolder Grand Hotel. That's where I'm staying. Would it be possible to share a cab? I will pay the fare."

Guiseppe stared at her for a moment, and then answered, "I'm sorry, but —" Before he had completed his sentence, the old woman had shown the driver her bags and begun climbing into the taxi. She inched her way onto the seat, until Guiseppe was forced to make room for her. What an inconvenience, he thought sourly. Being forced into sharing a cab with an old fossil like this. It was nearly unbearable. He turned away, faced the window, and remained in

123

that position throughout the entire drive. The old woman straightened her skirt, adjusted her perfectly combed grey hair and smiled with satisfaction as the taxi bounced over the cobblestone streets of Zurich.

In front of the giant old stone Dolder Grand, one of the city's oldest and most exclusive hotels, Guiseppe got out of the cab, ordered the bellman to handle his luggage, and without glancing back at the elderly woman, walked into the hotel.

The old woman paid the fare and muttered something that the driver considered surprisingly obscene for a woman of her age. Her bags were wheeled into the lobby and she stopped by the main restrooms, where she remained for nearly thirty minutes.

Madison McGuire smiled at herself as she stepped in front of the mirror, set a small bag on the counter, and removed the grey wig. She shook out the thick chestnut hair under the wig and carefully removed the made-up wrinkles. She then stepped into a stall where she changed into a conservative brown skirt, a white ruffled top and flat cream-colored shoes.

At the reservation desk she registered under the name of Paula Emerson. As soon as the bellman left her room, Madison attached the scrambling device to the telephone, ordered a direct line, and dialed the number she remembered for Anthony Cane, code name Sugarbaker.

"The accommodations are quite adequate here. Are you in the area?" she asked.

"Yes. We've been with you the entire time. Our post is just around the corner. Your friend has made two calls. One to the restaurant downstairs, the other to the Unione di Banche Switzerland. He inquired as to their street address and said he would stop by in the afternoon. Oh, yes, he also called the front desk and asked not to be disturbed for three hours. He's going to take a nap. So, Scorpion, you can relax and get some rest. I'll ring you if there are any changes. And by the way, his room is only three doors away from you. Number four-one-four."

"Thank you. I'll be in touch."

Madison unpacked a few items and rang the restaurant. She was hungry and exhausted. Although it was eight a.m. in Zurich, her inside clock told her it was three a.m. She wondered if Terry was sleeping peacefully in North Carolina, and smiled remembering the last few days they had shared together.

Minutes later Madison heard a voice in the hallway. *"Zimmer bedie'nung, bitte."* Room service had arrived with her breakfast. Madison answered in German and asked the man to leave the food in the hallway, an old habit learned from many years in the intelligence business. Never open the door at any request. Always wait, always stall.

She waited to hear the descending footsteps of the waiter outside before opening the door. There were none. An alarm sounded in her trained mind.

She moved silently across the old floor of the hotel and reached into her bag for her automatic. Quietly snapped the silencer into place and moved to the bathroom, turning on the shower. With the agility of a cat closing in on its prey, she moved quickly, easily across the room and flattened her body against the wall behind the door.

Then another sound . . . A footstep . . . Someone outside shifting his weight from one foot to another. Madison's heart rate increased and she felt the rush of adrenaline that always came in these situations. The automatic in one hand, she quietly released the chain lock from the door, and once again flattened herself against the wall. Within seconds the knob began to slowly turn and the door was eased open just enough for the intruder to see inside. Madison did not move or breathe.

The intruder leaned further into the room and saw the steam escaping from the bath. Assured that his victim was safely in the shower, he took two steps inside the room, leaving the door slightly ajar. Madison did not recognize the would-be assailant, but the weapon in his hand was familiar enough, an Ingram Mac-10, capable of tearing the room to pieces with just one 9mm blast . . . It was time to move.

The man was now less than three feet in front of her, and she knew it might be her only chance to save herself and take the man alive. That was imperative. He was her only key to who was trying to kill her.

Madison took a short step forward. The old floorboards creaked and the man spun around. Madison lashed out with her right foot, bringing it up under his wrist with all her strength. The wrist snapped and the Mac-10 flew across the room. The intruder pivoted on one foot, spinning full circle, and smashed the other into Madison's stomach.

She felt the air rush out of her body and she hunched over, her arms around her stomach, the automatic still in her hand. She tried to regain some control. The man withdrew a knife from inside the white service jacket and lunged towards her. Madison raised up and smashed an elbow under his chin. The knife hit the floor as he reeled backwards and began crawling desperately towards the Mac-10. Madison took careful aim and fired once, sending a bullet to the back of the man's knee. He screamed and rolled over.

Madison pounced on him. Holding her gun to his temple, she demanded, "Who sent you?" The man did not answer. His face contorted in pain and he shook his head violently. "Tell me now. Who sent you?"

"Please, please," he begged. "I'll tell you everything. I have no more weapons. Help me." Madison pressed the gun harder against the temple, and expertly ran one hand over his body, searching for more weapons. She rose slowly and picked up the gun that had flown from his hand.

The man struggled to prop himself against the bed. "My knee . . . My wrist, it think it's broken." He brought his wrist close to his mouth and held it there for a few seconds in pain, and then let it fall limply to the floor.

Madison kept the gun on him as she eased across the room and closed the door. "All right," she said. "I'll ask you only once more. Who sent you? How did you know where to find me?"

The man looked at her, a sickening smile crossed his face, and suddenly he began to jerk and convulse, gasping for air. Then he was still, his eyes wide, glazed. Madison ran to him. She raised his hand and saw a thin strap attached to the broken wrist. Only remnants of the cyanide capsule remained.

Madison fell back into a chair. Who wanted to kill her? Who was so powerful that the killer knew he must take his own life rather than face questioning? There was only one answer, and Madison cursed aloud.

She then went to the briefcase and extracted the tiny camera, took several shots of the killer's face. Then she placed a small piece of transparent tape on the man's fingertips and pressed lightly. Her next move would be to let Sugarbaker know she had an important drop, and get the man's photos and fingerprints to the agency. Then she must dispose of the body and return in time to maintain surveillance on Louis Guiseppe and figure out what business he might have with the Unione di Banche Switzerland.

Few would have expected to find the head of the CIA and the NOIS sitting in a plain sedan, parked on the side of a street in an upper-middle class neighborhood. But both had agreed that they should personally handle this particular problem.

It was nearly eighty-five degrees in Washington and the air was thick. Troy Delcardo leaned forward and let his head rest on the steering wheel, a trickle of sweat running down his face. He turned to Andrew McFaye, who was in the passenger's seat. "It's just so hard to accept. Hadden was one of our best. Since he became DDO he's accomplished some remarkable things. He had such a bright future. The stupid bastard. I can't believe he's been sabotaging our operations from the inside, that he's been acting as an errand boy for Club Twelve."

Andrew sighed, and dabbed his forehead with a handkerchief. "He's the reason they always manage to find Madison. We double-checked the tap from Gascongnie's telephone. It was Hadden's voice, all right. He called Gascongnie after the attempted hit on

Madison in Vail. Thank God he never knew who Madison was trying to recruit up there, or the Woodall kid would probably be dead by now." He shifted his plump body in the seat. "You know, it's funny but Madison suspected him the whole time. She was the one who didn't want Hadden in on Accounting Central."

Delcardo looked in his rearview mirror. "Here he comes," he said.

The two men watched as Mark Hadden pulled into his driveway and walked towards the house. Hadden was fumbling with his front door keys when he heard Troy Delcardo's voice. "Hello, Mark."

Hadden spun around, the panic in his eyes clear as he looked at the two men standing in his front yard. He quickly regained control. "So, what brings you two big shots to my humble abode?" he asked casually.

"Something's come up," Andrew said. "Can we talk inside?"

Mark Hadden smiled and nodded. "Sure." He pushed the door open and walked in first. "Damn, it's going to be a hot summer. I hate the humidity in D.C. You guys want a drink?" He walked towards the bar and bent down, presumably for ice.

"No thanks," Delcardo said as he and Andrew both took chairs in the living room.

Andrew leaned forward and rested his elbows on his knees. He looked at Hadden, who was still standing behind the bar.

Suddenly Hadden was aware of the awful pounding in his chest, and his eyes began to dart back and forth from Delcardo to Andrew. At the same moment he saw two more cars pull up outside his home. His eyes widened, but he laughed lightly in a feeble attempt to hide his panic. "Hey, what is this anyway?"

"Mark, we know you've been leaking intelligence to Club Twelve. We also know you were involved in the attempt on Madison's life in London and Vail." Delcardo went on, "I'd like to make this easy on you. I'm prepared to offer you a deal if you're willing to cooperate."

Hadden looked shocked. "You can't be serious. You don't really believe this do you, Troy? There's been some kind of mistake. I'm not —"

Andrew broke in. "We have the evidence, Mark. You might as well talk."

"You bastard," Hadden answered angrily, and turned to Delcardo. "I'm not the one you want."

"Come on, Hadden," Delcardo answered. "Don't make us take you by force."

Mark Hadden began to tremble and a purplish color crept into his face. He raised a hand from under the bar, exposing a .38 caliber revolver. Delcardo rolled out of his chair with surprising agility. Hadden fired in his direction but missed. Andrew McFaye pulled his weapon from under his coat and fired. The bullet caught Hadden in the center of the forehead. He hit the floor, blood running from his eyes and mouth.

A tall woman with bright blue eyes dressed in soft leather pants tucked inside high suede boots approached the desk of the Dolder Grand Hotel. She wore a fashionable suede cap, and just a few stray locks of blonde hair could be seen from underneath. She offered the hotel manager a genuine smile which was immediately returned. He had seen many such women in his hotel. Usually they were models there for a fashion shoot, or expensive wives who came for extensive shopping.

The woman glanced at the name plate in front of the man and said, *"Gutten tag, Herr Strauss."* She then leaned forward and spoke quietly. "Herr Strauss, I have some rather urgent business to discuss with you. Could we speak privately?"

The manager stared at her for a moment. Something about the woman was familiar, but he could not place her. "I am a very busy man. May I inquire as to what type of business you wish to discuss, Frau . . . ?"

"Emerson," Madison supplied. "The name is Emerson. Is that a familiar name, Mr. Strauss?"

The manager's eyes widened slightly, as she had expected. She continued, "If you don't want me to use the gun I have pointed at your chest, sir, I suggest you show me into your office."

The manager's eyes dropped to the handbag Madison had casually laid on the counter, her hand inside. "Of course, Madame. Please follow me."

They walked into his private office and as soon as the door closed Madison grabbed the manager's arm and twisted it painfully behind his back. Holding her pistol against his back, she spoke calmly, in German, "Do not underestimate me, Herr Strauss. If you make a sudden move I will kill you. Do you understand?"

The man nodded nervously, beads of sweat forming on his upper lip. Madison slowly released his arm. "Sit down, Strauss, and tell me how much you were paid, and by whom, to give out my room number."

"Please, Frau Emerson, I do not know what you are talking about."

Madison sat down across the desk from him, and laid the pistol in front of her. She studied him momentarily, then asked, "Do you have a family, Herr Strauss?"

"I have a wife and two children," he replied, wiping the sweat from his lip with a trembling hand.

"If you're honest with me today, you'll get to see your family tonight. Someone tried to kill me in my room only an hour ago. He was wearing a hotel employee jacket. Who sent him and how did he know where I was?"

"I don't know. I swear. I do not know who he was."

Madison picked up the pistol and pulled the hammer back until it locked into place. "I am becoming very impatient, Herr Strauss. I have nothing to lose at this point. I didn't come here to kill you, but the prospect is becoming more appealing by the minute."

The manager held both hands in front of his face. "No. Please, I am so sorry. I swear I don't know who he was. I was paid. It is against hotel policy to give out the room numbers of our guests, but I'm in a difficult situation right now and I needed the money . . . I saw no real harm in it. I did not know he wanted to kill you. I am a peaceful man."

"Did he ask for me by name?"

"No. He wanted to know if any women had come in alone. I could remember only one. You."

Madison laid down the pistol again and studied

the man. The truth was in his eyes. He was too frightened to lie again. The information was something of a relief. It meant that no one, save one lone gunman randomly checking hotel rooms, knew the name Emerson. The operation was still safe. They didn't know what cover she was using.

"Herr Strauss," Madison said at length. "If you continue to cooperate, not only will you see your family tonight, but you will be a richer man." She reached into her bag and extracted two thousand American dollars. "I work for the American CIA, Herr Strauss, and I hope this will guarantee your loyalty for a few days."

The manager nodded enthusiastically. "It's more than adequate."

Madison leaned back in her chair and smiled. "Good. There will be others looking for a woman alone. I want you to cooperate with them. Oh, you shouldn't give in too easily, but give them the room number and tell them I've stepped out, and that I'm registered under the name of Jones. I want you to be sure that the name Emerson does not appear anywhere on your register. Do you follow me so far?"

The man nodded, and Madison went on, "Now I want you to have my things moved directly across the hall. I'll naturally pay you for both rooms. The minute anyone comes in, you are to ring my new room immediately. And please, Herr Strauss, if you double-cross us we will be forced to terminate our agreement. Do I make myself clear?"

"Oh, yes. Very clear. I will see to it that your wishes are carried out immediately. Will there be anything else?"

Madison looked at her watch and then at the

133

manager. "Yes. Please have your kitchen send up some food. I haven't eaten in hours."

Louis Guiseppe exited the Unione di Banche Switzerland. Carrying a leather briefcase, he strolled casually down Zurich's main street, the Bahnhofstrasse, past the ancient boat landings and cobblestone alleyways. He walked several blocks to Neumarkt Street, and the Old Town section of the city, which had been perfectly preserved since the eighteenth century. He paused in Lindenhof Square and watched one of the lakeside city's many street performers, a young man playing classical guitar, the case open at his feet. Guiseppe tossed in a few francs and Madison watched in surprise. Could this be the same man who had refused to pay cab fare for an old woman? Whatever business Guiseppe had had with the bank apparently had put him in an unusually generous mood.

A few blocks away, Guiseppe walked into an office supply store and had several pieces of paper in his briefcase copied. Madison thought she saw a smile on the handsome face when he returned to the street.

Following from a discreet distance, Madison watched Guiseppe go back into the hotel. Stopping at a newsstand only a hundred yards away, she casually scanned a newspaper, sure that her disguise allowed her to blend nicely with the crowds on that side of Zurich. She felt a bump at her elbow. A tall man politely excused himself, and then said, "Lovely city, isn't it?"

Madison nodded, recognizing the voice immediately.

Sugarbaker saw the recognition on her face and continued, "I was here in March, but I'm afraid it rained the entire time." He paid for a paper and nodded. "Good day."

Sugarbaker had just used a prearranged code. The month of March referred to the American Embassy or Consulate. Rain signified a message. He was telling her to go to the Consulate for a message.

Odd, Madison thought. Operatives rarely risked approaching one another on the streets of any city, especially Zurich which was filled with intelligence types from the KGB to the Mossad. There were a hundred more secure ways to communicate without risking another agency monitoring their activities. It was merely good tradecraft. Why had Sugarbaker broken the rules? The only explanation was that the message was urgent.

Madison turned and walked to a nearby taxi stand. *"Dos Amerikaner Konsulat, bitte,"* she said and the taxi roared off over the bridge and up the hill.

Chapter 12

The heavy door slammed shut and the sound echoed through the basement room of the American Consulate. Hearing the lock click from outside the guarded room, Madison picked up one of the secure telephone lines and dialed. A female voice answered, "Go ahead, please."

"Scorpion, three-double-o-three," Madison replied and, after a ninety second wait, Andrew McFaye came on the line.

"We've had some new developments in the last

few hours. Hadden turned on us. He was a plant," Andrew said.

Madison's mind raced. *So, that's how they knew I was in Zurich.* "Did you interrogate him?"

"No," McFaye answered, the tension in his voice clear. "We never had the chance. He's dead. But we found some interesting literature in his house. We now know the identity of seven Club Twelve members. It's not enough to move on officially, but it's a start. Six of the names were already on our suspect list. Only one was a real surprise. It was Stewart Lawrence," he said, and his voice trailed off.

"Lawrence?" Madison repeated. "The advisor to British Intelligence? I've met him several times."

Andrew sighed heavily. "I have new orders for you, and they come straight from the top. We believe that Club Twelve has a meeting planned. Six out of seven of the names on Hadden's list are either in Switzerland, or on their way there. Guiseppe is one of them. Stay close to him. We think he'll lead you to the meeting ground. If we're lucky the rest of them will show and we'll have a positive I.D. on all the members."

"I doubt that," Madison said flatly. "It would be foolish for all of them to meet in one place. So many men of consequence would most surely attract attention."

"You're probably right, but stick with it anyway." Andrew paused, and Madison thought she noticed a reluctance in his voice, a hesitation normally not there. "Madison, we've just discovered that there seems to be a pecking order within the group. Apparently certain members have more power than others. We think the order is something like this: Peter Mueller of Germany, Islom Jabril of Israel, Stewart Lawrence of England, Louis Dumas of France, Hans Baaker of Belgium, and Louis Guiseppe. The other five members probably fit in between somewhere. We think that if the two senior members of the group are taken out of their rank it would create power struggles, unrest and disharmony among the group. This is where your new orders fit in. Take them out, Scorpion, both Mueller and Jabril."

Madison sat back hard in her seat. "Christ, Andrew, I'm not an assassin. There must be another way to —"

"No." Andrew broke in firmly, all the hesitation in his voice gone. "There is no other way. I told you, the orders come from the top, the Oval Office, Madison. You're the best we have for this kind of assignment, and we cannot involve others in the operation. You already have top clearance. Now, can we count on you?"

There was a threatening tone in his voice that Madison had not heard before. Was he trying to warn her? She had seen what happened to operatives with top clearance who could no longer perform in the field. Why should she be an exception? She was either a great asset or a dangerous liability. She swallowed hard. Her throat felt dry and swollen. "It's just so hard to justify a direct hit," she said quietly.

Andrew's breathing reflected his growing anger. "You are in no position to bring up moral issues. Do you think the things these men have done can be justified?"

"That isn't a fair question," Madison retorted.

"It's not just a moral issue. I'm not pretending to be innocent. There are other things to consider here. We know Mueller and Jabril are involved in funding terrorist organizations. They lead large groups of fanatics. Terminating two men of such consequence in the terrorist world could have a serious backlash. More chaos may erupt than we ever thought possible. I'm merely suggesting that we take time to look at this realistically. The ramifications are —"

"The order has been issued, and we're in no position to question it," Andrew said, his voice low, authoritative. "I'm going to tell you something I should have told you long ago. We've known all this time who is responsible for killing your father. He was gunned down by a Syrian hit team because he got closer than anyone ever has until now to exposing a member of Club Twelve. That member was Amal Bahudi, the leader of the United Arab Republic. He gave the order to kill Jake McGuire, and then he had his body hung on a post in Halab for all to view the American spy."

Madison felt her heart pounding. She pushed back the tears, and somewhere under the ache she felt her anger mounting. "Why do you tell me this now? Because I dare to question the sanity of my orders? Because it finally serves your purpose?"

"Can't you see that we need your hurt and your anger now?" Andrew demanded. "What's happened to your passion and your outrage? Find it, Madison, and pull yourself back together and carry out your orders. No questions. No mistakes. No bullshit. If you refuse I cannot support your decision or protect you. Do I make myself clear?"

139

Madison sat up in the chair, trying hard to push away the images of her father's body on a post in Syria. *The bastards . . .* "Yes," she answered suddenly. "Perfectly clear. Are Mueller and Jabril both in Switzerland?" she asked coldly.

"Mueller will be in Zurich tonight, our sources tell us. We aren't sure about Jabril yet."

Madison thought for a moment, and then asked quietly, "Where is Amal Bahudi?"

There was a long silence. Andrew answered at last, "He's in Zurich at the Carlon du Lac. I know what you're thinking, Madison, but remember Amal Bahudi isn't part of the assignment."

Andrew heard the line disconnect. He took a deep breath and leaned back in his chair at the Langley office. Those bastards will be lucky if any of them make it out of Switzerland alive, he thought without regret.

Madison leaned forward and ran a hand across her forehead and through her hair. A familiar burn emerged from within, one that she had not felt since meeting Terry. Perhaps Andrew had posed a valid question. Was she losing her anger? Her outrage? She had thought it a step forward, but now she saw that the agency could only view it as the loss of an effective operative, who only a year ago would have accepted orders to kill without question.

"Goddammit," she yelled aloud, and her words echoed through the secure room. It was as if two separate entities, in constant conflict, lived inside her. There was the Madison who longed for a life away from the killing, away from the hurt, the hate, the anger. A woman who yearned to spend all day lying in the sand. A woman who wanted to go to the market, learn to sculpt, to play the piano . . . Were there still people with such concerns? It was hard to believe when you lived in her world.

Then there was the other Madison. The cold professional who carried out orders efficiently, without emotion. The one who forced her to keep fighting until they all paid the price for taking so many lives. Jake McGuire, Elicia Peabody, Terry's Jonothan Shore, and countless others among the group that had fallen victim to Club Twelve. Would one personality ever allow the other to live in peace? Would she ever fuse them into one whole, caring person?

She knew the answer. There would be nights of calm sleep, uninterrupted by nightmares of Elicia being killed in the streets of London, of men and women fighting secret wars where there were no medals of valor for brave deeds, only when her mission was complete. She knew she could not turn her back and walk away now. It was time to either make an effort to end the madness, or die in the trying. Andrew had said it once: "It's the life we've chosen." Now, Madison saw no alternatives that she could live with. No right. No wrong.

Perhaps, she thought, when this was all over she would leave the NOIS. She would find a way to get out safely, disappear. It's a shame, she mused, that one must protect oneself from one's own government. A government to which she had given half of her life. And later, if Terry would still have her, they could try and build something together.

* * * * *

Thousands of miles away, in Buxton, North Carolina, Terry Woodall sat on the wooden deck of her new house, a book spread open in front of her, a bologna sandwich in her hand. She checked her watch and wondered what Madison was doing now. Was it daylight wherever she was? Was she in Washington, locked away in some antiseptic-looking room analyzing some secret writing? Was she in some faraway city following a shady character on unfamiliar streets? Was there another lover waiting somewhere to hear from her?

Terry sighed and took an unenthusiastic bite from the sandwich. *God, why doesn't she call?* She smiled and shook her head. "Give yourself a break, Woodall," she muttered aloud, and returned to her book.

On the way back to the Dolder Grand Hotel, Madison opened an envelope given to her at the consulate, and pulled out a picture of Peter Mueller and one of Islom Jabril. A strange and eerie feeling swept over her. The two men she looked at had just been given a death sentence without a trial. She put the photographs away and tried to push her feelings aside and concentrate on her orders. Suddenly a vague plan came into focus and Madison McGuire the professional, the operative, the paid killer, leaned back in her seat and closed her eyes.

Chapter 13

Madison returned to her hotel room and immediately made three telephone calls. The first was to the NOIS listening post which had been set up within a block of the Dolder Grand. Sugarbaker's agent reported that Louis Guiseppe had made a call to a local restaurant and reserved a table for nine o'clock. Madison then rang up that very restaurant and reserved a table in the name of Paula Emerson for eight-thirty.

Her third and last call was made to Dr. Phillip Kruger. The conversation was short, and Madison hung up knowing that by the end of the evening she would have the information she needed from Louis Guiseppe.

After finishing a dinner of fresh lake fish and spaetzli, Louis Guiseppe leaned back and watched in amusement as the restaurant patrons clapped along with a folklore show that had just begun on the lower level of the restaurant.

The restaurant, the Fischtube Zurichhorn, offered one of the best views in the city, and Guiseppe's table overlooked Zurich Lake. He ordered a cognac and peered out the wide window.

Zurich was an old city, equally divided by the water, and at night the glistening city lights formed a circle around the clear water and sparkled, Guiseppe thought, like a jeweled necklace. He liked Switzerland. The Swiss were famous for their secretive ways, their coded bank accounts, and their beautiful old cities. All of these things Guiseppe accepted with deep appreciation.

Guiseppe's drink was delivered. He accepted it with a nod and glanced around the restaurant. Two tables away he noticed a woman, sitting alone, facing the window. Something about her drew his attention. Something in the way she moved, slowly, deliberately sipping her drink, oblivious to all others around her. He studied her. The back was straight, but not tense. She held her chin tilted slightly upward, accenting a fine, straight nose and wide, dark eyes. *Who is she? Why is she so familiar?*

Suddenly, the woman turned and looked directly

144

at Guiseppe, held his eyes for a moment, and then turned away, uninterested.

A waiter approached the woman's table. "Frau Emerson?" the waiter asked and the woman nodded. "You have a telephone call."

"*Danke,*" Madison answered. "*Bringen das telephon hier, bitte.*"

The waiter bowed slightly and hurried away. Guiseppe watched, still trying to place her, and straining to hear her words as the waiter delivered the telephone to her table. Guiseppe held out his arm and stopped the waiter.

The waiter paused, "Another drink, sir?"

Guiseppe withdrew a fifty franc note from his pocket and laid it on the table. "Yes, I'll have another, and tell me, who is the woman with the telephone?"

The waiter smiled and quickly pocketed the fifty francs. "Emerson, sir. Paula Emerson, I believe. Will there be anything else?"

Guiseppe shook his head. He knew of this woman, of course. Emerson Designs had worked with Woodall Enterprises many times, but still he could not understand why she was so familiar. After all, they had never met.

His next drink was delivered, and he watched the woman as he drained it and ordered another. She was stunning, he mused, and he still had one long night alone in Zurich. Perhaps . . .

He stood and approached her table, greeting her with his most dazzling smile. "It's very nice to meet you, Ms. Emerson. I'm Louis Guiseppe." He extended his hand.

The woman turned and looked at him as if he

145

were carrying an infectious disease. Ignoring his outstretched hand, she said curtly, "That is fascinating news, Mr. Guespsky, but if you wouldn't mind, I prefer dining alone."

Guiseppe withdrew his hand and straightened his shoulders. He stood there a moment feeling more awkward than he ever had in his life, while the woman stared blankly at him. "You don't understand —"

"Mr. Guespsky," Madison said, knowing enough about Louis Guiseppe from the background info she had studied on the plane to know that above all he liked a challenge, "although I appreciate your attempts, no matter how feeble or inept they may be, I will remind you that this is not an American pick-up joint. You would do me a great service if you would slither back to whatever rock you crawled out from under."

"The name is Guiseppe," he said, trying to disguise his fury and embarrassment. "I'm afraid you have misunderstood my intentions. But, as long as I'm here let me ask you a question. Do all men slither as far as you're concerned, or is it just people in general that you don't like? You apparently have an over-inflated view of yourself. I merely wanted to meet you. I won't blame you for not recognizing my name. However, I should tell you that you should be more polite to your customers in the future. Now, if you'll excuse me, I have a rock waiting." He started away.

Madison stood. "Mr. Guiseppe, should I know you?" she asked, and Louis stopped, his back turned to the woman, a smile on his face. He returned to the table, and extended his hand once again. "Shall we begin again?" he asked. "I'm with Woodall Enterprises, Inc."

Madison gestured to the extra chair at her table. "Please join me. I owe you an apology, Mr. Guiseppe. It's just that —"

"Please call me Louis," he said, taking his chair. "No explanation is necessary. I'm sure a woman of your obvious charms is approached quite often." The charming smile returned. "Besides, that was the most stimulating conversation I've had with a woman in some time."

Madison returned the smile. "If you won't let me apologize, at least let me buy you a drink. Let's see, I would guess you to be a scotch man. Am I right?"

"Absolutely," Guiseppe lied, and Madison nodded to the waiter.

Within minutes of Guiseppe's first sips of scotch his head began to spin, and his elbow slipped off the table.

"Are you all right?" Madison asked.

"Just feeling the scotch a little more than usual," he answered. A drunken smile suddenly crossed his face, and he added loudly, "I want you to now I have a terrific erection right now."

Madison's eyes widened in true surprise and she glanced around the restaurant. Most eyes were on their table. Guiseppe reeled, and his head hit the table. He was out. Mission complete.

Madison stood and gasped in rehearsed surprise, and a small man with a pinkish bald head hurried to the table. "I am a doctor," he said in German. "Is there anything I can do?"

"I'm not sure, Doctor. He just fell over," Madison answered as the waiter returned to her table and offered his assistance. "Please get me both checks immediately," Madison ordered. "And help the doctor get this poor man to the hospital."

The waiter nodded, and he and Dr. Phillip Kruger began to drag the drugged body of Louis Guiseppe from the restaurant.

Thirty minutes later Phillip Kruger, Madison McGuire, and one of Sugarbaker's sub-agents who was dressed as a waiter, carried Guiseppe's limp body into the doctor's home and laid him across the couch. Assured that Guiseppe would be out for at least another hour, Madison and Phillip Kruger moved into the doctor's study.

Madison glanced around at the heavy bookcases packed with medical journals. The desk top was littered with open books, ink pens and papers several layers high. The unkempt study was in direct contradiction to the meticulous little man Madison knew as Dr. Phillip Kruger, but she guessed that he knew exactly where everything was on that desk, and, if asked, would go efficiently to the proper layer of clutter to retrieve the proper book or paper.

The doctor crossed the room, a tiny vial in his hand. "This should do nicely. Our guest will be happy to answer your questions."

Madison looked at Phillip and smiled. "The scotch and the drugs certainly had an interesting effect. Wouldn't you say?"

The small man chuckled, his amused eyes wrinkled to slits. "Yes. I must remember to tell the poor fellow that he announced with great pride to everyone in

the restaurant that he had a terrific erection."
Madison and the doctor shared a good laugh at
Guiseppe's expense, and Madison noticed the sparkle
in Kruger's eyes. He did love his work. Madison had
seen him, needle in hand, pry secrets out of even the
best trained minds without leaving a tiny memory, or
even a trace on the arm. Years ago she and Kruger
had drugged and questioned Yuri Androv, a KGB
operative. The information they obtained had led to
major intelligence breakthroughs in the electronic
surveillance fields.

Kruger and Madison returned to the room where
Guiseppe lay sprawled across the couch. He was
beginning to stir a bit, and Madison looked at the
doctor questioningly. Kruger smiled reassuringly. "It's
good that he wakes partially. His pulse is up. This is
good too. Chemicals can be very dangerous. If not
administered in the proper doses they can be lethal.
But, we will be careful, no?"

"Yes. Do be careful, Doctor. It's important that
this man lives. If you have any questions as to
whether or not he can take Pentothal —"

Kruger waved a hand. "Do not worry, my dear.
He'll do fine. It will not be a very attractive sight,
but he'll make it."

Madison nodded, remembering the times she had
seen chemical interrogations. It was never pleasant.
Many times the subject jerked in violent spasms,
foamed at the mouth, cursed, vomited and thrashed
about. Madison often wondered why Kruger seemed to
enjoy his specialty so much. In all other respects he
was a gentle man.

The doctor dabbed a spot on Guiseppe's arm with
antiseptic, tapped the air out of the syringe and

149

carefully slipped the point under the skin. He turned to Madison and smiled. "Going up," he said, and pushed the chemical into the vein.

Nearly an hour passed before Kruger or Madison were able to get anything from Guiseppe other than incoherent mumbling. At length he mumbled something, barely audible.

"What is he saying?" Madison asked the doctor.

Phillip Kruger held up one hand for silence and moved his ear closer to Guiseppe's mouth. "I believe he is saying Vaduz . . . Yes. That is it, Vaduz."

Madison smiled. "Of course. Vaduz, Liechtenstein. The meeting is in Liechtenstein. Now all we have to do is find out where in Vaduz and I'm on my way."

Chapter 14

It was nearly two a.m. in Zurich, Switzerland and Madison McGuire was exhausted. She had not slept since leaving North Carolina. Now she sat at Dr. Phillip Kruger's kitchen table drinking black coffee and smoking a cigarette, waiting for an automobile to be delivered by one of Sugarbaker's sub-agents.

The cup was barely empty when she heard the engine outside, and she watched through the window as the agent got out of the car and walked casually down the block, leaving the keys in the ignition. Madison recognized the automobile immediately. It had been sent to Zurich last year as a test car by the Science and Technology Department at Langley, and was apparently capable of extraordinary speed.

She climbed in the white Mercedes 450SL and examined the control panel. There was nothing very unusual about the vehicle, except that it was equipped with an onboard computer which displayed a city street map on its screen with a flashing dot to indicate the driver's exact location. The car was equipped with a mobile telephone. However, there were no death ray buttons or James Bond-type ejector seats. "No fun," Madison said aloud, and smiled as she started the engine.

She drove back to the hotel and circled twice before deciding to use the service entrance. She wasn't sure if the hotel was being watched, and she knew she was in no condition for a confrontation.

Once on the fourth floor, she crept silently down the long quiet corridor towards her room. Only yards away she heard a sound . . . A creak in the floor . . . A doorknob turning.

Moving quickly, Madison pressed herself against the wall only a few feet away from the opening door. It opened wider . . . An inch, a foot, two feet, and then a woman stepped out, wrapping a coat around her shoulders. Suddenly she stopped and turned. Madison's heart leaped when she saw the cruel thin lips and the black eyes of Helda Steiner, one of the most sought after terrorists in Europe, a killer and a former member of the Red Army Faction of West Germany.

Madison's hand was firmly on her pistol. She motioned to the killer. "Move back into the room. Very slowly."

Steiner's cold eyes blazed, the cruel face drawn and tight. "Move," Madison repeated, pulling back the hammer until it locked into place with a click. Helda Steiner turned slowly, took one deliberate step into the dark room, and then abruptly spun around, bringing a hand crashing down against Madison's wrist.

Madison reeled. She tried to keep a grip on her weapon but it was too late. The gun hit the floor, and at the same moment Madison saw the flash of silver in the dim light, felt a blade at her throat. She closed her eyes in defeat, sure that in another second she would feel the icy incision at her neck. It did not come.

Madison opened her eyes slowly, her heart racing, and saw the killer's thin lips pull into a rigid smile, heard the thick German accent. "I will save you for later, coward," Steiner whispered, and bolted down the dim corridor.

Madison took a deep breath and fell back against the wall. Why had Steiner saved her? Why had she run?

Still a bit shaky and considerably puzzled, but nonetheless determined to get to Liechtenstein and find the Club Twelve meeting, Madison went back to her room, changed into comfortable shoes and clothes, gathered her things and left the old Dolder Grand Hotel.

She dialed Sugarbaker's number from the mobile phone before leaving the city limits of Zurich. He answered sleepily. Madison began angrily, "Why wasn't I informed that Helda Steiner was in Zurich at the very hotel where I've been staying?"

"Scorpion? Good Lord, woman. Do you never

sleep? Helda Steiner in Zurich? It's impossible. I know everyone who comes into this town. We've had no intelligence on Steiner."

"Someone is not giving you reliable information, my dear Cane. Steiner is here all right. We've just shared a very close encounter."

"My God, old girl. Are you all right? Are you injured in any way?" Anthony Cane asked.

"Only my pride," Madison answered. "She let me go when she could have killed me."

"That doesn't sound like the Helda Steiner we know. How very odd," he muttered, more to himself than to Madison.

"Let headquarters know she's here, would you? Be sure all your agents are alerted. The next one of us she bumps into may not be so lucky."

Max Rudger, firearms specialist and gunsmith extraordinaire, started at the sound of his telephone ringing in the middle of the night, rolled out of bed and walked through the house in his underwear. "Well, I'll be damned," he said in a thick Irish brogue. "Been thinking about you, Madison. Had a feeling you were close, and here you are by God. Well now, will you be dropping by?"

"Yes. I'm very close. Would you mind terribly?" Madison asked from her mobile phone.

"Of course I wouldn't mind. Come on, old girl. I'll heat us up a bit of coffee."

Max Rudger was a large, burly man with the rough scarred face of a soldier of fortune. He and Madison McGuire had met eleven years ago in

Ireland, and had taken to each other at once. They were an unlikely pair — Max rough and unpolished, Madison terminally British, but they were loyal friends.

He answered the door wearing faded jeans and no shirt. His stomach was considerably larger than Madison remembered, and a good portion of it hung over his belt. His smile was broad and sincere. "Well now, just look at you. A sight for sore eyes, you are. It's been a long time, Madi." He hugged her so tightly she was barely able to breathe. He pulled away and put one giant hand on each shoulder. "I'm so sorry, Madison dear, about Elicia. It's a bloody crying shame . . . I hope you'll be staying on a few days." He led her towards a small kitchen table covered with a red checkered tablecloth.

Madison sat down and smiled. "I'm sorry to say this isn't a social call, Max. In fact I'm in a bit of a hurry."

Max leaned back hard in his chair and shook his head. "Now isn't that just like you. I haven't seen you in almost two bloody years and you want to talk business."

Madison smiled. "I'm afraid so. But, I'd love a cup of that coffee you promised."

Max poured the thick black liquid through a strainer into their cups. "So, what is it I can do for you?"

"I need a rifle," Madison answered. "Probably a bolt-action. Something accurate but not too loud."

Max Rudger considered her suspiciously for a moment, then returned to the table and straddled a chair facing Madison. "And just what are you up to now, Madison McGuire? You're going to get yourself

155

in trouble one day, you know." He looked over his cup at her, his bushy eyebrows lowering in concern.

"I assure you, sir, I am as capable as you are. My survival instincts are very good."

Max seemed to find this uproariously funny. Madison could not understand why. "All right then Miss Capable Woman. Let's make our way downstairs."

They walked down a narrow, dark stairway into a basement. Madison paused at the base of the stairs while Max pulled the string on a bare light bulb. The room was lined with heavy glassfront cases, all filled with a wide array of weaponry. The basement air was thick and heavy, and smelled of cleaning fluid and gun metal.

Walking around a long wooden table in the center of the room, a table covered with grease rags and stray disassembled pieces of metal, Max opened a case, withdrew a rifle, and quickly, with no warning, tossed it to Madison. He threw his head back and laughed heartily when Madison automatically caught the weapon and positioned it without thought. "Very good," he said, smiling. "Still haven't lost your touch, I see."

He crossed the room, pointing to the weapon in her hands. "This little babe can shoot right along with the most accurate bolt-action. It's semi-automatic with an accuracy of two tenths of an inch at a hundred yards. What do you think?" he asked, sounding more like a proud father showing off his daughter to a potential suitor than a gun seller.

Madison studied the weapon for a moment. "I've used the AR-15 type before, but never this Ultra Match model."

"I've made a few modifications," he announced proudly. "It has a folding stock. Very handy for someone in your business, wouldn't you say? I also put a spacer at the rear to give it the proper pull, and a target scope that magnifies twenty-four times."

"What kind of ammo?" Madison asked, seeing Max's delight in having the opportunity to display his expertise.

"You'll get the best results using a .223, 55 grain." He paused and Madison saw the slight sparkle in the big man's bright blue eyes. "Madi, you've never seen anything like this one. Pluck the hair off a snail's ass at a hundred yards, it will."

Madison smiled at that, and asked, "How much?"

Max Rudger chuckled. "Now, that's what I like, a lady who gets right down to business." He rubbed his thick mustache and peered at Madison through heavy brows. "Let's say, just for you, fifteen hundred, American."

Madison's eyes widened. "This thing isn't worth five hundred in the States."

"Well now, you're not in the States, are you?" he said slyly.

Madison smiled and dug deep into the pocket of her jeans. "You're still a bandit, Max Rudger, but I love you."

After one more cup of coffee Madison left Max Rudger's small farmhouse, but not before he gave her a strong hug and said, "Remember, dear Madison, if you ever need a place to go, my house is your house."

* * * * *

Louis Guiseppe walked into the side entrance of an empty storage warehouse in Vaduz, Liechtenstein, and stood for a moment, giving his eyes time to adjust to the dim light, his head still spinning from the scotch he had consumed the evening before, although he could remember none of it. He saw a long table in the center of the warehouse, and counted several empty chairs. He heard a voice and squinted to make out its origin.

Peter Mueller said, "Glad you could make it, Louis." He walked towards Guiseppe, a hand extended.

Louis Guiseppe accepted the hand. "I'm sorry I'm late. I haven't been feeling well. Where are the others? I only count five."

A small round man with sharp eyes stood and glared at Guiseppe. "Did you really think we would all come? This is risky enough. I must insist on knowing what this is all about."

Guiseppe turned and looked at Mueller questioningly. Mueller smiled. "This is Hans Baaker, Louis, and to my right we have Amal Bahudi, Louis Dumas, and you know Sir Stewart Lawrence."

Each man nodded as he was introduced. Bahudi and Dumas chose to lean back out of the dim light, their faces shaded. Guiseppe persisted. "When do I meet the others?"

Mueller displayed a patient smile. "When we all agree that you are ready, my friend. Patience is a virtue you have yet to learn. Please, sit down, Louis, and tell us why we are here."

Guiseppe laid his briefcase on the table in front of him, pulled out a stack of papers and tossed them to the center of the table. He addressed the men with confidence. "Gentlemen, this is a record of Club Twelve dating back to nineteen fifty-two. It names ten of our members, their backgrounds, and documents the Club's activities in the last twenty-six years. This file has enough valid information in it to put you all away for a very long time." He paused and watched as the others shifted uncomfortably in their seats. "However, I have no intention of using this information against you. I brought it here as a gesture of good faith, a symbol of my loyalty. This file came from a safety deposit box belonging to the late Marcus Radcliffe." He paused again briefly to allow the others to exchange glances and whispers. "I risked my neck to get this file. I've saved us from the one man who could destroy our group to prove I'm worthy of your trust. Now, I think I have the right to demand to meet the others and be told who the secret member is that's not on this list."

Hans Baaker's fat jaws quivered in anger. He shouted, "You will demand nothing. You are an arrogant American fool. You risk exposure for nothing. You killed Radcliffe for nothing."

The confusion on Guiseppe's face was clear. "What are you saying? Don't you understand what I did? What I brought you today?"

Stewart Lawrence broke in calmly. "Mr. Guiseppe, I'm afraid Hans is right. You see, we knew this file existed. We knew Radcliffe was going to deliver it to American Intelligence. What you apparently did not know was that we have a man in Washington. Once the file got to him it would have gone no further. The contents would have been replaced with information of little value, and Radcliffe would have been dismissed as a paranoid old fart. The original information would have been destroyed immediately. So, you see, you took the risk for nothing, and it *was* a risk, my boy."

Guiseppe's face flushed. "Why wasn't I told? Why don't you keep me informed?"

"Trust takes time, Louis," Peter Mueller answered. "Perhaps if you had told us of your plan we could have prevented you from taking the risk. We function as one unit. If it's glory you want you're in the wrong place. However, your efforts were noble and we will take this into consideration. Now, if you have nothing else to share with us, you may go."

"You can't just dismiss me like a child."

Mueller walked to Guiseppe and touched his arm firmly. "We will be in touch. We have a large shipment coming from your company in a few weeks. We'll talk before then. Goodbye Louis."

Louis Guiseppe grabbed his briefcase angrily and hurried out.

Mueller looked at Steward Lawrence. "Do you think he made copies of the file?"

"Most certainly," Lawrence answered.

Amal Bahudi's black eyes flashed. "We will have to dispose of him very soon."

The others nodded their agreement.

Outside, Madison was positioned on one of the low warehouse rooftops only fifty yards away from the meeting. The information she and the doctor had obtained from Guiseppe the night before had been accurate, and Madison had found her way there with ease. So far she had managed to photograph the four

160

guards outside and everyone who had entered the warehouse. She recognized several of the men: Stewart Lawrence she knew from London, Peter Mueller from the photograph given her at the Consulate, and she guessed that Amal Bahudi was the dark man in the white robe. She did not recognize Hans Baaker, and was careful to get a close-up of his face.

Thirty minutes after Guiseppe stormed angrily out of the building, the side door opened and Peter Mueller walked out with Amal Bahudi. Madison flattened her body against the rooftop and pulled the semi-automatic assault rifle close to her. Slowly, she raised it to her shoulder and looked through the scope, Peter Mueller's chest in her sights.

Madison knew she must do what she was sent for. It was now or never. Her finger twitched and then tightened around the trigger. Beads of perspiration formed on her forehead and over her lips. Her heart raced. Her head pounded. She applied more pressure to the trigger and felt it begin to give.

Then there was a thunderous boom, and another. The sound of a rifle being fired from only yards away. Madison started and missed her mark. Her shots ricocheted off the warehouse below. She looked over the edge of the roof. Peter Mueller and Amal Bahudi both lay in a pool of deep red blood.

Madison heard the running footsteps. She heard voices from below, orders being given and guards scrambling about in a panic. She turned in time to see a figure running across an adjacent rooftop. A woman — wearing a khaki shirt and pants. She carried a rifle close to her, and most incredibly, her hair was very red. Just before the woman jumped

161

from the rear of the warehouse, Madison caught a glimpse of her face. It was the killer Helda Steiner in a red wig.

Madison was stunned. Why was Steiner there? Why had she shot Mueller and Bahudi? And why, in God's name, was she wearing a red wig?

The guards below piled into automobiles and roared around the warehouse looking for the killer. Once the area was clear, Madison took off the tight gloves she wore and discarded the rifle. She found her automobile and headed out of Liechtenstein, still asking herself why Steiner had been there.

Thirty miles away Madison stopped at a Post Telephone and Telegraph office and sent a coded message to Andrew McFaye in Langley. She explained, as best she could, what had happened in Liechtenstein, and also reported that she had several photographs which she would deliver to the usual drop site in Zurich in the next twenty-four hours.

She climbed back in her car, but something told her not to return to Zurich. Something told her it wasn't safe. She drove towards Max Rudger's house.

Chapter 15

Max had only to see her face when she stepped into his house to know that Madison McGuire was near total exhaustion. He took her arm and led her to the bedroom, tucked a blanket tightly around her, and watched as she drifted off to sleep.

She did not stir until the next morning, and even then it took Max's hand on her shoulder and the smell of strong coffee to wake her.

"We've got eggs, toast, coffee and some damn good conversation in the kitchen if you're up to it," Max said cheerfully, and then left her to herself.

Madison wandered sleepily into the tiny kitchen and sat down. Without a word Max filled her coffee cup, piled a plate with food and pushed it in front of her.

Madison accepted it silently but gratefully, and ate with enthusiasm. At length Max inquired, "You want anyone to know you're here?"

Madison shook her head.

"Well, someone wanted to know. That fancy car of yours had a tracing device on the underside."

Madison laid down her fork and looked at him. "Is it activated?"

Max smiled and the blue eyes twinkled. "Oh, yes. It was a live one. Don't you be worrying about it though. Right now it's stuck to the underside of a Zurich taxi. I made a little trip into the city while you slept."

Madison, finishing her breakfast, pushed her plate aside. "Thanks, love." She was still trying to piece the puzzle together in her mind.

Max watched her quietly for a moment. "Tell me what happened after you left London. Did they try to put you on the shelf?"

"Almost. They stuck me behind a desk for a while."

"You glad to be back in the field again?" Max persisted.

Madison sighed and lit a cigarette. "I don't know, Max. It's funny in a way. I wanted to get back out here so bad. Now . . . I'm beginning to wonder if I'm not getting too old for this kind of work."

"Ah, hogwash," Max replied with a smile. "You're barely in the prime of your life, Madison. Maybe you're just feelin' a bit guilty. It happens to the best soldiers, you know. In the dark and still of the night when those images run before our eyes, we wonder if what we're doing is right or wrong. I know how it is. I questioned myself so many times during my IRA days."

Madison smiled and took a sip of coffee. "I wish I were that noble. No, Max, I don't think it's guilt getting to me. I'm not that moral, you understand. I'm just tired, and I'm losing my nerve."

"Is that what I see that's eating away at you? Is that what's on your mind?"

Madison went on to explain the bizarre events in Liechtenstein. About Helda Steiner killing Mueller and Bahudi, about Steiner going out of her way to be seen, about the horrible red wig the killer wore, about the encounter in the hotel with the terrorist.

Max listened quietly, occasionally rubbing his thick mustache and twisting up the corners in thought. When Madison was finished, he said, "Looks like a clean frame-up to me, Madi. It's obvious she wanted everyone to think it was you who killed those men. After all, you are a bit of a legend in your own time. No one really knows what you look like, but there's a story about an American agent with red hair. And only a few of us know you don't take your red hair into the field." He paused in thought and then finished, "Christ, don't ya see? It's perfect. She couldn't kill you in that hotel because if you were dead you couldn't take the blame for the Liechtenstein killings."

Madison looked at him in disbelief. "That's absurd. What would be her motive?"

Max leaned back and propped his feet up on the table. His blue eyes glowed with excitement, the challenge to think and plan and use his mind again — something he was very good at. "Perhaps she doesn't work alone. Perhaps she has been hired to do the job on you."

Madison thought about that for a moment. "She just killed the two men who finance the Red Army's activities and a handful of Islamic terrorist organizations. Who else could she be working for? And why would she kill men who are essentially on her side?"

"Let's backtrack a bit. Peter Mueller is the man you were supposed to take out, right?" Madison nodded. "Okay. So how did the Syrian get involved in this? If this is a set-up and someone in Washington wants you taken out, then there must have been a reason for killing Amal Bahudi along with Peter Mueller. Is there any personal connection between you and the Arab?"

Madison stared at him for a moment. "What makes you think there's a connection?"

"If there isn't, then why would you kill him?"

"I didn't kill him, Max. I bloody well told you that," Madison snapped. "I didn't even want to accept the hit on Mueller. But, when they told me about —"

"Max sat up straight. "Told you about what, Madison. What is it?"

"Andrew told me Bahudi was the one who had my father executed in Syria," Madison answered quietly.

"Holy Mother of God," Max mumbled. "And upon hearing this you accepted the orders? They set you up. I'm willing to bet on it."

"Who set me up? And why?" Madison asked, frustrated.

Max leaned back and answered quietly. "That, my dear, is what we're going to have to find out. In the meantime you're to stay here where you'll be safe. The car's hidden in a shed so no one can see it. Now, I think I'll be taking a ride into Zurich. I'll see what I can find out. Need anything?"

"Some cigarettes and a local paper, and a *Washington Post* if you can find one."

Max stood up and found his keys. He gave Madison a quick peck on the cheek. "You got it, love. See you soon."

Troy Delcardo walked into Andrew McFaye's office, his long drawn face showing more tension than usual. Approaching Andrew's desk, he handed him a decoded wire from Switzerland. "What do you think?" he asked impatiently, and before Andrew could reply, he went on. "I think it's bullshit, Andy. She lost her head out there and took out Bahudi and Mueller. Then she made up a story about this woman, Helda Steiner, to cover her ass."

Andrew lit his pipe; the smell of cherry tobacco filled the room. "That doesn't sound like the Madison I know. I've never known her to lose her head on assignment. And even if she did, Troy, she sure as hell wouldn't allow herself to be seen. Madison's a pro all the way."

Troy pulled up a chair and sat across from Andrew. He leaned forward, his eyes narrowed. "Are you saying you believe this ridiculous story? You really think Steiner put on a red wig and killed those two men? Come on, Andrew. I think your number one

167

girl just lost her shit, went nuts, and then ran like hell."

"Madison never goes into the field with red hair. Never. You know that. She'd be a target for every glory-seeking fanatic and enemy agent on the street. Stratton told me when he met her at the air base a few days ago her hair was chestnut brown."

There was a knock on the door, and Marshall Stratton walked in, a sheet of paper in his hand. "This is the report on Helda Steiner," Stratton said sadly. "She was seen in West Germany yesterday morning. There's no way she could have been in Vaduz, Liechtenstein at the same time."

Marshall walked out of the office and Troy studied Andrew's reaction to the information. "I don't have to tell you, Andy, that we have a big problem. Someone leaked it to the press. The nosy bastards were outside my home this morning. They asked if I'd seen the headlines and if I approved of political assassination. They wanted to know if we sent our agent to kill Mueller and Bahudi. The shit has really hit the fan. Syrian Intelligence says they'll pick up every agent we have over there and charge them with spying unless we hand her over and make a public apology. The Germans want her to stand trial in their country, and every fanatic faction in the Middle East wants our ass. They're promising to strike back against all U.S. citizens in their countries and across Europe. And the President called. He wants to see us this afternoon. Have any idea what the fuck we're gonna tell him?"

"Madison didn't do this, Troy. It's not her style. That's what I'm going to tell President Boone."

Madison crossed the small kitchen and picked up the telephone. She knew it was a risk, knew that Terry's phone could be tapped, but she needed to hear her voice. She would keep her calls to under a minute, rendering them untraceable, until she found out exactly what was going on within the agency.

Terry answered, and Madison began, "Hello, darling. I only have a few seconds to tell you that I love you and I'm thinking about you."

Terry sighed. "It's so good to hear your voice. Are you all right? Are you coming home soon?"

Madison smiled. "I'm fine, and I hope I'll be home very soon. I just wanted to hear your sweet voice. I'm sorry I can't stay on longer. Goodbye, love."

Max Rudger did not return from Zurich until very late in the afternoon. His face seemed pale and more tired than usual. Madison watched him walk from his truck to the house, and knew immediately that his mood was serious. He entered the house, a large, imposing figure, and frowned in Madison's general direction.

"Sit down, Madison," he directed, crossing the kitchen and pouring two shots of whiskey. He downed one and slid the second in front of Madison. "Drink it. You're going to be needin' it."

Reading his face, Madison followed his lead and tossed the shot glass back, feeling the warm whiskey in the back of her throat. "What's wrong?" she questioned, only half wanting to know whatever news he had.

169

He tossed a newspaper in front of her and walked to the sink, staring at her as if he could read the effect of the words she was about to see.

Madison stared at the front page of the *Washington Post* in disbelief.

U.S. INTELLIGENCE OFFICER WANTED IN SHOOTING DEATHS: CIA AND NOIS DENY KNOWLEDGE

Below the bold type was a three-column article devoted to the incident and the two who were murdered. Next to the article was a small composite sketch of a woman seen by several witnesses. The woman looked very much like Madison McGuire.

Max returned to the table and refilled Madison's glass. She drained it.

Terry Woodall sat up in bed unable to sleep. She considered, with some amazement, the incredible events which had taken place in her life in the past few weeks. She had met Madison, lost her very best friend, been recruited by a government agency, left her home and Harvard, and now she sat alone in a beach house on the coast of North Carolina. Had anyone told her a few weeks ago that she would be doing what she was doing now, she would have thought them insane.

She had felt restless since her conversation with Madison, so much so that the quiet in her new home had disturbed her to the point where she had gone out and purchased a nineteen-inch color television.

After wrestling it up a flight of stairs, she had installed it in her bedroom.

She pointed the remote control, heard the popping and cracking, and sat in front of the glowing screen, stunned. She stared at the television almost stupidly for several moments, trying hard to digest the information on the screen. She let out an audible gasp and raised the volume. The face on the screen was one she recognized well. The lips were a bit too thin, but the face was undeniably that of her lover.

The picture faded, quickly replaced by a brief interview with the Secretary of State, Alexander Pratt. He was saying, "This administration did not order, nor has is ever participated in political assassination. At this time we have no real evidence to suggest that the killer is one of our agents. Whoever carried out this savage act acted on their own, without our knowledge. I assure you we are anxious to get to the bottom of this."

The newscaster went on to explain that the two men killed were Peter Mueller, the head of the West German labor party, and Amal Bahudi of the United Arab Republic.

Terry leaped for her telephone and fumbled to find the number Madison had left her. "My name is Terry Woodall. I'd like to speak with Andrew McFaye," she said to the man who answered. Seconds later another voice came on the line. "Mr. McFaye?"

"I'm sorry," the voice answered politely. "Mr. McFaye is not in. Could I help you, Terry? This is Marshall Stratton."

"Marshall," Terry said, remembering him from Vail, from the mountain. "Madison gave me this number in case I had a problem . . . I just saw the

171

news. There must be some mistake. Madison couldn't have killed those men."

There was a brief pause, and then Field Agent Stratton asked, "Have you spoken with Madison?"

Terry's ever-increasing panic told her to lie. "No," she answered flatly. "But I know Madison wouldn't have done that."

"You realize, Terry, that this is classified. If you've seen the news or read the papers you know we haven't released her name. You must not, under any circumstances, speak to anyone about this. Do you understand?"

"Of course I understand. I just want to know what you guys are doing. You must know it's a mistake. Are you protecting her?" Terry demanded.

"I'm sorry but I'm not authorized to answer your questions, Terry. You understand," Marshall said.

"Where's McFaye?" Terry asked.

"He isn't in, but I'll be glad to give him a message if you'd like." He asked again, "Did you say you had spoken with Madison?"

Terry flushed with anger and frustration. "Fuck you, Marshall." She slammed down the receiver.

Louis Guiseppe took a seat in the Frankfurt airport and leaned back with a sigh. A newspaper which he had not yet got around to reading was folded on his lap. He felt uncharacteristically gloomy today. His entire trip had been a disaster. Starting in that damned restaurant, he thought. Getting drunk in front of the most intriguing woman he'd met in some time. He'd made an ass of himself. Then

172

Liechtenstein. Being dismissed like a child from a meeting of adults who had no time for him. Louis Guiseppe didn't care if he ever saw Switzerland again.

He checked his watch impatiently, and shook the fold out of his newspaper. A moment later he lowered the paper in utter horror, and muttered, "Paula Emerson. Holy shit. Paula Emerson is a spy." He had recognized the small sketch in the paper. Within the next few minutes his mind began to perceive the entire, horrible plot. And he knew he had unwittingly played a role in the assassination of Peter Mueller and Amal Bahudi.

Chapter 16

Madison McGuire picked up the telephone and dialed. When the voice answered at Langley, she began efficiently. "This is Scorpion, three-double-o-three. I know this conversation is being recorded. I'll give you ten minutes to run the voice checks before I call back, and then I want to be patched through to Andrew McFaye's office immediately. If it takes longer than thirty seconds I will disconnect the line and it's your butt. This is a red code emergency." Madison replaced the receiver and looked at Max, who was smiling at her from the kitchen table.

"You're a tough ole broad, you are," he said with a sly narrowing of his eyes.

Madison returned the smile and sat down beside him. "You realize of course that you're taking quite a risk by keeping me here. You're a good friend, Max."

Max Rudger smiled and waved a hand. His blue eyes twinkled. "Now don't you be gettin' mushy on me, Madison. It's too bloody much for me coming from you."

Madison smiled again and studied the big man briefly. He was a strange sort, she mused, a bit of a loner, a man who rarely talked about himself. Madison knew he had once been married, but he had been a rowdy young man, always drinking and brawling, and she guessed that it had ended his marriage. One year after he became a single man again, he had joined the IRA, and several years later had become disillusioned. He had once told her, when she questioned him about leaving the IRA, "There's no glory in the fight anymore. No honor, no need to be strong and brave. Just killing and more killing. There's nothin' noble about that."

She looked at him now, and asked, "Max, did you ever think of taking another wife?"

"Thought about it a lot. But I'm too set in my ways, too old and fat. Besides, who needs a woman around, always needin' to be taken care of, always gettin' in the bloody way."

Madison considered this for a moment. "You

know, old boy, not all women need taking care of. Perhaps if you weren't such a chauvinist you could find someone."

Max looked up surprised, and laughed aloud, a devilish sparkle in his eyes. "Why, Madison McGuire, you wouldn't be proposin' to me, would you now?"

Madison smiled and reached across the table, good-naturedly tousling Max's hair. She checked her watch. Eight minutes had elapsed.

She picked up the telephone, gave her identifying code numbers to the answering voice, and was patched through at once. "Field agent Stratton. Go ahead, please.

"Marshall, it's Madison. I asked to speak with Andrew. What's going on?"

"McFaye and Delcardo had a meeting with the President this afternoon. Things are pretty crazy down here right now. Tell me where you are and I'll make sure you're brought in safely."

"Oh no, my friend. Not until I know what's going on." Madison checked her watch. She had talked for thirty seconds. Not enough time for an international trace.

"All right," Stratton said. "Give me a phone number and I'll have him call you the minute he comes back in."

"I'll call again." Madison replaced the receiver thoughtfully.

Max watched as she walked silently back to the table and fell into a chair. "You think they've cut you loose, don't you?"

"Yes," Madison answered, and Max thought he

saw fear in Madison McGuire's eyes for the first time since he had known her.

Troy Delcardo, Andrew McFaye and Alexander Pratt sat in the Oval Office awaiting John Boone, the President of the United States. The heavy door opened and the President walked in. The three men stood, but he waved a hand. "Keep your seats, gentlemen," he said, barely looking at them, and not bothering with the usual amenities. They sat in uncomfortable silence. John Boone removed his jacket and tie, undid the first two buttons on his shirt, and then shuffled through a stack of papers on his desk. Occasionally he ran a hand through his thick blond hair and grimaced slightly at something he read. At length he laid the papers on his lap and leaned back in his chair, propping his feet on the edge of his desk.

"We have one hell of a problem," he muttered, his gaze shifting between the three men. "We gave this assignment to Scorpion on your recommendation, Andrew. And Troy, you supported this decision. How could you both make such a tragic error in judgment? What the hell went wrong?"

"Mr. President," Andrew began. "I believe someone has gone out of their way to set up my best operative. Scorpion had nothing to do with this. She didn't blow the hit on Mueller and she did not kill Bahudi. It's not her style. Scorpion is the best, most productive deep cover operative we have in the field. I believe her report. I believe that Steiner is responsible."

John Boone turned to Troy Delcardo. "What does the CIA have to say? Do you have any intelligence that would tell us who's at the heart of this operation?"

"Well, sir, there are any number of people who would like the U.S. to look like the Great Satan. The most urgent problem on my mind right now is who the hell leaked all this to the press. We apparently have a leak at top level."

"Yes," the President answered pensively. "But that is something we'll have to deal with at a later date. Right now we have to decide what I'm going to say to the American people. Even if we take the word of your operative and believe that someone set us up, I still have nothing to tell the public. We can't announce publicly that we wanted to kill Mueller but we just never got the chance. I suppose we could stick to our story and deny everything, but that won't do a thing to repair diplomatic relations with Syria and Germany, and it won't help protect our citizens when they travel abroad."

"Mr. President," Alex Pratt broke in, his Texas drawl slow and clear. "Let us deal in facts for a moment. The U.N. is on our backs, NATO is threatened because of the uproar in Germany, England is being threatened with terrorist attacks simply because they support us, Syria and Iran want our ass. We've been forced to double security at our embassies, and the Swiss have mounted a monstrous search for Scorpion. Now, the way I see it, we don't have many options. Everyone wants a quick response.

We can bring Scorpion in, put her on the box, and if we find she's telling the truth, we can go to our people and tell them honestly that we had nothing to do with it. But that won't satisfy the fanatics that want blood, and simple denial won't repair diplomatic relations. On the other hand we could give her some compensation, release her, destroy her files, and send her on her way to make out alone. However, if an adversary agency gets hold of her, drugs and questions her, we've got real problems."

"What is your point?" the President asked impatiently.

Troy Delcardo broke in. "I think what the Secretary is trying to say is that this agent has been in the field for many years. She's had access to eyes only information, and she's worked with our networks all around the world. Scorpion could single-handedly destroy networks that have taken years to develop. If another agency got her and found out what she knows, our entire intelligence community could be compromised."

The President sighed, and rubbed his temples lightly. "So, you're saying that we can't leave her out there, and we can't bring her in?"

"That's exactly right," Alex Pratt agreed. "We only have one reasonable option, Mr. President. Scorpion must be eliminated."

Andrew sat up in his chair. "Now just wait a minute. This agent has devoted half her life to government service. And you want to terminate? You're a sonofabitch, Pratt," Andrew spat.

John Boone repressed a smile. Delcardo turned to Andrew. "I'm sorry, Andy, but I have to agree. We'll lose a good operative, but we won't risk compromising networks that we couldn't replace in a hundred years. I see this as necessary to maintain national security."

"Speaking from a diplomatic point of view, sir," Pratt said, "I think we should go public and say we've discovered that the Liechtenstein killer is an ex-agent who was released some years ago. We say she escaped our surveillance and disappeared for over a year. And we're searching for her and intend to prosecute. In the meantime, we stay in touch with her, tell her it's all nothing more than a PR campaign, and we want to bring her in, give her a new identity and send her on her way. When we find her, we eliminate her and everyone is happy."

Andrew laughed aloud. "She'll never go for it. She'll sense a trap. I suggest we get another opinion. How about bringing Marge Price in on this one?"

"I'm sorry, Andrew," the President said sadly. "But we just don't have time for a lengthy analysis. I'm supposed to go on national television tomorrow night."

John Boone studied the men in front of him. He had the face of a kind man who regretted the decision that had just been made. "We have no choice. Right or wrong, our only alternative is to terminate Scorpion." He looked at each man gravely. "God forgive us."

Andrew McFaye left the White House, walking slowly, his head down. He used the rear exit in order to avoid the press, and asked the driver of the military sedan to drive him straight home. He climbed into the car, leaned his head back, and closed his eyes.

Oh, Madison, I never thought it would end for you

this way. It's too late now. I can't turn back . . . Oh,
God, what kind of monster have I turned into?

"Mr. McFaye. You're home, sir," the driver was saying, but Andrew did not hear.

The driver climbed out of the car and opened the rear door. "You're home now, sir," he repeated. Andrew looked at him blankly for a moment, and then stepped out of the car and walked towards his house.

Terry Woodall picked up her telephone and dialed the home offices of Woodall Enterprises, Inc. It was time to begin to fulfill her commitment to the NOIS. There was no turning back now. She waited while her call was transferred to her father's office, feeling as if she were about to commit treason against her own father. His secretary answered.

"Anne, this is Terry. Is Dad in his office?"

"Hello, Terry. He's in there but you'll have to hold. This place is a madhouse today," Anne complained.

Terry smiled. Anne always voiced the same complaint. "What's going on there?" Terry asked, not really wanting to know the details of her father's secretary's day.

Anne lowered her voice and almost whispered. "We have a lot of people in from a computer security company. Your father's been very unhappy with them. Someone broke into our computers and nearly got to the government files. Probably a competitor."

Terry let a slight gasp escape, and at the same instant images of Jonothan Shore and the burning building vividly flashed before her, and her mind seized the images with a sort of morbid tenacity, her features drawn into a rigid immobility. It was then, thankfully, that Anne interrupted her torpid state with, "Oh, they're coming out. Hold on."

She barely had time to begin to assimilate the information or grasp its meaning before her father came on the line with a hearty, "Where you been, kid? I tried to call you last week in Boston."

"I'm not in Boston, Dad. I'm taking a break from school."

There was a brief silence, before Woodall made a quiet response. "You haven't dropped out have you?"

"I'm just taking a break, Dad . . . Listen, I really called to tell you that I've decided to take the job. Can I start in the fall? September maybe?"

"Hey, that's the best news I've had in a while. You can start whenever you want. I'm glad you changed your mind. I can hardly wait to tell Louis."

"I'm not sure Louis would share your enthusiasm," Terry answered, and then added, "So, what's going on there? Anne said something about someone breaking into your offices, I think," Terry embroidered.

"No. Nothing like that. Just some hacker in Cambridge trying to get into our computers. No big deal."

"So, you traced him. Did you report him?"

"No. Louis had a talk with him. He won't bother us anymore," Woodall answered.

So, Terry thought, it's true. And I never even suspected.

When Terry hung up, all her feelings of guilt had vanished. Family loyalty was not a consideration. They had murdered Jonothan Shore, that was all that mattered to her now.

Chapter 17

Madison scanned the classifieds, hoping against hope to see a message buried there somewhere from her agency, some word or phrase telling her it was safe to come in. Nothing.

She walked to the telephone, her only link now to the outside world, and dialed Andrew McFaye's private number. A number that only a few were given access to, that only Andrew answered.

After several rings, a voice answered. Not

Andrew's voice. Madison's mind searched for some reason. Where was Andrew? Was he ill? Hurt?

"Andrew McFaye, please." she said.

After a brief pause, the voice responded. "I'm sorry. Mr. McFaye is in conference. May I say who's calling?"

"No. You may not," Madison snapped. "Give him this message: Red code, Scorpion. And bring him to the phone quickly."

"Hold please."

Madison checked her time. She had less than thirty safe seconds to stay on the line.

Then the voice was back, "I'm sorry, but Mr. McFaye cannot be disturbed. Would you leave a number?"

Madison disconnected the line and lowered herself slowly into a chair. What did it mean? She felt a hand on her shoulder and looked up to see Max Rudger standing beside her. He knelt down close, and Madison said, "I just don't understand it, Max. Andrew has never refused a call from me. Ever. You know what they're doing, don't you? They're turning me loose. It's unbelievable. The bastards."

"Ah, they're just tryin' to decide what the hell to do with you. Don't you see? You could be very dangerous to them right now. We're talking about people with political considerations. They're afraid to touch you. You're too hot. I'll bet you that your buddy Andrew is tryin' to sway them. Just give it a little time, and let things cool down a bit."

He patted her knee reassuringly and stood up. "I came in here to tell you the President is giving a speech tonight. We'll have it live on satellite, if we can stay awake. It'll be damn near three in the bloody mornin' by our time."

John Boone faced the nation from behind his presidential podium, the round face and the famous wide smile more weathered and stern than usual.

He denied, with complete and convincing resolve, his administration's involvement in any attempts at political assassination. He did, however, acknowledge that the men who were murdered were suspected supporters of terrorist activities.

Madison, who stared at the television solemnly, could not fault the man for his denial. She understood his position. She had no delusions about the job that she had accepted or the oath she had taken eighteen years ago. Some things, as every agent knew, were beyond the comprehension of the general public. Covert operations must remain covert at all costs.

It was the President's next declaration that caused her to swallow hard and sit up, gripping the sofa cushions until her knuckles were white. His intelligence agencies, he reported, had uncovered vital information in the last few hours, and to his profound regret he now knew that the Liechtenstein killer was a former intelligence officer who had been relieved from her post nearly three years ago after displaying unstable behavior.

A photograph appeared on the screen. Madison's

I.D. badge at Langley headquarters. Under the photograph her name and her date of birth.

The President continued, "Last year we received an intelligence report out of London which told us this woman had been killed. We now know this report was falsified, and we're investigating our sources. We now believe the woman has left Switzerland and is in hiding in the Middle East with a group of known terrorists whose leader is the infamous Abu Nidal. I appear before you, the American people and the people of the world, asking for your assistance in bringing this woman to justice. Already Syria, Germany and England have agreed to aid us in our search."

Madison leaned forward and turned off the television, and then sank back into the sofa.

"Ah, don't you be worrying now, Madi. It's just their way of gettin' the heat off themselves until they can reel you in safely. It's a bloody public relations campaign," Max stated flatly.

Madison looked at him for a moment. "No. Something's wrong, Max. I feel it. It's more than that. They've turned me loose. I'm a dead woman unless I get out of here. It's only a matter of time before they get into their computers and find out you're living outside Zurich. It won't take long to figure out that I must be here."

Max thought about that for a moment. "You get some sleep. In the mornin' we'll go dump the car, and then I'll arrange to get you a fresh passport and get you out of here. Any particular place you want to go?"

"London," Madison answered. "I have contacts there. I've got to track down Helda Steiner. She has the answer to this puzzle."

Thirty-six hours later, Madison McGuire arrived at London's Heathrow airport. Security was tight in London, as it had been in Zurich, and all the passengers coming in from Switzerland were subjected to special scrutiny. She was traveling as Greta Belz, a woman twenty years older than herself. It had not been difficult for Madison to assume the stance and personality of an older woman. She was an expert at those subtle changes that allow one to melt into a crowd. She wore a navy blue floral dress with a bit of padding underneath, which gave the impression that she had a full, round stomach. She prayed silently that she would not be searched, since the padding under her dress was filled with NOIS money she had taken to Switzerland. Max had managed to convert the money to Swiss francs, and then back to American dollars so that the serial numbers could not be traced. Still, Madison knew that a woman stuffed with over twenty thousand dollars would most certainly be subjected to questioning.

She moved through the gates at the airport, avoiding direct eye contact with the men who studied the faces of the passengers as they filed out into Heathrow. She was only a few feet from freedom when she heard a voice.

"Wait just a minute, please." A man touched her arm lightly.

Madison looked up at him. She made her voice

small and shaky, and spoke with a heavy German accent. "There is some problem?"

"Do you mind if I have another look at your passport, please?" the Englishman asked, and Madison produced the passport that Max had acquired for her. The man studied the passport, and then Madison's face, his eyes tracing the lines in her face which she had painstakingly applied.

Then another man approached. He looked at Madison, and then leaned to speak into the other man's ear. They exchanged whispers, and Madison hoped the trembling in her knees and the perspiration on her forehead would not give her away. The man looked at her again. This time he smiled politely. "My apologies for detaining you Mrs. Belz. Enjoy your visit."

"*Danke,*" Madison said, trying to hide her relief, and moving slowly towards her freedom. Suddenly, she heard from the loud speaker: "Mrs. Greta Belz, please meet your party at the reservation desk."

Madison kept walking slowly, resisting the urge to run, ignoring the announcement. She knew there was no party waiting for her at Heathrow. She could see the double glass doors now, the exit to the airport, only yards away. Then one of the men from the gate ran to her, touching her arm lightly and turning her around. "Mrs. Belz, you're being paged. The reservation desk is that way." He pointed. "Would you like me to walk with you?" he asked helpfully.

"No. I'll find my way. Thank you, again," Madison answered, and started towards the desk, not knowing what she would find there, or if she would now get out of Heathrow alive.

Then she felt herself being spun around. Felt

arms seize her. It was over, she thought sadly, turning to see the man's face. He was bearded and sandy-haired and looked to be in his thirties, and to her surprise he offered her a sincere smile.

"Mother," he said loudly enough for all around to hear. "It's good to see you. How was your trip?" He hugged her tightly, whispering in her ear. "Call me Peter. Max sent me. Everything is all right."

Arm in arm, mother and son, they exited Heathrow Airport and climbed into Peter's Mercedes. He looked at her and grinned. "Hope I didn't give you too much of a start. Max told me you might need some assistance." He spoke with a British accent.

Madison smiled. "I only wish Max would have shared this with me. I'm afraid you gave me a bit of a jolt."

Peter looked at her, surprised. "You're English. I assumed from the name that you were Swiss or German." He paused. "Greta, I'm sorry to say I'm not in a position to give you further assistance. Being in a rather delicate situation yourself, I'm sure you understand I have my own people to protect. I'll be more than happy to drop you somewhere. But then I'm afraid we must go our separate ways."

"Of course, Peter," Madison answered. "You can drop me at the West End tube station. I'll find my way from there."

For the second night since the President's address to the nation, Terry Woodall lay in bed unable to sleep, and stared up at the ceiling, feeling more helpless than she ever had in her life.

190

Madison, what have they done to you? I know it's a lie. It's all a terrible lie . . . Why are they doing this to you? To us? I feel so goddamn helpless . . . I love you . . . I want you home safe, with me . . .

Terry got up and crossed to the window. Looking out on the water, she remembered the nights she and Madison had spent in this bedroom. Remembered waking to find Madison naked, standing at the window staring out at the same water, the ever-present cigarette in her hand, her body silhouetted in the light, her skin glistening perfection.

Terry leaned her forehead against the window and let the tears fall freely until finally, out of pure exhaustion, she made her way to the bed and fell asleep without turning back the sheets.

At first light she collected her newspaper from the driveway and walked back into the big, empty house. Over coffee, she scanned the paper, looking for the latest information on the government's rogue agent. Her only consolation was in knowing that Madison was still free. Her heart told her Madison was alive.

She searched her memory, trying to remember everything Madison had told her about her life, anything that might tell her where Madison was hiding. Suddenly she sat up straight. England. Of course. It was only logical. Madison had spent most of her life there. She knew people who could help her and hide her, she knew the countryside and the cities.

Chapter 18

That night Terry stood at her front door, balancing a bag of groceries with one arm and fumbling with the front door key. Once inside she set the bag on the counter and suddenly stopped all movement. A sound behind her. Someone breathing . . . A footstep. Her heart leaped to her throat. She spun around to see a man standing behind her. He reached into his jacket and Terry closed her eyes, unable to speak, unable to scream, terrified.

"Relax, Terry," said the booming voice. "I apologize for scaring you."

Terry opened her eyes slowly. The man reached for his identification. Still trembling, she asked, "Who are you? What do you want?"

"My name is McFaye. Andrew McFaye. I thought we could talk."

Terry relaxed slightly, but the adrenalin was still surging and quickly turning her fear to anger. "Jesus Christ, McFaye. You scared the hell out of me. How about calling first next time." She walked to the refrigerator and poured herself a glass of wine, without offering one to her uninvited guest.

"I got a message that you called," he said.

"I'm not interested in talking to you anymore," she stated. "I called when I thought you were Madison's friend."

She took a sip of wine and studied him over the glass. "You know, Andrew, Madison told me you had been like a father to her, that you were a man who could be trusted. How could you let this happen? How could you people do this to her? I know Madison well enough to know she isn't a murderer. I know you're all lying. Why? Did she find out something she wasn't supposed to know?"

Andrew looked at her calmly and crossed the room, positioning himself in a kitchen chair. "Let's talk about that, Terry. How well *do* you know her? How much do you know about the person inside? How much do you really know about her life?"

Terry took a chair across from him. "What are you getting at?" She was annoyed.

Andrew ignored the question. "Let me tell you

193

something, Terry. Those two dead men were both members of Club Twelve. One of them, the Syrian, was the man who killed Madison's father nearly twenty years ago. Jake McGuire was a CIA agent at the time of his death. If you're looking for a motive, you've got one now."

Terry braced herself. "Oh, my God," she muttered.

Andrew went on. "Did she ever tell you about Elicia Peabody?" Terry shook her head. "She was Madison's lover of five years in London," Andrew said. "Elicia was killed mistakenly. Madison was the target, and she was sure that Club Twelve was behind the hit. So you see, Terry, Madison has a lot of hate for these men. I understand this is hard for you to accept. I could hardly believe it at first. I think she has just been pushed too far. She's lost her balance, and for good reason when you consider what she's been through. Then, there was another attempt on her life in Vail, and another in Switzerland. I think it was the final straw that broke the camel's back."

"What are you saying?" Terry demanded. "That Madison lost it? Turned into a killer? That's ridiculous."

"Is it?" Andrew let his eyes rest on Terry. "Madison McGuire has been in the field for eighteen years. Try and imagine the kind of stress that could produce. Eighteen years of running, hiding, killing. Eighteen years of deception. You can't even grasp it, can you? No . . . Of course you can't. Eighteen years ago you were still sucking on fudgesickles and watching *Captain Kangaroo.*"

194

"What do you want from me?" Terry asked coldly.

"I want you to let her know everything is going to be all right. Tell her I'm working out the details and we'll bring her home soon."

"I haven't talked to Madison. I don't know where she is," Terry replied, taking a sip of her wine.

"You *will* hear from her. She trusts you, she cares for you. She told me that herself . . . Terry, we don't want to hurt her. We want to find help for her. Psychiatric help. We'll give her a new life, a new identity, money, anything she wants. This is for her own protection. She's a danger to herself and everyone around her right now. You've only seen the tender, loving side of Madison. Believe me, there is another side."

Terry stared at him in disbelief. "That is the biggest, smelliest bag of crap I've ever heard. Surely you don't expect me to believe that."

Her telephone was ringing. "Excuse me." She walked to the telephone in the living room.

"Hello, darling," Madison said.

Terry quickly collected herself. "Mom, hi. I was just thinking about you."

Madison heard the fear in her lover's voice. She understood. "You have company. The Agency?"

"That's right," Terry answered casually, turning to look at Andrew.

"I'll call again tomorrow. I just wanted you to know that I'm all right, darling. Please, don't believe the reports you hear about me. It's not true. And Terry, don't trust anyone."

"All right, Mom. Goodbye."

Terry walked into the kitchen, glared at Andrew for a moment, and then ordered, "Get out of my house. You're a bastard."

Madison, still dressed as Greta Belz, hung up the public telephone on Oxford Street in London, and walked towards the West End tube station. So, she thought, the Agency has made contact with Terry. There was little doubt in her mind now that Terry's phones were tapped, that they had Terry under surveillance, that they were counting on Madison getting in touch with her. Madison knew she would have to use extreme caution when next she phoned Terry.

The street was narrow like many London streets, and filled with tourists and locals anxious to visit Oxford Street shops and department stores. Madison looked up at the tall buildings that sat close to the street, a friendly mixture of Tudor, Victorian, and Georgian architecture rising high above the crowds. She allowed herself a smile, almost forgetting for a moment all the madness in her life. There was something wonderfully comforting about Europe, the unavoidable sense of history one feels when surrounded by buildings and traditions that have outlasted the centuries.

At the tube station, she boarded a train to Tracadero Center in the heart of Piccadilly Circus. Tracadero was an enclosed shopping complex and she knew she would find shops where she could purchase suitable clothes. She remembered that there was a rent-a-car office near its north end.

Her business in the center did not take long. In an hour she had managed to buy the clothes and rent a car.

She drove north on Portabello Road and fifteen minutes later saw what she was looking for. She parked the rented automobile at the rear of the Portabello Inn and walked around to the front entrance, knowing that inside she would find Mary Plitchard — a woman Madison had known for nearly ten years, a constant source of underground information, a friend she could trust.

In her early days Ms. Plitchard had been known as Walkin' Mary, a prostitute who, it was said, had walked those old streets for years with her head held as high as any of the wealthy in Knightsbridge. It was widely rumored that in her purse Walkin' Mary packed a five pound brick and was known, on more than one occasion, to hurl it like a hand grenade at the windshields of autos filled with rowdy young men who stopped to make vulgar comments.

Mary Plitchard, it had turned out, was a shrewd businesswoman, and had carefully squirreled away nearly every shilling she had ever earned on those streets, and in her retirement she had purchased the Portabello Inn.

Mary glanced up casually when the door opened. She saw a tired-looking woman with grey hair walk slowly to the counter.

Madison smiled. Mary had not changed. Her hair was still a mess, ratted and teased into a platinum mane, but she seemed at home in the shabby surroundings of the Portabello Inn. Seeing that there was no one in the lobby, Madison removed the wig and shook out her hair, which was almost back to its natural red. She raised her head and said, "Hello, Mary."

Mary Plitchard's jaw dropped slightly as a hint of recognition crossed her round face. "Well I'll be. Am I seeing a ghost? I heard you left this world, dearie. What was it that brought you back? I tell you, if I could get out of it I would, mind you. With all the constables always wanting something for free, and with prices going up."

Madison crossed behind the desk and gave Mary a hug which was returned with genuine affection. "Good to see you, Mary. How's your business?"

"It's a bloody stinking business, Madison dear. I tell you, I don't know why I ever bought this bleeding inn. But you didn't come here to hear about my troubles, did you now? I bet you got some troubles of your own. I been wonderin' if it was you they been lookin' for. I couldn't believe my eyes when I saw that picture in the papers. The bloody bastards, always coming up with some story to suit their purpose." Her face was twisted in anger. "You run along to my apartment and get yourself cleaned up. You look like hell. You'll be wantin' some food and a bath. I close up in an hour and I'll come along."

Mary watched Madison walk down the hall towards her flat, and shook her head. "Bloody bastards," she repeated.

Madison entered the small flat and looked around. Every wall, every surface in the flat was covered with something — pictures, paintings, sheet music, old newspapers, mugs and glasses. On an old upright piano in the far corner two cats lounged leisurely. Madison pushed away a stack of papers and sat down in a comfortable old chair which was covered with a rose floral-patterned fabric. Her first action was to reach for the *Times* and go to the classifieds, pure habit. She scanned the columns, hoping for some message. Once again there was nothing. She sighed and rested her head on the back of the chair.

By the time Mary Plitchard walked in, Madison had bathed, dressed and located the food.

"All right then, dearie," Mary said. "What can I do for you?"

"I need some information on a woman named Helda Steiner. I'm not even sure she's in England. I'm afraid I can't even point you in the right direction, but I've got cash, and I've got time as long as you'll let me take a room here."

Mary offered her a broad smile, exposing yellowing teeth. "I never got why you stayed in this business, Madison. They're a rotten lot, you know. You're the only one of them I ever trusted . . . I'll send some runners out and we'll see if we can find your Helda Steiner."

"A warning, Mary," Madison said. "The woman is dangerous. It will take your best people to find her without being seen."

Madison settled on a price with Mary Plitchard. Five thousand dollars, American, plus a week in advance for the room. After all, Mary had a business to run, she had told Madison gently.

Chapter 19

Madison opened her eyes and shivered in the damp, cool English morning that had somehow managed to seep into her room at the Portabello. At the knock on her door she automatically reached for her shoulder holster and gun, forgetting momentarily that she had been forced to leave her weapon with Max in Switzerland.

Mary Plitchard spoke through the closed door in a low whisper. "Come have a bite, dearie. Plenty of eggs and kippers downstairs, and the lobby's empty."

Madison shuddered slightly. She loathed kippers.

"Thanks, Mary. Coffee is fine. Be right down." She rose reluctantly from the soft mattress, brushed her teeth and attempted to shake off the stiffness that had come with hours of immobility. Opening the door, she checked both ends of the hallway before heading down the stairs and into Mary's flat.

"Mornin'" Mary said cheerfully, pushing a cup of coffee and a copy of the *Times* in Madison's general direction.

Madison accepted the coffee gratefully, and turned troubled eyes to the newspaper, her anticipation of its contents turning to both dread and exasperation. Today, for some reason unknown to her, she did not go directly to the classified advertisements, but instead gazed hopelessly at the front page. "How could they know?" she mumbled to herself at the news report that the rogue American agent was now believed to be in England. The newspaper also declared that a reward of twenty-five thousand pounds had been offered for information leading to her capture.

Madison returned the newspaper to Mary's coffee table without bothering to check the classifieds. "Do you know a discreet gun seller, Mary," she inquired, suddenly faced with the possibility that agents would be actively looking for her in London.

The pawn shop sat in a row of dingy brick buildings with mud stains at their base from the frequent and sometimes heavy London rain. The shop was cluttered with a wide array of junk and collectibles. The robust man behind the counter was

201

nearly bald, with a strong, wide jaw. Madison did not guess him to be a friendly sort at all.

She approached the counter, her hair tucked under a riding cap, rose-colored spectacles neatly placed on her small nose. "Mr. Malone?" she inquired in her strongest cockney.

"Yes?" the robust man answered. "And who might you be?"

"Mary Plitchard sent me. Might I have a moment of your time?"

The big man smiled, exposing a blackened space where there had once been a tooth, and called out to a back room: "Robbie, come here, boy, and watch for customers. I'll be a few minutes."

A younger man emerged from the back, his hands plunged deep in the pockets of his jeans, his face displaying irritation and boredom all at once. He took his place behind the counter and stared curiously at Madison as Malone led her into an adjoining room and closed the door.

Madison's business with the gun seller was concluded in a matter of minutes. She found a comfortable holster and, to her surprise, an American government model 1911A1 Auto Ordinance Thirty-Eight Super with a five inch barrel and a loaded weight of only forty-four ounces.

The only unexpected complication came upon reentering the shop and finding young Robbie huddled close to the door.

"Get back, man," Malone ordered, and then looked at Madison apologetically. "Nothin' to worry about, mum," he muttered. "He's my son. A nosy sort, but a fine lad really."

* * * * *

It was a gray day in London and the sky threatened rain. Still Madison was glad she had chosen to walk the fifteen blocks to the pawn shop. Her muscles begged to be exercised, and with each block she felt a tiny bit of the tension release.

Public phones in London were notorious for their service problems, and it was not until she stepped into the third red phone booth that she found one which could actually supply her with a dial tone.

Madison checked her watch when she heard the ringing, and when Terry answered, she began at once. "Listen carefully, darling. I know your line is monitored. We have approximately two minutes. Who visited you last evening and what did they say?"

"It was Andrew," Terry answered. "He wanted me to give you a message . . . Madison, I don't trust him."

"Please, Terry, just give me the message," Madison urged.

"He said they want to bring you home. He's working out the details."

Madison let out a relieved sigh.

Terry continued, "There's something wrong though. He told me that you'd lost it, that you were dangerous. Don't you see? He tried to turn me against you. He said they wanted to help you, that you needed psychiatric help . . . Listen to me. He was lying. They'll kill you if you turn yourself in. Oh, God, Madison. I'm so afraid."

"All right, sweetheart. Don't worry. I'll be fine. I'll be careful. I love you."

"Oh, Madison, please —" The line went dead before Terry could finish. She replaced the receiver slowly, fell to her knees and cried.

Madison leaned against the inside of the telephone booth, letting her head rest against the glass, Terry's words swirling round her brain. *He said you'd lost it, that you're dangerous . . . Psychiatric help. He was lying . . . They'll kill you . . . Lying.*

Madison raised both hands to her head and held it firmly, as if somehow she could erase those terrible words. *Why Andrew? Why are you doing this to me?*

She opened the door of the booth and stepped out, her balance unsure, her head still reeling. Suddenly she felt a hand on her shoulder, and spun around to see Robbie, the gun seller's son, smiling, his hand in the pocket of his jacket.

"Can't really yell for a constable, can you?" he said, the small brown eyes narrowing as he spoke.

Madison shook his hand off her as if it carried some infectious disease.

"What do you want?" she demanded, and started walking slowly, cursing herself for lingering so long in the phone booth.

"I know who you are," he said, walking next to her. "Thought you and me could work something out. I could take you to Whitehall right now and get twenty-five thousand pounds, you know. But, I wouldn't want to do that."

Madison saw an alleyway a few yards in front of them, and continued towards it, her pace steady, her mind racing. "I'm afraid I don't know what you're talking about."

He threw back his head and laughed, a disgusting sound, pulling a newspaper from under one arm.

"Let's see now. It's McGuire, isn't it? Madison McGuire. That's it. Well then, Madison McGuire, you'd be smart to deal with me."

Madison sighed, and turned to him as they walked. "All right then, Robbie. You've got me." She surveyed the street, watching to see if he was alone, looking for anyone in the crowds who was out of place or out of step. There was no one, she realized. The little fool had come alone.

She stepped into the alley. Robbie followed for another twenty yards, before Madison spun around, slammed her elbow under his chin and rammed a fist into the boy's kidney. He gasped, a bit of blood escaping his mouth. She withdrew the Thirty-Eight Super and held it firmly under the young man's chin. "You didn't really think this out, Robbie," she said. "You should have never come alone. I could kill you now with one short blow to the throat. No gunfire. No noise. No one would know. You little bastard. Did you think I'd pay you to keep quiet?"

Robbie trembled helplessly. "I wouldn't have done it. I wouldn't have turned you over," he said, coughing away the blood in his mouth.

"I want you to turn around and walk very slowly back home. It's your lucky day, Robbie. You can live. Just remember, I have friends. I know where you are and you'll be the first to pay if anything out of the ordinary happens to me while I'm in London. Understand?"

"Yes," Robbie answered, nodding rapidly, his knees buckling under him.

Madison put the gun back in its holster. "Go," she ordered, and the boy turned and walked away.

Madison kept a watchful eye on him for several

blocks. He moved at a normal pace, never stopping, never turning. Fortunately he did not know that she could have never killed a boy his age. He had probably soiled his pants, she mused. She turned to walk back towards the Portabello Inn.

Halfway there she had an idea. It was time to find out what was happening. She was tired of running, tired of not knowing the truth. She decided to take the offensive.

She stepped into another phone booth, got a dial tone the first time, and rang the American Embassy in London. She knew of a man who had been posted to that Embassy two years ago. Madison had heard that James Phillips, the man who now held the position of London Station Chief, was an honest man.

"I want to go home, Mr. Phillips," Madison said when he came on the line. "What the hell is going on?"

"Scorpion?" James Phillips muttered more to himself than to Madison.

"That's right. There's no point in trying to trace the call. I won't be on that long. Just listen. I want to arrange a meeting with someone from the agency. Someone I can trust. I'll meet with one of two men. Andrew McFaye or Marshall Stratton. No one else. I want to know who signed my death warrant, Phillips. I want a normal life again. If they try to trick me, if anything happens to me, you tell them that I have files kept in a very safe place. If I die or disappear, those files will hit the newspapers. I'll call you back tomorrow and tell you where I want to meet. Goodbye Mr. Phillips."

"Scorpion, wait. You don't understand. No one wants to kill you. We've been trying to bring you in safely. The whole thing is just a P.R. ploy. But we can't protect you unless you come in."

The line went dead. "Damn it," Phillips said, and immediately put in a call to Langley.

Terry Woodall walked back to her house after going into Buxton and using a pay phone to call the airlines. She had made her decision. She would go to Madison, find her somehow, help her somehow.

With no particular plan in mind, she walked to her bedroom and started packing hurriedly. She had a six o'clock flight to New York, and then to Heathrow.

It never once occurred to her that she might be leading the enemy straight to Madison.

Chapter 20

No one could have been more surprised to see Max Rudger walk through the doors of the Portabello Inn than Mary Plitchard. She looked up at him, stunned.

"Hello, Mary. Still keepin' a room for me?" he asked casually.

Mary smiled cheerfully. "Just look at you. Still handsome as ever. How are you, old boy?"

Max set his suitcase down with a thud. "I'll be lookin' for a mutual friend of ours, Mary. What have you heard of her? Is she safe?"

Mary surveyed him suspiciously. "It has been a long time, old boy. How can I be sure you're still on the same side?"

Max crossed behind the counter and grabbed Mary Plitchard, planting a wet kiss on her lips. "Ah now, Mary. You always trusted me. We had some devilish good times together. Did ya miss me?"

Mary smiled and pulled away. "You haven't changed a bit, Max Rudger. Still using that bloody charm to get what you want. I'll make this agreement with you. If I see her I'll let her know where you are."

Max tossed back his head, and a huge booming laugh escaped. "Aren't you the sly one," he said. "You can tell our friend that I'm stayin' right here. That is if you have a room for me. Hell, I'll even pay in advance. What more could you want? A handsome, strong man like me, payin' in advance and all."

Mary handed him a room key. "Now, be off with you. I've got a business to run."

Fifteen minutes later Madison McGuire walked through the door of the Portabello. Mary barely looked up, tilted her head to the side towards her own flat. Seeing that someone was in the lobby, Madison took the hint and walked to Mary's apartment, keeping her head low and her stride steady as she went.

Mary followed presently, and handed Madison a small scrap of paper. "Try this address," she said. "Your Helda Steiner *is* in London, old girl. It's said she's stayin' with a friend. Probably restin' up to go out and start up more trouble."

Madison looked at Mary and smiled. "You're a miracle worker, Mary Plitchard. Thank you so much."

Mary shrugged. "You paid for it, dearie. I was just doing my job. By the way, Max Rudger was here lookin' for you. That devil. I wouldn't tell him nothing, naturally. Didn't know if you wanted to see him."

Madison's eyes widened. "Max? Here in London? Where is he?"

Mary smiled. "He said I could still trust him, but you never know. I'll have you know he tried to sweet-talk me, he did. But I acted like there wasn't a tongue in me head."

Madison took Mary's shoulders, the excitement clear in her voice. "Tell me. Where is he?"

"Number ten," Mary answered with a smile, and on those words Madison bolted out of the flat without bothering to check the lobby, taking the stairs two at a time.

Max opened his door, and Madison fell into his arms. "Glad to see me, are you, Madi? Well, the feelin' is mutual. When I saw the papers, I knew I couldn't leave you to yourself. I was hoping I could help out a little."

"You shouldn't be here, Max. There is no reason for you to get involved."

"The way I see it, I'm already involved. Now you and I have to put our heads together and figure out how we're going to get you out of this unholy mess you're in . . . And don't you go tellin' me it's none of my business. I care about you. You'd do the same for me, wouldn't you now?"

"She's in London, Max. Steiner is in London. I've got the address, but she's just visiting so I have to move on it soon."

* * * * *

Behind closed doors on the seventh floor of
Langley headquarters an emergency meeting was in
progress. Alarmed by the information they had
received via top priority cipher from James Phillips in
London, four strategists and one operative sat in Troy
Delcardo's office contemplating the macabre business
at hand.

There was so much to consider here tonight. Who
could be sure how one would react under abnormal
stress? Even the most dependable professionals could
be pushed into unpredictable and erratic behavior.
Madison McGuire had become just that — erratic and
unpredictably dangerous. At least, that was the
conclusion of all but one of the individuals in this
room.

Gerold Rutledge, head of the State Department's
clandestine activities group, traced the lines at the
corner of his mouth with his index finger in thought.
He shifted in his chair and cleared his throat. "I see
that your principal agent in London recommends we
take her threats seriously. He believes she's capable
of releasing information that could hurt us. He's
worried about his own network being torn apart."

Andrew McFaye added thoughtfully, "Oh, yes.
Madison can be quite convincing. However, I see it as
a bluff. I don't believe for a minute that she could
have seen this kind of thing coming and stashed away
eyes only files. It's not her style."

Marge Price's stern face looked drawn and tired.
She lit a cigarette and inhaled deeply. "Frankly, I
don't believe any of this." She held up Madison's file

and let it drop back onto the desk top. "It's completely out of character. Over the last ten years I've done semi-annual evaluations of this operative. She has been nothing if not professional and well-balanced even under the most extreme circumstances. I cannot accept the reports I have in front of me. It says here she may be suffering from hallucinations? She imagined seeing a woman who apparently was not in the area at the time? A terrorist? This is completely inconsistent with her past behavior. Gentlemen, one does not become a hallucinating, paranoid schizophrenic overnight. In my opinion the threat she made to Phillips was nothing more than a cry for help. This woman is not a traitor and she's not a murderer. She wants to come home. She's fighting to prove her innocence."

Troy Delcardo sighed. "That's crap, Marge. She isn't trying to prove her innocence. She's trying to ruin our credibility by releasing embarrassing information. We can change codes, we can warn networks, we can even alter all our procedures to protect our people. But we can't change the past, and that's what she's threatening us with. We've made some mistakes, and Scorpion is going to strangle us with them. We can't afford that. I say we send Marshall over there, bring her back alive and find out if she's bluffing about the files."

"You people don't listen," Andrew shouted suddenly. His breathing was heavy and uneasy.

Marge Price and Troy Delcardo exchanged uncertain glances. Andrew had not been himself lately.

"You people don't listen," he repeated angrily.

"I'm telling you Madison doesn't have classified information stored anywhere but in her brain. You want to send Marshall? Fine. Let him go. But we cannot bring her back alive. It's going directly against Presidential orders —"

Gerold Rutledge broke in. "Yes, but Andrew, in light of these new circumstances —"

"Fuck the circumstances. She's just buying time." He lowered his voice and managed to collect himself. "I know you're all surprised. It's true I didn't want to go along with this, but now I see what she's doing. We have to consider what kind of damage this woman could do if she's allowed to continue. The lives of many come before the life of one disappointing, treasonous operative who's flipped her lid completely. Madison McGuire is dangerous and she must be eliminated."

Troy Delcardo studied the man beside him. He wondered if he were in Andrew's position if he could make the same decision. This woman was someone whom Andrew had once loved and guided. He marveled at his colleague's commitment to his government.

There was a knock on the door. A woman entered and handed a computer printout to Andrew McFaye. He studied it for a moment and then looked around the room. "It's the Woodall kid. She made reservations for a flight to London. That makes our job easy. She'll lead us right to her."

Terry Woodall arrived at Heathrow at seven a.m. London time. She collected her luggage quickly, and

213

headed out the front entrance where she flagged a taxi. "What are the biggest newspapers here?" she asked the driver.

"Well, mum," he answered thoughtfully, "there's the *Times* and the *Mirror* and . . ."

Terry interrupted. "That's fine, take me there, please."

"The *Times* or the *Mirror,* mum?" the driver inquired.

"Both. And then the Intercontinental Hotel."

The driver waited, meter running, as Terry walked into the huge old building that housed the *Times of London* offices. She spoke with a small, prim woman who directed her up the stairs and down the hall to where a man, a neat mustache on his upper lip and his spectacles firmly on his nose, sat behind a counter. "I'd like to run a personal," Terry said.

"Pardon me?" the man answered, looking up at her.

"An advertisement," Terry answered impatiently. "You know, in the personals."

"I see," he answered slowly. "I'm afraid they're not yet open for business. You'll have to wait."

"How long?" Terry demanded.

"Pardon me?"

"How long before they open?"

"Why, just a few minutes, mum," he answered, and Terry gave him an exasperated sigh, pushed past him and headed on down the hallway, searching for the correct department. The man behind the counter picked up his telephone and pressed one digit. "Higgins," he said. "There is a most unpleasant American on the way to see you. I'm afraid I could not detain her. She was rather insistent."

214

"Yes," Higgins answered with a sigh. "Aren't they all."

Minutes later Terry Woodall left the *Times* offices and headed for the *Mirror,* where she was prepared to be just as insistent. After all, she mused with a smile, no one ever said Americans were particularly polite.

Max Rudger walked into Madison's room rubbing his stomach. "What say we grab some pub-grub and take a drive to our friend Helda's house?" He paused and looked Madison up and down. "You look like the devil, old girl. Had any food lately?"

"I seem to have lost my appetite," Madison answered, slipping on her shoes.

"Well now, you're just going to have to find it because I haven't lost mine."

An hour later Max and Madison sat a few hundred yards away from Helda Steiner's address, Madison peering through binoculars, Max finishing the pork pie he had purchased from a pub on the way. He wiped his mustache and then his hands, and complained, "That is the worst blasted food I've ever eaten. You people just don't know how to eat. Londoners are sweet, polite little chaps, though, I give you that." He seemed to think this one of his funnier statements, and snickered to himself. He cleared his throat, and straightened up a bit. "Any movement?" he asked.

"A shadow behind a curtain. Someone's in there, but no one's coming in or out. No cars. Let's wait a while and see if we can get a look at the exits and windows."

215

Max reached into the back seat for another pair of binoculars. "Don't worry, old girl. We'll know every bloody inch of that place by the time we move in. I'll be pickin' up everything we'll be needin' for the job tomorrow. When the fireworks start she won't know what hit her. By the way, Madison. I've got a friend up near Oxford with a nice little cottage. I think we can rent her out for a few days. She owes me a favor. We'll be needin' a place to stow Steiner, mind you. I think she'll like a country cottage."

Chapter 21

The intelligence they had gathered was, in Madison's opinion, well worth the five thousand dollars she had paid Mary Plitchard. There was no doubt that Steiner was in the house. They had seen her go in there once.

Max and Madison returned to the Portabello. Madison went straight to her room. Max said he had errands to take care of.

Madison sat on the single mattress and looked around the room. Its dingy walls and the permanently stained sheets only added to her melancholy. So, she thought grimly, this is what eighteen years of serving your country gets you . . .

She leaned back again and closed her eyes. Sleep would not come.

Walking cautiously down the steps of the old inn, she leaned around to see Mary Plitchard on a stool behind the counter, a newspaper spread out in her lap. Madison smiled when she saw Mary's head nod slightly. Moving silently down the stairs Madison slid the paper from Mary's lap.

Once back in her room, she opened the paper and was relieved to find that reports about the rogue American agent had finally been moved to the second page. She didn't bother to read them. Instead she went straight to the classified advertisements. Scanning the columns as usual, she muttered something barely audible and closed the paper. She was a fool to keep looking, she thought, knowing in her heart that she had been betrayed, that they had abandoned her.

Suddenly she opened the paper again. What had she just seen? Something had caught her eye. Something that she had nearly overlooked. Reading it again and again, her heart beat fast, and a smile slowly creased her face.

M. From the mountains to the shores of N.C.,
and now in Intercontinental London.
Waiting. I miss you. T.

She looked up from the paper. "Terry," she said aloud, and bolted for the door. Finding Mary still asleep, she sneaked past into Mary's flat and went to the telephone. "Operator, I need the number for the Intercontinental Hotel, please." Madison committed the number to memory, and dialed as quickly as she could. "Do you have anyone registered under the name of Woodall, initial T.?"

"Yes. I can ring that room for you. Please hold." Madison hung up. She had found out what she needed to know.

The door to Mary's flat swung wide open and Max walked in. Madison turned and gave him a wide smile.

"Now just what are you up to, Madison McGuire? I know that look in your eyes."

Madison suddenly realized that there had not been time to tell Max about Terry. Oh, he was well aware that she was a lesbian. She had made that very clear several years ago when Max, after three shots of strong whiskey, had become overly affectionate. Since then he seemed to have accepted the fact reluctantly. Madison smiled and took his hand. He sat beside her and she went on to explain how she and Terry had met, and then, "Although we are very different people, Terry and I, you'll like her, Max. She's young, early twenties, but she's bright, sincere, witty. I fell in love with her so quickly . . . And now she's come all this way to find me. I can hardly believe it. She figured out where I was and how to communicate with me. The funniest thing is, I'll bet she's traveling on NOIS money."

Max laughed. "Glad she's on our side." He paused, and became serious. "She must love you very much." He then stretched and added casually, "Although, I can't see what the devil it is about you.

219

You're skinny as a rail . . . Must be your money she wants. Can't be your brains. Not with you acting the fool like this."

"And what, my dear fellow, would that mean?"

"Christ, woman, are you so blinded by your lust that you can't smell a trap? How long's it been since you got laid anyway?"

Madison thought about that. "I only called the hotel to find out if she was truly registered there. I won't try to see her today. I know they'll be watching her." She paused and smiled. "There are ways to get around surveillance, and you're going to help me, you dear sweet man." Madison leaned forward and kissed his cheek.

He sighed and nodded. "I have a feeling I'm going to regret this," he said quietly. "Now, if you can see your way clear to thinking about business, we have some planning to do. I got the cottage. It's about thirty miles northeast and off the main road. Everything we need is there, but I could use your help puttin' together the explosives. Nothing fancy. Just some fireworks. I say we take Steiner sometime in the early mornin' hours before dawn tomorrow."

"Yes," Madison answered thoughtfully. "We should move right away . . . I wonder when she'll make her move on Lawrence."

"Lawrence?" Max repeated.

"Stewart Lawrence. It's just a gut feeling. She already took out Bahudi and Mueller, and now she's in London. It makes sense she'd go after Lawrence now. It looks like she's going for all the top brass in the group . . . Listen, why don't you sleep for a couple of hours? I'm going to have a bath. Then we'll go to the cottage and put our fireworks together."

Max stretched and yawned. "Sounds good," he answered sleepily.

Madison bathed quickly, went upstairs and changed into jeans and the blonde wig. She then opened Max's door quietly and checked his breathing. Sure that he was asleep, she found her car keys in the pockets of his pants, and crept quietly into the hallway.

Max watched her with one opened eye. He rolled over and got out of bed, pulled on his pants, and muttered, "Bloody stupid woman."

Mary Plitchard was not thrilled with the prospect of Max Rudger using her car. But when she heard that Madison might be in trouble, she lent it willingly. Max, upon seeing the condition of the vehicle, an old painted-over London cab, wondered why Mary cared at all what happened to it. The rented car was still in the parking lot, so Max lay down in the front seat of Mary's old car and waited for Madison.

It took only a few minutes before she was in the car and traveling east on Portabello Road. Max tailed her from a discreet distance.

Madison parked the car at an apartment building, got out and went inside. Twenty minutes later she stepped into her newly leased flat. It was a dump, to be sure, but it would suit her purpose here today.

Finding no working telephones in the apartment building, Madison crossed the street and picked up a public telephone. Seconds later James Phillips from the American Embassy was on the line. "Scorpion?" he asked.

"That's right, Phillips. Is Stratton with you?"

"Yes. We've been waiting for your call. What are your instructions?"

"Tell Marshall that I want him checked into the Oxford Hotel within the next thirty minutes. I'll contact him there."

James Phillips complained, "But that hotel is nearly twenty minutes away, and with traffic —"

Madison interrupted abruptly. "Thirty minutes. No more." She hung up, looking at the front of the Oxford Hotel.

Marshall Stratton and James Phillips hurried across town towards the east end of Oxford Street.

"She wants you where she can see you," Phillips said, annoyed. "She'll be out there somewhere and we won't know where. It gives her a distinct advantage. Do you think she'll meet you there?"

Marshall Stratton turned his attention to James Phillips. "She'll wait to see me alone. I have instructions to play it by her rules for a while."

"Listen, Stratton," Phillips broke in angrily. "This is my territory. My network is the first she'll blow apart if she gets away. What if we can't get to her in time? What if she smells a trap?"

Stratton got out of the car, turned back to the passenger's window and spoke quietly. "You're paranoid, Phillips. Have a little faith. What do you think they teach us at Langley? Listen, once I activate this little device you'll know exactly where I am all the time."

He leaned towards Phillips, pointing as he spoke. "If we don't get her this time we'll never have another opportunity. I don't want any John Wayne stuff out there. For God's sake don't show up with the fucking British Army or you'll blow it. Give me some time alone with her. This is my baby, Phillips. I want no interference. Understood?"

Madison watched out the window of the newly leased apartment as several vehicles pulled up in front of the Oxford. She counted fifteen men piling out and surrounding the hotel. Then she saw Marshall Stratton and James Phillips enter the lobby. After waiting ten minutes, Madison walked downstairs and into the resident manager's apartment where she knew there was a telephone; she had heard it ring only moments ago. She reached into the short jacket she wore, withdrew a hundred dollars and handed it to the surprised manager. It was enough. He left his apartment and his telephone to her without question.

Madison rang the Oxford and was transferred to Stratton's room. She said, "I really am surprised at you, Marshall. I mean all those cars and spooks out there. It's a rather feeble attempt at surveillance, wouldn't you say?"

Marshall laughed, and James Phillips looked at him as if he were insane. "You didn't give us much time, Madison." His voice became low and serious. "How are you?"

"As well as can be expected considering the circumstances, I'd say. But then, why would you care, Marshall? You've been sent here to, shall we say, terminate my contract."

"I came here to talk," Stratton answered nervously. "Maybe we can work things out. Give it a chance. You could be back at Langley in a few hours."

Madison thought about that for a few moments. "All right. We'll talk. But first you're going to have to get rid of all those troublesome men. I counted fifteen. Phillips makes sixteen. I expect to see them leaving within the next five minutes. Phillips is to leave the automobile with you . . . Oh, and Marshall, don't lose your perspective. Just because I'm on the defensive doesn't mean I'll make errors in judgment. I can assure you I am not alone. If those men don't stay at least ten blocks back, I promise you that my next call will be to the *Washington Post*."

Stratton turned to Phillips and waved a hand. "I'll clear the area at once."

"When I get word they're gone, I'll ring you back." Madison hung up.

Stratton turned to Phillips. "She wants all of you out of here. She has back-up. Someone has the place staked out. Clear the area at once. She'll call me back when she knows we're following her instructions."

Phillips glared at Stratton. He resented like hell this young smartass fresh from The Farm giving him orders. He turned to walk out, and heard Stratton say, "Oh, Phillips. You'll have to ride with one of your men. I need your car." James Phillips slammed the door behind him.

Marshall Stratton sighed, and lowered his large frame onto the bed. He was not pleased with his assignment. He deeply regretted being the one chosen to eliminate another operative, especially one he cared about. But, it was always discouraging to hear of a colleague who had tipped over the edge. Fortunately it was not that common. The CIA and the NOIS had had extraordinary success in filtering out the bad ones. Still, a few did slip through. Stratton had never thought Madison would be one of the ones who sold out, or lost their balance, who turned on the agency, forgetting all their commitments, their code of silence. Some had had complete breakdowns. Others, like Madison, became intoxicated by the power and the games. These were the killers.

Stratton shook his head in disbelief and stretched out on the bed.

Chapter 22

The activity in front of the Oxford was not lost on Max Rudger, who watched from the corner near the apartment house into which Madison had disappeared. He allowed himself a chuckle, watching the men piling into cars quickly and leaving the hotel. *Dumb bastards might as well wear sandwich signs with SPOOK written across them.*

He wasn't completely sure what was going on, but the picture was beginning to take form. All but one of the men who had arrived at the Oxford were now gone or leaving. Madison, he guessed, was probably watching from the apartment window. Suddenly it hit him, and he slapped his forehead with a flat hand. *The bloody fool is going to be meeting with one of those spooks. And with no back-up, mind you. Christ, Madison. What are you thinking about?*

Max strolled casually to the borrowed car and climbed in. Something told him it would be time to move very soon.

Madison made her phone call and gave Stratton directions to a small park near a school. She knew the park well. The school had been the one where her Elicia had taught. She knew it had two exits, both visible from the south end, and she reasoned that if anything went wrong she would be able to get out. Madison told Stratton that he must follow her directions exactly, and if he strayed from the route she had given him the meeting would be cancelled. She knew there would be several traffic stops on the way, and that was what she was counting on.

Peering out the window of the cheap apartment house, Madison watched in amusement as Stratton climbed into Phillips' car and drove away, apparently forgetting that in England, forward traffic moves on the left-hand side of the narrow streets. Presently she heard the inevitable car horns blasting and voices shouting, as Stratton attempted to negotiate his way back to the correct side of the road. This he managed without incident.

Madison waited two minutes and then left the apartment, climbed in the rented automobile, and followed a shorter route to the park. Five minutes later she pulled up to a nearby intersection and checked her watch. It would take Stratton another two minutes to reach the same intersection. She withdrew the .38 Super and snapped a silencer into place.

The navy blue sedan was nearly in the center of the intersection when Madison aimed and fired, blowing out the two rear tires. The sedan swerved abruptly and came to a stop. Once again horns blasted, and the vehicle behind Stratton rammed a parked bus to avoid a head-on collision with an oncoming automobile. Even more chaos had erupted than Madison had counted on.

She gunned the engine and pulled alongside the blue sedan just as Stratton, red-faced and cursing loudly, stepped out to inspect the tires. Seeing that both his rear tires had been flattened, he immediately spun around. Madison, moving to the passenger's side of the vehicle, pushed the door of her own car open and pointed the .38 at Stratton. "Get in," she ordered. "You drive."

Stratton climbed into the driver's seat, and Madison immediately reached inside his coat and withdrew his gun from the shoulder holster. "Where to?" he asked sullenly.

"Straight on," Madison answered, and then added. "All right, Marshall. Where is it?"

"Where is what?" Stratton asked, concentrating on taking a curve, and scraping the sides of the tires on the curb. "Jesus, how the hell is anyone supposed to drive on these streets?"

Madison, holding her gun in her right hand, ran her left hand over Stratton's clothing. She then raised the collar on his jacket and jerked off what appeared to be a loose button.

"This is what I was looking for. Christ, I may be crazy, Marshall, but I'm not stupid. Did you think I wouldn't know you were wearing a tracking device? Give me a little credit."

She looked at him. "So, was that the plan? They surround the meeting ground and gun me down in case you couldn't do it?"

Stratton kept his eyes on the road. His silence had answered Madison's question.

"Take a right here," she said, and Stratton obeyed, running over another curb as he did so. Madison shook her head, and turned to see if anyone was following. There was a dark taxi in the distance. "Pull over here. In front of the school."

Minutes later Marshall Stratton and Madison McGuire walked across the playground. Keeping a close eye on Stratton and the two roads that circled the park, Madison walked to a small log structure that had been erected for the children, and leaned against it. Stratton did the same.

"You want a cigarette?" he asked, reaching into his pocket slowly.

Madison looked at him suspiciously. "You don't smoke, Marshall," she said holding out her hand. "Let's have them."

He handed her the cigarette pack and she inspected them closely. There seemed to be nothng unusual about them; they were of a uniform size and shape, and no foul odor was obvious, but Madison guessed they were loaded.

The Science and Technology Department had long

experimented with cigarettes and cigars loaded with poisons and tranquilizers. It came under the heading of unconventional weaponry, and had first been used in a CIA plot to assassinate Castro. At that time, Madison recalled, they developed poison cigars, exploding seashells, fountain pens that injected their user with infectious disease, and even wetsuits dusted with bacteria. All had failed as a useful device against Castro. But this kind of weaponry had been effective on a number of other victims. Madison did not want to be one of them.

"What's happened to you, Madison? Why did you do it? Killing Bahudi is one thing, but why expose yourself? Why expose your government? What went wrong? Too much pressure?"

Madison tossed the cigarette pack aside and extracted one from her own pack. "I see they've convinced you too. I want to tell you something, Marshall. Not that it would make any difference. I know now that they intend to kill me, but I want you to know this. I want you to live with it . . . I was set up. I never even got a shot off in Liechtenstein. Helda Steiner killed those men. She used a loud bolt-action, she wore a red wig, and she was very obvious. Think about it. Do you really think I'd risk my life in order to expose myself? Why would I? Come on, man. It's not logical. I am as sane as anyone in this bloody, stinking business."

She leaned back and took a long drag from her cigarette. "You know what really disturbs me, Marshall? It isn't just that I'll probably be killed here in London. It's not even that my country turned its back on me. It's that there is someone inside our headquarters, a member of Club Twelve, and I can tell you I most certainly won't be the last casualty. There'll be many others . . . Christ, I don't know what happened. I suppose I got too close to something. I don't even know what the hell I did to sign my own death warrant. Maybe it was my insistence on going back into the field. Perhaps if Andrew could have talked me into staying inside this would have never happened."

She took a deep breath, and Marshall took a long look at her. "You're telling the truth," he muttered quietly. "Oh, my God."

"And if you believe that, my dear fellow, you'll be the next one on their list."

"Madison, listen to me," he said, urgency in his voice. "There is one person in Washington who may be able to help you. She's an advisor to the NSC and the President. I met her last night at Langley. Her name is Marge Price. She was the only one there who didn't believe you were capable of this."

"What about Andrew?" Madison asked.

Marshall looked down at the ground. "I'm sorry," he answered.

Madison stared at him for a moment, unable to accept what she had just heard. Then they both heard the screeching of tires in the distance. They drew closer . . .

Marshall turned to Madison, his eyes wide, panicked. "It's a trap, Madison. Run."

Madison quickly looked to the street and then back to Marshall. "Come with me."

He smiled and shook his head. "Get the fuck out of here. Go."

Madison reached in her jean jacket and tossed Marshall the revolver she had taken from him in the car. She then ran across the playground and into her automobile. She made it to the corner before she saw the line of vehicles moving towards her. She swerved right, drove across the playground, and hit the street with a solid bump.

Before the others could follow, an old taxi pulled from a parked position and blocked their way. Several of the vehicles slammed into one another from the sudden stop, and the taxi driver got out and smiled. He yelled at the men running towards him. "Sorry. The bleeding engine has stalled," he said with a shrug of his wide shoulders.

Madison turned to look, and saw Max Rudger standing in front of the taxi, a satisfied grin on his face. She gunned the engine and took off. By the time the cab was pushed out of the way, Madison was well out of reach.

James Phillips and one other man ran towards Stratton, who was leaning casually against the log playhouse, a hand inside his jacket pocket. Suddenly he turned towards them, his face crimson with anger, his body trembling. "Liars," he screamed and opened fire.

James Phillips and the other man hit the ground rolling, returning his fire.

Stratton started to shoot again, but a bullet to the chest stopped him.

Max Rudger looked on in complete and total astonishment.

A tall man approached James Phillips. "We lost her. Couldn't even get the plate numbers."

"Idiot," Phillips spat. "Get over there and get that goddamn taxi driver's name and address. I'm not sure he wasn't part of this whole fiasco."

The tall man turned and looked towards the street. "He's gone, James."

Terry Woodall called the front desk for the third time since she had checked in this morning. "Are you sure I don't have any messages?"

"Yes, Madame. As I told you before, if you receive any calls we will ring your room directly. Will there be anything else?"

"No." Terry slammed down the receiver.

Max Rudger walked into the Portabello Inn, his face flushed with rage. He stormed up the stairs, ignoring Mary Plitchard, and banged on Madison's door. She opened the door and returned to sit on the bed without looking at him.

"Just what in God's name did you think you were doin' out there?" There was no answer. "You bloody fool. You could have gotten us both killed. I should turn you over my knee . . ."

Madison looked at him. Her eyes blazed. "Shut up, Max. Just go away and leave me alone."

"Ah," he said, throwing his hands in the air. "So now you're wantin' to be alone, are you. Well it's a damn good thing I didn't leave you alone earlier today, isn't it? You'd be splattered all over the blessed streets right now."

Madison crossed the room deliberately. She pushed a stiff finger against Max's chest. "What the hell do you want me to do? Thank you? Is that what you're looking for? Well then, Max. Thank you very much. Okay? Is that enough gratitude or shall I fall to my knees?"

Max grabbed both her shoulders and shook her. "What is it, Madi? Tell me, damn you, woman. This isn't you. What's wrong?" He felt her go limp, felt her knees buckle, and he pulled her close to him, letting her head rest on his wide chest.

She cried. Max could not remember ever seeing Madison McGuire cry. His heart went out to her in a spasm of grief. "Oh, Madi. You've been through so much. I'm sorry for all of this mess."

She looked up at him, her eyes wet with tears. "Marshall told me Andrew agreed with their decision to terminate me. It's so unbelievable, Max. Ever since my Dad died Andrew and I have been very close. He always supported me, always seemed to love me. Now he wants to kill me. Why? Why would he buy into this?"

Max held her tightly. "It's okay. Just let it all out. We'll find a way to get through this thing. Don't forget you've got a lovely lady waitin' for you on the other side of town. And tonight we'll grab Steiner and get to the bottom of this mess."

An hour later they were at the cottage northeast of London planning their raid on the terrorist's house.

They worked methodically on the explosives, using the knowledge they had both gained over the years, Madison in Intelligence, Max with the IRA. Madison was beginning to believe that Max's cause had been the nobler one.

When they were finished, Max looked at her. "I've got to run out for a while. Be back in an hour or so.

Will you be all right?" Madison nodded and Max walked out.

Terry Woodall had spent the entire day inside the hotel room, restless, waiting, hoping. It was nearly 9:00 p.m. when her dinner arrived from room service. The steak, the most costly she had ever purchased, was a pathetic example of English cooking. She recalled her father once telling her that the English had an almost mystical way of taking a perfectly good cut of meat and reducing it to crisp fragments in a matter of minutes. Terry stabbed at the meal with her fork, uninterested.

Then, a knock on the door, barely audible. Terry sprang to her feet and swung the door open with such force that the maid on the other side started. "I'm sorry," Terry said. "I was waiting for . . . Can I help you?"

"Yes, mum," the small woman answered in a thick cockney dialect. "I'm to give you this." She handed Terry a small piece of paper and disappeared quickly down the hallway.

Chapter 23

Madison was alive and safe, the note read, and then it instructed Terry to leave her room, go to the rear service entrance of the downstairs car-park, being careful to avoid the lifts.

Pushing a heavy door open that led into the downstairs garage, confident that if anyone had her room under surveillance they would not know she had left it, Terry stepped into the parking garage. It was at that moment she saw the two men, one at the far side of the building, one pacing through the center; each had wires running from his ears down into his coat. The ear pieces told her they were government men, but she had no place to run, no place to hide.

She took a step backwards, deciding to return to the stairwell . . . Then, a huge hand covered her mouth and part of her nose, the other arm gripped her in a bear hug. She gasped for breath and made one attempt to break free, but the hand, the arm tightened around her, guiding her silently to a small dark space in the shadow of the stairs where she was held flat against the wall, her eyes darting about, her heart racing.

The sound of heels clicking against the concrete floor moved closer as one of the government surveillance men passed, and the grip that held her tightened even more in a warning she understood. She did not move, did not breathe.

As the sounds of the heels became more distant, the hand loosened its grip, but Terry knew it was ready to cover her mouth again at the slightest peep. She made none, and presently she heard a voice whisper, "It's all right. I'm a friend of Madison's."

Terry gasped to catch her breath and turned to get a look at her assailant, finding it necessary to cock her head back to look into the tall man's face. The scar across the cheek, the nose that was slightly oversized and looked as if it had been broken one too many times, and the sheer size of the man before her, startled her.

He handed her a cap, a pair of wire-rimmed glasses, and a navy-blue coat, the type she had seen American sailors wear. "Slip these things on and stuff your hair under the cap," the big man instructed, and Terry obeyed, afraid to do anything else.

237

"Now, follow me. Walk slowly, casually. Understand? And try not to look so bloody terrified. It's a long walk from here to the car."

At the gate they stopped, the big man showed his ticket to the attendant, the wooden rail lifted, and the cream-colored Renault moved cautiously away from the Intercontinental Hotel.

Madison heard the car pull up in front of the cottage. She recognized the sound of the engine. She was sitting on the sofa, her feet propped on a small table, her hands busily, skillfully assembling a detonator for the explosives she and Max had crafted, her lap covered with newspaper and stray pieces of clipped wires.

Seeing the figure out of the corner of her eye, and knowing at once it was too small to be her friend Max Rudger, Madison started and spun around, the .38 in her hand. The paper and wires on her lap hit the floor. Madison's jaw dropped in astonishment. Terry was standing there, smiling. Another second did not pass before they were in each other's arms.

Max Rudger stood at the door, and at length he offered, with a grin in his voice, "I see you won't be needin' me for a while. You've got two hours, Madi, and then we've got a job to do." He turned and went back to the car and drove away.

They stood at arm's length in the center of the living room, looking at each other tenderly. "I never thought I would see that beautiful face again," Terry said. "God, I love you, Madison." Tears welled up in her eyes, spilling down flushed cheeks.

Madison took a long look at the face she had longed to see, the beautiful dark eyes, the full, red lips. She pulled Terry close to her, and there, without thought, without planning, they made love, slowly, tenderly.

Andrew McFaye pulled into his long driveway, and sat there for a moment trying to calm himself. The telephone call he had received before leaving the office had sent shock waves over him. He had been told to expect visitors at his home today.

He climbed out of the tan Mercedes and walked slowly towards his house. He was greeted at the front door by a man he did not know, but he recognized the small man standing in the center of his den — the white baggy pants, the drawn, brown face.

"Ah, Andrew, my friend. It's good to see you after such a long time," said Islom Jabril. "I regret imposing on you in this way." Andrew stood there a moment, trying to get his bearings, staring blankly at Jabril. "Islom, you have to leave. You cannot come to my house like this. We cannot be seen together."

The old man, now the leader of Club Twelve, sat down and laughed at this, his brown face creased into a thousand folds and wrinkles. "If the home of the Chairman of the NOIS is not safe, I ask you, where in this world can we go?"

His expression quickly took on a troubled look. The old eyes studied Andrew. "We must talk, Andrew. The group has been very disturbed by the intelligence we have received on your agent, Scorpion. Our friends Amal and Peter are dead. She took their lives, yet she lives. Many in our group believe she did not act alone out of a personal vendetta as you reported. They believe someone gave her the orders to kill our friends, someone who wishes to strip us of our power. Perhaps someone in our own circle."

He paused, and the small brown eyes burned through Andrew like tiny torches. "Perhaps even you, my friend," he added as Andrew shifted uncomfortably. "Of course, I do not subscribe to this theory. I told them you had been a loyal member for twenty years. One day, if you are patient, you will take command of our group. You *can* wait for your power, can't you, Andrew?" He paused again. "Still, it is hard to understand why this woman is allowed to live."

Islom Jabril stood up, balancing himself on the back of a chair, his frail body uneasy with his own weight. "Find her, my friend, and see to it that she is eliminated. This will prove you are still our friend."

Two men walked out of Andrew's kitchen. He assumed they were Jabril's bodyguards until he looked at their faces and recognized one immediately. *Is it some kind of warning? Why has Jabril brought this man to my house?*

"How foolish of me for failing to introduce the two of you. Louis has long wanted to meet you, Andrew."

Louis Guiseppe held out his hand and Andrew accepted it reluctantly. "I'm sure Mr. McFaye recognizes me. After all, he had his agent follow me in Zurich."

At this statement Andrew released Guiseppe's hand. Jabril studied them both for a moment before saying, "We will leave you to your business now, Andrew. Please, do stay in touch."

Andrew McFaye stood at his front door and watched them leave, his knees weak under his weight, his stomach sick, his head pounding violently. *Had they discovered the truth?*

He walked to the mahogany bar and poured a tall, warm glass of bourbon. Sweat rolled off his forehead and down his ruddy cheeks as he drained the glass. He had to find Madison. The Club would never trust him again if he failed. "Dammit," he shouted, "it was never supposed to go this far."

If Madison would have just left it alone. But no, she kept pressing on relentlessly until she had nearly exposed the entire group. Two years ago she had taken off on her own in London and placed herself undercover in the middle of a giant weapons sale that had led to Amir Ansari of Pakistan and Islom Jabril. It was only a matter of time, she had reported, until she would identify the rest of the members. And on that day Madison McGuire had unwittingly become the enemy of Andrew McFaye.

After the hit had failed in London, and Madison's lover was mistakenly killed, Andrew had had no choice but to bring her back to the States. He had his position at the NOIS to consider, and the eyes of government officials were on him. At that point he considered her to be no real threat. If the hit had failed in one way, it was a success in another. Madison would return to the States defeated, hurt, devastated by her loss. He would keep her inside, encourage her to retire early, to take her pension and live a normal life again. But Madison had surprised him. Her resolve and conviction were even stronger than before.

It had been the day she stood in his office threatening to leave the agency and pursue Club Twelve alone if he didn't put her back in the field that he had suddenly come upon the idea. At first it had been merely a dull and fleeting thought, but presently it had grown into what Andrew perceived as the most brilliant scheme of his life. Why hadn't he seen it before, he'd asked himself on that day. He could use Madison's anger, use her hate to eliminate the oldest members of the group, leaving only himself to take control.

It had made perfect sense. Madison was the best. She was quick, agile, and she never missed. But, he would have to work her into it slowly, and plan another operation as a diversion. That operation was Accounting Central — an operation that he had never intended to take place.

The entire plan had almost been destroyed when that idiot, Mark Hadden, took it upon himself to take a contract out on Scorpion and have her killed in Vail. However, once again Andrew had recovered from the setback and produced evidence to incriminate Mark Hadden.

Employing Helda Steiner had been a stroke of genius, he mused. With Steiner running around Europe killing everyone in sight, it would not be difficult to convince the government that Madison had gone totally and completely insane. Of course, Helda Steiner would also have to eliminated one day. Still, that was no great loss. Steiner was a radical fanatic, a killer with no particular allegiance to anyone or anything, except perhaps the highest bidder.

In the beginning he had had his regrets, his share of sleepless nights over the decision to kill Madison in London. He had loved her once when she was very young. But priorities changed. There was survival to consider. What was love compared with power? A useless and painful emotion.

Madison was so much like her father. Never giving a thought to personal gain or power, mindlessly serving a government that would use them all until they were too old to perform, and then toss them aside with a pension that was barely enough to eat on.

"Fuck them," he muttered under his breath, and poured another drink. "I want more. I deserve more. I'll have it all." He tossed the drink back. His laughter echoed through his empty house.

It was not one of the nicer neighborhoods in London. In fact it could hardly be called a neighborhood at all. On this particular street there was but one small house at the end of the street. The city dump, which emitted the most sickening of odors, stood at the front of the half-mile long street.

Madison and Max drove down a small hill, into the dump, and parked. They stepped out of the vehicle, both wearing black pants and shirts, their forms blending into the darkness of the unlit street.

Working quickly, Madison snapped a four-inch-wide belt around her waist. It held a six-inch knife blade, one pack of homemade ammonia-based explosives, one canister containing a stun grenade, and a syringe loaded with a heavy tranquilizer protected by a plastic case. She checked the .38 Super once more and stuffed it into its holster. Giving Max a nod, she took a deep breath and they started down the street, keeping low to the ground, zigzagging through the edge of the woods and across the street.

With surprising agility for a man of his size, Max went about silently driving metal shims into the sides of the windows, making sure they could not be opened from the inside. Once this was done he returned to Madison, who was at the rear of the house. "We got lucky," he whispered. "She's the only one in there. She's in the left rear."

Madison nodded and moved quickly, placing a blob of the explosives on the rear corner of the house. At Max's signal they both began counting in their minds, from sixty backwards, and Max disappeared around the front of the house.

Forty eight . . . Forty seven . . . Forty six . . .

Max attached his explosives to the right side of the front porch and drove a thick metal shim under the front door. The weathered wood of the porch creaked its objection to his weight, and one of the inside lights was immediately extinguished. He dove off the side of the porch and crawled on his belly towards the cover of the shrubbery.

Twenty three . . . Twenty two . . . Twenty one . . .

The second and only remaining light in the house was turned off. The surprise was lost. Helda Steiner knew they were there.

Ten . . . Nine . . . Eight . . .

Madison rolled over and over the dew moistened grass to get into position.

Three . . . Two . . . One . . . Zero . . .

She touched two wires together on the homemade detonator.

A sudden and violent detonation engulfed the entire back yard in a blue-white light. Then, a second explosion from the front told Madison that Max had placed his explosives well. Using the front yard explosion as a diversion, Madison ran to the back door and flattened herself against the house. She waited there, her heart pounding with excitement, waiting for Steiner to make her escape, knowing that the back door was her only way out.

Madison withdrew the syringe from her belt. Another full minute passed and still Helda Steiner had not shown herself. Madison noticed a small fire beginning on the side of the house where the first explosives had gone off. She envisioned Helda Steiner inside, overcome with smoke and heat, unable to escape. She could wait no longer. Steiner was her only key to this horrible puzzle and she couldn't risk losing her.

She stepped back and smashed her right foot into the door, just below the doorknob. It swung open. Madison flattened herself against the house once again, half expecting an eruption of gunfire. She dove into the kitchen, sliding across the tiled floor, rolling over and over — a moving target.

Then, a quick prism-like reflection shot through the room, something mirrored in the flames from the rear of the house. Where had it come from? Madison whipped her head around just in time to catch a glimpse of the assassin's black eyes in the dim light. She lunged towards them and suddenly there was an icy, metallic incision. It cut through her shirt and sliced across her shoulder in one precise stroke.

Madison pivoted and lashed out with her right foot, slamming her attacker against the wall. She grabbed the killer's head with both hands and savagely slammed her knee into the woman's face. Steiner slid down the wall in a heap, her blood soaking the floor.

Madison withdrew the syringe and knelt to administer the drug, fighting the dizziness that comes with rapid loss of blood. The killer suddenly surged towards her, slashing wildly, and again Madison felt the blade crease her flesh. Blood erupted from two places, soaking her clothing. First cold and then fire-like gashes sent throbbing shock waves to her brain. The numbness was beginning to roll over her. She felt her fingers and hands beginning to tingle. The killer rolled over and disappeared into the dark smoke that was now filling the tiny house.

Madison crawled to the wall and leaned against it, breathing heavily, trying to cover her mouth and nose to keep out the thick smoke . . . Then it came. A sudden, blinding flash of light. Madison saw Helda Steiner silhouetted behind a small machine gun. The sound and light filled her eyes and ears, and the raw, sweet smell of her own blood penetrated her nostrils.

Madison dove to the right, leveling her gun at the blinding light, knowing now that any hopes of taking the killer alive were gone. It was kill or be killed. Her own gunfire was lost in the deafening sound of the machine gun blast. Madison rolled through the small kitchen, trying to avoid the lethal spray of bullets. One grazed her neck. She yelled and grabbed at the wound. And then, finally it came. A crash from the front of the house, just as the flames were growing ever closer to the kitchen. *Max, thank God.*

Madison heard an empty clip hit the floor. The killer had emptied her weapon. Madison slowly climbed to her feet and stumbled, half dazed, through the smoke-filled kitchen.

"Madison, get down," Max screamed, and Madison fell to the floor, feeling sick and terrified.

She turned to see Helda Steiner lunge towards Max, her bloody knife held high. Madison, unable to stand, crawled towards the front door. She plunged the needle violently into the back of the assassin's knee and pushed the drug under the skin, into the vein.

A savage, hollow scream filled the darkness as the assassin turned to the source of the pain. Max administered the final blow to the side of Steiner's neck and she dropped to the floor.

Madison rolled over onto her back and grimaced in pain, feeling the wounds that her mind would not allow her to accept earlier. Max withdrew his flashlight and quickly examined the damage. "Holy Mother of God," he mumbled quietly when he saw Madison's condition and the thick red pool of blood that had formed around her.

He stuck his flashlight in his mouth to free his hands and picked Madison up, carrying her into the front yard, away from the flames and smoke. He hurried back into the house and pulled Steiner out into the yard, then moved quickly to Madison. He began cutting away her clothing, his entire body trembling. A yell coming from deep within the big man died out unheard and became a sickening dryness in his mouth. He put his hand on her forehead. "You're going to be all right, old girl. The

247

wounds aren't deep but you're losing a lot of blood. We've got to get you out of here. I'm going for the car. I'll be right back."

Max ran as fast as his legs would move him, his heart racing with fear. *Oh, Madison. Don't die. Please don't die on me.*

Chapter 24

Max tied Helda Steiner's feet and hands, gagged her, and dragged her limp body across the yard and stuffed it into the back of the car.

Breathing heavily, he returned to Madison's side, aware for the first time of the sound of sirens in the distance. Madison was staring blankly up at the sky. He tore his shirt and wrapped it around the wounds, and slid one big arm under her waist and helped her to her feet. Madison wrapped her arm around him with surprising strength. She was still reasonably aware. But her right arm hung limply, helplessly at her side, and Max wondered sadly if that arm would ever be completely functional again.

At the car, he raised her gently into the front seat. Her eyes met his for a moment and she managed a weak smile. "We got her, Max. We got her," she whispered.

He leaned forward and kissed her forehead lightly. "You bloody lunatic," he said, and walked around to the driver's side.

Madison was barely conscious. She wanted to reach out for him, wanted to let him know she was all right, but she could not find the strength. She tried to speak again but all that came out was a strange cracking noise.

What followed was a blurred, distorted mass of images in her mind, perceptible and recognizable only in an indefinite way which Madison could not comprehend . . . She was in a vehicle. Of this she was sure. She felt the forward motion and with each surge, each curve and bump, a wave of pain registered in her brain. Everything seemed out of place and time, slow and hazy as if she were peering through a soft focus lens. Images trailed before her, sounds and voices in the background, vague and indistinct. Then, movement again. Pain again.

When she woke she was staring at a low, timbered ceiling, hazy and understated through the fog in her mind. Where was she? What had happened? She tried to move, but something prevented her. She turned to inspect the unseen restraints, but the pain shot through her and forced her to lie still.

Blinking several times, she fought to focus. Then

a face appeared in front of her. A face she recognized. But her brain could not respond to the images.

"Hello darling. How are you feeling?" Terry asked, softly.

Madison attempted to croak out a sound, but it sounded so ridiculous even to her that she closed her mouth again.

"It's okay," Terry said. "We'll talk later. Here . . . Can you suck on this straw? It's water. It'll help."

Madison drank thirstily, quickly draining the glass of its contents. She sighed and let her head fall back onto the pillow. Terry dabbed her forehead with a cool cloth, and kissed her face gently. "Do you remember what happened?" Terry asked.

"Ah, hell she remembers," boomed a voice behind her. It was Max. "It was one of her finest moments. The old girl just wouldn't give up. A woman possessed, she was. Crawling along the floor with every ounce of her strength to —"

Terry interrupted that brief reminiscence with a look. He stepped back, and said, "Sorry . . . I suppose this isn't the best time to talk about it. How are you, old girl?" he asked, walking towards the bed and leaning over.

Madison uttered her first words. "How long have I been down?"

"Three days," Terry answered.

"What about . . ."

"Steiner?" Max asked. "Oh we took care of the bloody bitch. I got a doctor up here. He patched you up and gave Steiner an injection that made her sing. We got a full confession, and we got it on tape. Everything from Liechtenstein to London, and a few

251

things in between we didn't even know about. Terry and I tied her up and took her to Peter. Remember Peter from the airport? He's the one who met you there. Anyway, as soon as we give him the word he'll see to it that Steiner's delivered to Scotland Yard. She's wanted for so many crimes across Europe they'll be keeping her for a long while."

"Who hired her?" Madison asked in a low, hoarse voice.

"Later, darling," Terry answered. "Right now we need to get some food in you. Try and be patient. We've got copies of the tapes. We'll hear them tonight. I promise."

Madison nodded and smiled faintly.

Terry took Max's arm and escorted him from the bedroom. He stood there in the hallway looking down at the floor, and for the first time Terry realized how useless he must feel. After all he and Madison had been through together, he must now feel alienated. She smiled and patted his shoulder. "Listen, I've got some soup in the kitchen for her. Would you take it to her and be sure she eats? She's right-handed you know. That means you'll probably have to feed her."

Max's face lit up like that of a child's. "I think I can handle this assignment."

Madison's initial reaction to Steiner's confession tapes was complete denial. She could hardly accept that Andrew, a once loved and trusted friend, had betrayed her and everything she had always believed he stood for. After several minutes of quiet contemplation, Madison looked at Max and then at

Terry. Her words were even, measured. "I want to see him. I want to look into his eyes. I want him to tell me why."

"Come now, Madison. Haven't you been through enough hell? No point in pushin' yourself anymore, is there?"

"I can't leave it at this," Madison explained quietly. "It just doesn't seem real this way. I don't know how to explain it. It's like when you lose someone you really care about. It doesn't seem real until the funeral . . . There's something so final about funerals . . . Do you understand? I have to confront him."

A vague plan began to take shape in her mind. She looked at Terry. "Darling, I want you to do something for me. There's a woman in Washington named Marge Price. She works for the State Department. Do you think you can find a way to get to her and take her these tapes?"

Terry and Max exchanged uneasy glances. "I suppose I could find her, but why?"

"Marshall told me Price would help me. Apparently she doesn't believe that I've flipped. If we could convince her that I really am innocent and that Andrew is behind all this, maybe we could go home. Maybe I could stop running."

Max sighed and crossed one foot over his knee. "Sounds like you'd be giving them a chance to set another trap for you. It's too risky."

"What would you have me do then, Mr. Rudger?" Madison asked sarcastically. "Have the two of you hide me for the next twenty years? How long before one of us makes a mistake? Do you think I want to spend my life as a fugitive? That's no way to live. It wouldn't be fair to any of us. I can't be much of a friend to you, Max, or a lover to you, Terry, until my life has some kind of order again." She fought back tears. "That bastard." Then she said, "I need some air. I'm going outside. I feel fine now. I just need some air."

Terry started to follow, but Max touched her arm gently and said, "Let her be. She's needin' some time." Terry nodded and sat down beside him.

An hour later Max, Madison and Terry sat in a conspiratorial huddle in the living room of the cottage. Madison picked up the phone and dialed Andrew's private number. She listened for the voice to answer, and handed the phone to Max, who had already attached a tiny suction cup listening device to the receiver and plugged the other end into the tape recorder.

"Gutten abend, Herr McFaye," Max said in his best German accent. "I'm a friend of Helda's."

"Who is this?" McFaye demanded with enough slur in his words for Max to guess that he had been drinking.

"I know what you did, Helda told me everything."

There was a long pause. "I don't know who you are or what you want, but I don't intend to continue this conversation any —"

"Do not be so hasty, Herr McFaye. Does the name Club Twelve mean anything to you? And would it be so unusual for someone like Helda to document her activities?"

"What do you want?" Andrew asked angrily.

254

"I want the same things you want. Money, power. Perhaps we could make some financial arrangements in order to assure my silence."

After a brief pause, McFaye answered, "Where can I meet you?"

"I will contact you again," Max answered. *"Gutten abend."*

Max replaced the receiver and offered Terry and Madison a wide grin.

At London's Heathrow airport, Terry was well aware of the surveillance on her. It had begun immediately upon her return to the Intercontinental Hotel where she had collected her luggage and called for a cab. The surveillance did not particularly concern her, however. The danger that she might lead them to Madison had passed for now, with Madison safely tucked away in a cottage miles away from London.

In a matter of hours Terry Woodall arrived in Washington, D.C., checked into a hotel and went directly to the State Department Building. She was detained there by a security officer who insisted on knowing her business. "I want to see Marge Price. It's very important. My name is Terry Woodall."

The officer instructed her to wait while he walked to the telephone, spoke quietly for a moment and then returned. "I'm sorry, but we have no one by that name in this building."

Terry stared blankly at the man until, strangely, her attention was drawn to the opening doors of an elevator several yards away. A woman inside, a woman with grey-brown hair, a stern face, pale grey eyes. Exactly the woman Madison had described.

Terry pressed past the guard and ran to the elevator, feeling in her purse for the tapes. The woman, upon seeing Terry rushing towards her, pushed a button inside the elevator.

"Please, Ms. Price. You have to listen to me. My name is Terry Woodall."

The elevator doors began closing and the security guard held one of Terry's arms.

"Please, just take these tapes. They explain everything."

The elevator doors closed abruptly.

It was nearly 8:00 p.m. when Marge Price left the building and flagged a taxi. Terry appeared behind her. "Please, all I want is to give you these tapes. Madison didn't kill those men. We know who did it. Please," Terry pleaded.

Marge Price did not alter her stride one bit. She did not turn, she did not slow.

Terry persisted. "You're our only hope. Can't you see that an innocent woman is going to be murdered if you don't help? Marshall Stratton told us you would help. He believed her, Ms. Price."

At this Marge Price whipped her head and looked at Terry for the first time. She answered hesitantly. "I'll listen to the tapes, but no promises."

Terry watched the taxi drive away, and for the first time had real hope. She was halfway across the street before she heard the footsteps running behind her and the voice yelling, "Watch out!"

She turned and saw the vehicle speeding towards her. She felt someone push her out of the road. She heard the screeching of tires and turned in time to see the man who had just saved her hit the hood of the car and roll off limply into the street.

A large crowd had gathered by the time the police and ambulance arrived. Terry explained, as best she could, what had happened. It was a light-colored car. No. She did not know the make or model. No. She hadn't had time to get the tag number.

The telephone in the hotel room was ringing when Terry walked in. Marge Price identified herself.

"Thank God it's you," Terry said urgently. "Someone just tried to kill me. I'm sure of it. I was nearly run down in the street after we talked. And then a man appeared from nowhere and pushed me out of the way."

"Are you sure, Terry?" Marge Price asked in tones of astonishment.

"Yes. I'm sure the car meant to hit me."

"Stay there. Don't move. I'm sending a car for you." Marge Price hung up.

Chapter 25

The house was forty-five minutes from D.C. The men on its front steps and grounds, Terry was informed, were FBI agents put there for everyone's protection. Terry tried not to dwell on the fact that *everyone* needed protection.

Marge Price greeted Terry at the door and led her down a long foyer and into what appeared to be a rather large study, then went about the business of preparing refreshments for both of them. "Since we last spoke we've collected a great deal of information about the accident in front of State." She spoke casually as she dropped ice into the glasses. "We have a make, model and partial tag number on the vehicle that almost hit you."

"That's great. Do you know who it was yet?"

"Let's just say we have an idea," Price answered vaguely, finishing her business at the bar and joining Terry on a long couch.

"What about the tapes?" Terry asked anxiously.

Price lit a cigarette and leaned back, crossing her legs. "I have to admit I was rather skeptical about the Helda Steiner tape, Terry. We can't even analyze the voice until we get a speech sample on her. But the other tape, the one with McFaye and the anonymous man threatening to expose him, didn't present the same problems. Getting a sample of McFaye's voice was fairly simple. We know now that you're telling the truth, Terry. The fact is we've been a little suspicious of Andrew lately."

"Thank God," Terry muttered. "That bastard."

"I couldn't agree with you more," Marge said. "However, there are some things we have to discuss. This is an extremely sensitive issue. We have a top ranking government official who has been basically acting as a double agent —"

"Ms. Price," Terry broke in, "if you're concerned that I may go to the press with this information or something like that, let me ease your mind. My sole interest lies in getting Madison McGuire home safely and cleared. Once this is done I would just as soon erase the whole nightmare from my memory forever."

"I see," Marge Price answered, a faint smile crossing her face. "Would you sign a statement saying that you'll never disclose any of this information?"

"Of course. On condition that you arrange to

bring Madison home and clear her of any charges. We don't care what you tell the public. All we want is to be left alone. No more government interference in our lives."

"Unfortunately, Terry, it isn't that simple. Madison will have to endure a long debriefing after her last assignment. You see, we still don't have enough evidence on McFaye for a conviction. Knowing Madison and Andrew's history, we feel she could draw a confession out of him. We would like her to see him, wearing a wire. Do you think she'll agree?"

Terry smiled. "I think she'd be happy to have that be her last official act."

Madison was issued diplomatic clearance and given instructions to board a plane from Heathrow to Dulles airport.

Max Rudger walked with her to the gate. Her right arm was still stiff, but free now from the sling she had worn for over a week, and she felt strong, confident again. "You're a dear, sweet man, Max Rudger. I don't know how to thank you for all you've done," she said at the gate, hugging the big man tightly.

He pulled away and dabbed tears from the corners of his blue eyes. "Take care of yourself, love. And take care of Terry too. She's too good for you, you know."

Madison smiled. "I know . . . Goodbye, Max."

* * * * *

260

They did not make love that night after Madison's return; in fact they hardly spoke. Instead they lay in bed quietly holding each other, both still unable to fully comprehend all that had happened, all they had been through.

For the last several weeks Madison McGuire had lived on a diet of pure stress, fed to her by a cruel, power-hungry man. She would need time to heal, time to forgive, time to learn how to live again.

The next day was cloudy and rainy in Virginia. Appropriate weather, Madison mused, for the gloomy business at hand.

She and Terry sat in the back seat of a military sedan, a lead car with three field agents in front of them. The tail car held two agents and Troy Delcardo.

Madison shifted in her seat and made some adjustments to the wires attached to her chest and stomach. She turned and looked at the tail car. "Testing. One, two, three." Troy Delcardo gave her a thumbs-up.

The three automobiles pulled to the end of Andrew's half-mile long drive and stopped. Madison climbed out of the car, followed by Terry.

"How much time do you think you'll need?" Troy Delcardo asked.

"I don't know. Fifteen minutes, perhaps more or less. I just don't know," Madison answered and turned to Terry. "Don't worry. I'll be all right. You'll be able to hear everything that goes on. It's completely safe."

* * * * *

Andrew McFaye was sitting in his favorite chair, near the fireplace. Madison moved directly to the end table in the center of the room, opened its drawer and extracted the revolver she knew Andrew kept there. She turned and looked at him.

The once comforting, tender man now seemed a menacing, sullen figure, sitting there with his head down, fleshy fists clenched. He looked up at her, half intoxicated, his prominent, heavy lidded eyes swollen, the round face flushed. "How did you get here?" he demanded.

Madison stood in front of him. "It's all over, Andy. We all know. They're outside waiting for you."

Andrew brought his hands to his head, letting his elbows rest on his knees. "Oh, God," he mumbled.

Madison looked at him without emotion, without pity, without hate. "Why, Andrew? Just tell me why you've done this. You're not the man I knew. The honest, loving man I knew as a child would never have done this. He would never have killed those men for his own gain. He would never have tried to kill me. Christ, Andy, how many others were on your hit list?"

Andrew shook his head and laughed quietly, reaching for a half-empty glass beside him. "I wanted more, Madison. Much more than you've ever allowed yourself to dream about. You know, you make me laugh. Standing there with all your fucking righteous indignation. Let me tell you something," he went on, his voice becoming louder, his anger increasing. "We live in a world where countless thousands die every day. In a world where there is only fear. Indignation

262

is a luxury my dear, pure Madison . . . Don't you see what we could have accomplished? I could have been at the head of a group that could change the world, relieve it of the burden of its old ideals, free it of its garbage. But you'll never understand that, will you? You're too goddamn squeaky clean. You remind me of your father. Always on some fucking crusade."

He paused and Madison saw a strange, distant glint in the red-rimmed eyes. "Jake was like that. He always thought he was better than everyone else. He thought he had some great calling. Well, let me tell you something. Jake was a fool. The same kind of fool you are. A blind, idealistic fool."

Madison glared at him. She felt her thumb pulling back the hammer on her gun. It clicked into place and her finger tensed on the trigger. "You bastard," she blurted in disbelief. "You killed him, didn't you? You exposed him so Bahudi and his men could find him. You were the leak all along."

Andrew smiled and Madison stepped back, staring at him. Madness in and of itself was completely and totally terrifying to her — it could not be bought, or bribed, or talked out of a person. Now, she perceived sadly, this madness had become as much a part of Andrew as his eyes or mouth or nose. Her hand trembled holding the gun, her finger twitched, her stomach turned.

"Are you going to kill me now, Madison? Can you kill me?" Andrew asked, still smiling.

Madison walked to him and placed his revolver in front of him. "Living or dying is a decision you'll have to make," she said quietly, and turned and walked out.

Only seconds after she had closed the front door

and stepped onto the sidewalk, she heard the cough of his weapon. She paused briefly, and then slowly walked towards the car.

The administration took full advantage of this most convenient way out that Andrew McFaye had chosen for himself.

The *Washington Post* headlines the next day read:

CHAIRMAN-NOIS DIES SUDDENLY
OF HEART ATTACK

Epilogue

A cool autumn wind whipped off the water, promising a bitter winter. Marge Price and Terry Woodall sat in the kitchen of the beach house in Buxton, North Carolina. Occasionally Terry glanced out the window to see Madison sitting on the beach, staring thoughtfully at the whitecapped waves.

"How is she?" Marge asked.

"Distant sometimes, thoughtful. But I think she'll be okay. We're comfortable here . . . I think a little bit of the wall chips apart every day."

Marge smiled and patted Terry's hand. "Be

patient. It will take time. How does one return to a normal life overnight? The memories of the constant fight, the survival, the pain, they'll take some time to go away. You know, every month when I come down here for her examinations, she's a little more relaxed. Not so stretched. Hang in there, Terry. She'll be fine in time."

Terry smiled. "So, what's happening with my dear brother, Louis?"

"He's cooperating nicely. He's been offered a reduced sentence for the murder of Jonothan Shore because he turned over the Club Twelve file he took from Radcliffe. England wants him for Radcliffe's murder, but we'll keep him here under a witness protection program. He's agreed to testify against all of them, providing we protect him after he serves his time."

"What about the others?" Terry asked.

"Well, two people from Defense are in jail and two have been dismissed for their suspected involvement in a bid-rigging scheme with WEI. Your father, as you know, wasn't involved in Club Twelve, but his company will have to pay a substantial fine for rigging the contracts and they won't be able to bid on any government contracts for three years. And, we have the remaining members of Club Twelve in custody in their own countries . . . Except Islom Jabril. He seems to have disappeared."

Terry studied her for a moment. "Do you think we should be concerned about Jabril? Do you think Madison is in any danger?"

Price smiled. "No way. The moment he surfaces we'll have him. The two of you are in no danger." Marge stubbed out her cigarette and took a last sip

266

from her coffee cup. "Well, I should hit the road. I'll see you next month. Say goodbye to Madison for me, and don't worry, she'll be just fine. She's a tough one, you know."

Terry put her arm around Marge's shoulder and walked her to the door. "Thanks, Marge. Thanks for everything. See you next month."

Terry watched Marge leave, and then walked to the deck. Madison was still sitting on the beach looking out at the water "Hey!" Terry yelled down to her.

Madison turned and smiled up at her. "Come join me."

Terry mimicked a shiver. "What? Are you nuts? It's too cold down there."

Madison laughed and stared at her for a moment. Terry's dark hair was blowing behind her, the light shining through it. The delicate triangular face that moved her so was smiling down at her, and Madison thought she knew exactly where she wanted to begin the rest of her life.

A few of the publications of
THE NAIAD PRESS, INC.
P.O. Box 10543 • Tallahassee, Florida 32302
Phone (904) 539-5965
Mail orders welcome. Please include 15% postage.

CLUB 12 by Amanda Kyle Williams. 288 pp. Espionage thriller featuring a lesbian agent!	ISBN 0-941483-64-9	$8.95
LESBIAN QUERIES by Hertz & Ertman. 112 pp. The questions you were too embarrassed to ask.	ISBN 0-941483-67-3	8.95
THEME FOR DIVERSE INSTRUMENTS by Jane Rule. 208 pp. Powerful romantic lesbian stories.	ISBN 0-941483-63-0	8.95
PRIORITIES by Lynda Lyons 288 pp. Science fiction with a twist.	ISBN 0-941483-66-5	8.95
DEATH DOWN UNDER by Claire McNab. 240 pp. 3rd Det. Insp. Carol Ashton mystery.	ISBN 0-941483-39-8	8.95
MONTANA FEATHERS by Penny Hayes. 256 pp. Vivian and Elizabeth find love in frontier Montana.	ISBN 0-941483-61-4	8.95
CHESAPEAKE PROJECT by Phyllis Horn. 304 pp. Jessie & Meredith in perilous adventure.	ISBN 0-941483-58-4	8.95
LIFESTYLES by Jackie Calhoun. 224 pp. Contemporary Lesbian lives and loves.	ISBN 0-941483-57-6	8.95
VIRAGO by Karen Marie Christa Minns. 208 pp. Darsen has chosen Ginny.	ISBN 0-941483-56-8	8.95
WILDERNESS TREK by Dorothy Tell. 192 pp. Six women on vacation learning "new" skills.	ISBN 0-941483-60-6	8.95
MURDER BY THE BOOK by Pat Welch. 256 pp. A Helen Black Mystery. First in a series.	ISBN 0-941483-59-2	8.95
BERRIGAN by Vicki P. McConnell. 176 pp. Youthful Lesbian– romantic, idealistic Berrigan.	ISBN 0-941483-55-X	8.95
LESBIANS IN GERMANY by Lillian Faderman & B. Eriksson. 128 pp. Fiction, poetry, essays.	ISBN 0-941483-62-2	8.95
THE BEVERLY MALIBU by Katherine V. Forrest. 288 pp. A Kate Delafield Mystery. 3rd in a series.	ISBN 0-941483-47-9	16.95
THERE'S SOMETHING I'VE BEEN MEANING TO TELL YOU Ed. by Loralee MacPike. 288 pp. Gay men and lesbians coming out to their children.	ISBN 0-941483-44-4	9.95
	ISBN 0-941483-54-1	16.95
LIFTING BELLY by Gertrude Stein. Ed. by Rebecca Mark. 104 pp. Erotic poetry.	ISBN 0-941483-51-7	8.95
	ISBN 0-941483-53-3	14.95
ROSE PENSKI by Roz Perry. 192 pp. Adult lovers in a long-term relationship.	ISBN 0-941483-37-1	8.95

AFTER THE FIRE by Jane Rule. 256 pp. Warm, human novel
by this incomparable author.   ISBN 0-941483-45-2   8.95

SUE SLATE, PRIVATE EYE by Lee Lynch. 176 pp. The gay
folk of Peacock Alley are *all* cats.   ISBN 0-941483-52-5   8.95

CHRIS by Randy Salem. 224 pp. Golden oldie. Handsome Chris
and her adventures.   ISBN 0-941483-42-8   8.95

THREE WOMEN by March Hastings. 232 pp. Golden oldie. A
triangle among wealthy sophisticates.   ISBN 0-941483-43-6   8.95

RICE AND BEANS by Valeria Taylor. 232 pp. Love and
romance on poverty row.   ISBN 0-941483-41-X   8.95

PLEASURES by Robbi Sommers. 204 pp. Unprecedented
eroticism.   ISBN 0-941483-49-5   8.95

EDGEWISE by Camarin Grae. 372 pp. Spellbinding
adventure.   ISBN 0-941483-19-3   9.95

FATAL REUNION by Claire McNab. 216 pp. 2nd Det. Inspec.
Carol Ashton mystery.   ISBN 0-941483-40-1   8.95

KEEP TO ME STRANGER by Sarah Aldridge. 372 pp. Romance
set in a department store dynasty.   ISBN 0-941483-38-X   9.95

HEARTSCAPE by Sue Gambill. 204 pp. American lesbian in
Portugal.   ISBN 0-941483-33-9   8.95

IN THE BLOOD by Lauren Wright Douglas. 252 pp. Lesbian
science fiction adventure fantasy   ISBN 0-941483-22-3   8.95

THE BEE'S KISS by Shirley Verel. 216 pp. Delicate, delicious
romance.   ISBN 0-941483-36-3   8.95

RAGING MOTHER MOUNTAIN by Pat Emmerson. 264 pp.
Furosa Firechild's adventures in Wonderland. ISBN 0-941483-35-5   8.95

IN EVERY PORT by Karin Kallmaker. 228 pp. Jessica's sexy,
adventuresome travels.   ISBN 0-941483-37-7   8.95

OF LOVE AND GLORY by Evelyn Kennedy. 192 pp. Exciting
WWII romance.   ISBN 0-941483-32-0   8.95

CLICKING STONES by Nancy Tyler Glenn. 288 pp. Love
transcending time.   ISBN 0-941483-31-2   8.95

SURVIVING SISTERS by Gail Pass. 252 pp. Powerful love
story.   ISBN 0-941483-16-9   8.95

SOUTH OF THE LINE by Catherine Ennis. 216 pp. Civil War
adventure.   ISBN 0-941483-29-0   8.95

WOMAN PLUS WOMAN by Dolores Klaich. 300 pp. Supurb
Lesbian overview.   ISBN 0-941483-28-2   9.95

SLOW DANCING AT MISS POLLY'S by Sheila Ortiz Taylor.
96 pp. Lesbian Poetry   ISBN 0-941483-30-4   7.95

DOUBLE DAUGHTER by Vicki P. McConnell. 216 pp. A Nyla
Wade Mystery, third in the series.   ISBN 0-941483-26-6   8.95

MEMORY BOARD by Jane Rule. 336 pp. Memorable novel about an aging Lesbian couple. ISBN 0-941483-02-9   9.95

THE ALWAYS ANONYMOUS BEAST by Lauren Wright Douglas. 224 pp. A Caitlin Reese mystery. First in a series. ISBN 0-941483-04-5   8.95

SEARCHING FOR SPRING by Patricia A. Murphy. 224 pp. Novel about the recovery of love. ISBN 0-941483-00-2   8.95

DUSTY'S QUEEN OF HEARTS DINER by Lee Lynch. 240 pp. Romantic blue-collar novel. ISBN 0-941483-01-0   8.95

PARENTS MATTER by Ann Muller. 240 pp. Parents' relationships with Lesbian daughters and gay sons. ISBN 0-930044-91-6   9.95

THE PEARLS by Shelley Smith. 176 pp. Passion and fun in the Caribbean sun. ISBN 0-930044-93-2   7.95

MAGDALENA by Sarah Aldridge. 352 pp. Epic Lesbian novel set on three continents. ISBN 0-930044-99-1   8.95

THE BLACK AND WHITE OF IT by Ann Allen Shockley. 144 pp. Short stories. ISBN 0-930044-96-7   7.95

SAY JESUS AND COME TO ME by Ann Allen Shockley. 288 pp. Contemporary romance. ISBN 0-930044-98-3   8.95

LOVING HER by Ann Allen Shockley. 192 pp. Romantic love story. ISBN 0-930044-97-5   7.95

MURDER AT THE NIGHTWOOD BAR by Katherine V. Forrest. 240 pp. A Kate Delafield mystery. Second in a series. ISBN 0-930044-92-4   8.95

ZOE'S BOOK by Gail Pass. 224 pp. Passionate, obsessive love story. ISBN 0-930044-95-9   7.95

WINGED DANCER by Camarin Grae. 228 pp. Erotic Lesbian adventure story. ISBN 0-930044-88-6   8.95

PAZ by Camarin Grae. 336 pp. Romantic Lesbian adventurer with the power to change the world. ISBN 0-930044-89-4   8.95

SOUL SNATCHER by Camarin Grae. 224 pp. A puzzle, an adventure, a mystery — Lesbian romance. ISBN 0-930044-90-8   8.95

THE LOVE OF GOOD WOMEN by Isabel Miller. 224 pp. Long-awaited new novel by the author of the beloved *Patience and Sarah.* ISBN 0-930044-81-9   8.95

THE HOUSE AT PELHAM FALLS by Brenda Weathers. 240 pp. Suspenseful Lesbian ghost story. ISBN 0-930044-79-7   7.95

HOME IN YOUR HANDS by Lee Lynch. 240 pp. More stories from the author of *Old Dyke Tales.* ISBN 0-930044-80-0   7.95

EACH HAND A MAP by Anita Skeen. 112 pp. Real-life poems that touch us all. ISBN 0-930044-82-7   6.95

SURPLUS by Sylvia Stevenson. 342 pp. A classic early Lesbian novel.	ISBN 0-930044-78-9	7.95
PEMBROKE PARK by Michelle Martin. 256 pp. Derring-do and daring romance in Regency England.	ISBN 0-930044-77-0	7.95
THE LONG TRAIL by Penny Hayes. 248 pp. Vivid adventures of two women in love in the old west.	ISBN 0-930044-76-2	8.95
HORIZON OF THE HEART by Shelley Smith. 192 pp. Hot romance in summertime New England.	ISBN 0-930044-75-4	7.95
AN EMERGENCE OF GREEN by Katherine V. Forrest. 288 pp. Powerful novel of sexual discovery.	ISBN 0-930044-69-X	8.95
THE LESBIAN PERIODICALS INDEX edited by Claire Potter. 432 pp. Author & subject index.	ISBN 0-930044-74-6	29.95
DESERT OF THE HEART by Jane Rule. 224 pp. A classic; basis for the movie Desert Hearts.	ISBN 0-930044-73-8	7.95
SPRING FORWARD/FALL BACK by Sheila Ortiz Taylor. 288 pp. Literary novel of timeless love.	ISBN 0-930044-70-3	7.95
FOR KEEPS by Elisabeth Nonas. 144 pp. Contemporary novel about losing and finding love.	ISBN 0-930044-71-1	7.95
TORCHLIGHT TO VALHALLA by Gale Wilhelm. 128 pp. Classic novel by a great Lesbian writer.	ISBN 0-930044-68-1	7.95
LESBIAN NUNS: BREAKING SILENCE edited by Rosemary Curb and Nancy Manahan. 432 pp. Unprecedented autobiographies of religious life.	ISBN 0-930044-62-2	9.95
THE SWASHBUCKLER by Lee Lynch. 288 pp. Colorful novel set in Greenwich Village in the sixties.	ISBN 0-930044-66-5	8.95
MISFORTUNE'S FRIEND by Sarah Aldridge. 320 pp. Historical Lesbian novel set on two continents.	ISBN 0-930044-67-3	7.95
A STUDIO OF ONE'S OWN by Ann Stokes. Edited by Dolores Klaich. 128 pp. Autobiography.	ISBN 0-930044-64-9	7.95
SEX VARIANT WOMEN IN LITERATURE by Jeannette Howard Foster. 448 pp. Literary history.	ISBN 0-930044-65-7	8.95
A HOT-EYED MODERATE by Jane Rule. 252 pp. Hard-hitting essays on gay life; writing; art.	ISBN 0-930044-57-6	7.95
INLAND PASSAGE AND OTHER STORIES by Jane Rule. 288 pp. Wide-ranging new collection.	ISBN 0-930044-56-8	7.95
WE TOO ARE DRIFTING by Gale Wilhelm. 128 pp. Timeless Lesbian novel, a masterpiece.	ISBN 0-930044-61-4	6.95
AMATEUR CITY by Katherine V. Forrest. 224 pp. A Kate Delafield mystery. First in a series.	ISBN 0-930044-55-X	8.95
THE SOPHIE HOROWITZ STORY by Sarah Schulman. 176 pp. Engaging novel of madcap intrigue.	ISBN 0-930044-54-1	7.95

THE BURNTON WIDOWS by Vickie P. McConnell. 272 pp. A
Nyla Wade mystery, second in the series. ISBN 0-930044-52-5 7.95

OLD DYKE TALES by Lee Lynch. 224 pp. Extraordinary
stories of our diverse Lesbian lives. ISBN 0-930044-51-7 8.95

DAUGHTERS OF A CORAL DAWN by Katherine V. Forrest.
240 pp. Novel set in a Lesbian new world. ISBN 0-930044-50-9 8.95

THE PRICE OF SALT by Claire Morgan. 288 pp. A milestone
novel, a beloved classic. ISBN 0-930044-49-5 8.95

AGAINST THE SEASON by Jane Rule. 224 pp. Luminous,
complex novel of interrelationships. ISBN 0-930044-48-7 8.95

LOVERS IN THE PRESENT AFTERNOON by Kathleen
Fleming. 288 pp. A novel about recovery and growth.
ISBN 0-930044-46-0 8.95

TOOTHPICK HOUSE by Lee Lynch. 264 pp. Love between
two Lesbians of different classes. ISBN 0-930044-45-2 7.95

MADAME AURORA by Sarah Aldridge. 256 pp. Historical
novel featuring a charismatic "seer." ISBN 0-930044-44-4 7.95

CURIOUS WINE by Katherine V. Forrest. 176 pp. Passionate
Lesbian love story, a best-seller. ISBN 0-930044-43-6 8.95

BLACK LESBIAN IN WHITE AMERICA by Anita Cornwell.
141 pp. Stories, essays, autobiography. ISBN 0-930044-41-X 7.95

CONTRACT WITH THE WORLD by Jane Rule. 340 pp.
Powerful, panoramic novel of gay life. ISBN 0-930044-28-2 9.95

MRS. PORTER'S LETTER by Vicki P. McConnell. 224 pp.
The first Nyla Wade mystery. ISBN 0-930044-29-0 7.95

TO THE CLEVELAND STATION by Carol Anne Douglas.
192 pp. Interracial Lesbian love story. ISBN 0-930044-27-4 6.95

THE NESTING PLACE by Sarah Aldridge. 224 pp. A
three-woman triangle—love conquers all! ISBN 0-930044-26-6 7.95

THIS IS NOT FOR YOU by Jane Rule. 284 pp. A letter to a
beloved is also an intricate novel. ISBN 0-930044-25-8 8.95

FAULTLINE by Sheila Ortiz Taylor. 140 pp. Warm, funny,
literate story of a startling family. ISBN 0-930044-24-X 6.95

THE LESBIAN IN LITERATURE by Barbara Grier. 3d ed.
Foreword by Maida Tilchen. 240 pp. Comprehensive bibliography.
Literary ratings; rare photos. ISBN 0-930044-23-1 7.95

ANNA'S COUNTRY by Elizabeth Lang. 208 pp. A woman
finds her Lesbian identity. ISBN 0-930044-19-3 6.95

PRISM by Valerie Taylor. 158 pp. A love affair between two
women in their sixties. ISBN 0-930044-18-5 6.95

BLACK LESBIANS: AN ANNOTATED BIBLIOGRAPHY

compiled by J. R. Roberts. Foreword by Barbara Smith. 112 pp.
Award-winning bibliography.   ISBN 0-930044-21-5   5.95

THE MARQUISE AND THE NOVICE by Victoria Ramstetter.
108 pp. A Lesbian Gothic novel.   ISBN 0-930044-16-9   6.95

OUTLANDER by Jane Rule. 207 pp. Short stories and essays
by one of our finest writers.   ISBN 0-930044-17-7   8.95

ALL TRUE LOVERS by Sarah Aldridge. 292 pp. Romantic
novel set in the 1930s and 1940s.   ISBN 0-930044-10-X   7.95

A WOMAN APPEARED TO ME by Renee Vivien. 65 pp. A
classic; translated by Jeannette H. Foster.   ISBN 0-930044-06-1   5.00

CYTHEREA'S BREATH by Sarah Aldridge. 240 pp. Romantic
novel about women's entrance into medicine.
                                          ISBN 0-930044-02-9   6.95

TOTTIE by Sarah Aldridge. 181 pp. Lesbian romance in the
turmoil of the sixties.   ISBN 0-930044-01-0   6.95

THE LATECOMER by Sarah Aldridge. 107 pp. A delicate love
story.   ISBN 0-930044-00-2   6.95

ODD GIRL OUT by Ann Bannon.   ISBN 0-930044-83-5   5.95

I AM A WOMAN by Ann Bannon.   ISBN 0-930044-84-3   5.95

WOMEN IN THE SHADOWS by Ann Bannon.
                                          ISBN 0-930044-85-1   5.95

JOURNEY TO A WOMAN by Ann Bannon.
                                          ISBN 0-930044-86-X   5.95

BEEBO BRINKER by Ann Bannon.   ISBN 0-930044-87-8   5.95
          Legendary novels written in the fifties and sixties,
              set in the gay mecca of Greenwich Village.

VOLUTE BOOKS

JOURNEY TO FULFILLMENT	Early classics by Valerie	3.95
A WORLD WITHOUT MEN	Taylor: The Erika Frohmann	3.95
RETURN TO LESBOS	series.	3.95

These are just a few of the many Naiad Press titles — we are the oldest and
largest lesbian/feminist publishing company in the world. Please request a
complete catalog. We offer personal service; we encourage and welcome
direct mail orders from individuals who have limited access to bookstores
carrying our publications.